Praise for the Novels
of Michelle Rowen

"I've been bitten and smitten by Michelle Rowen."
—*New York Times* bestselling author
Sherrilyn Kenyon

"Michelle Rowen never disappoints! I love her work!"
—*New York Times* bestselling author Gena Showalter

"What a charming, hilarious book! Frankly, I'm insanely jealous I didn't write it."
—*New York Times* bestselling author
MaryJanice Davidson

"Rowen's foray into a new dark, gritty world is a brilliant success . . . [and] an adrenaline rush!"
—*New York Times* bestselling author Larissa Ione

"Michelle Rowen's books never fail to thrill."
—Bitten by Books

"Sassy and exhilarating . . . epic and thrilling."
—Fresh Fiction

"Should leave readers breathless."   —*Kirkus Reviews*

"I have never read a Michelle Rowen book that I did not adore."
—Enchanted by Books

BLOOD BATH & BEYOND

AN IMMORTALITY BITES MYSTERY

MICHELLE ROWEN

AN OBSIDIAN MYSTERY

OBSIDIAN
Published by New American Library, a division of
Penguin Group (USA) Inc., 375 Hudson Street,
New York, New York 10014, USA
Penguin Group (Canada), 90 Eglinton Avenue East, Suite 700, Toronto,
Ontario M4P 2Y3, Canada (a division of Pearson Penguin Canada Inc.)
Penguin Books Ltd., 80 Strand, London WC2R 0RL, England
Penguin Ireland, 25 St. Stephen's Green, Dublin 2,
Ireland (a division of Penguin Books Ltd.)
Penguin Group (Australia), 250 Camberwell Road, Camberwell, Victoria 3124,
Australia (a division of Pearson Australia Group Pty. Ltd.)
Penguin Books India Pvt. Ltd., 11 Community Centre, Panchsheel Park,
New Delhi - 110 017, India
Penguin Group (NZ), 67 Apollo Drive, Rosedale, Auckland 0632,
New Zealand (a division of Pearson New Zealand Ltd.)
Penguin Books (South Africa) (Pty.) Ltd., 24 Sturdee Avenue,
Rosebank, Johannesburg 2196, South Africa

Penguin Books Ltd., Registered Offices:
80 Strand, London WC2R 0RL, England

First published by Obsidian, an imprint of New American Library,
a division of Penguin Group (USA) Inc.

First Printing, August 2012
10 9 8 7 6 5 4 3 2 1

PUBLISHER'S NOTE
This is a work of fiction. Names, characters, places, and incidents either are
the product of the author's imagination or are used fictitiously, and any
resemblance to actual persons, living or dead, business establishments,
events, or locales is entirely coincidental.
    The publisher does not have any control over and does not assume any
responsibility for author or third-party Web sites or their content.

If you purchased this book without a cover you should be aware that
this book is stolen property. It was reported as "unsold and destroyed" to
the publisher and neither the author nor the publisher has received any
payment for this "stripped book."

To Bonnie Starling

Acknowledgments

Thank you so much to my agent, Jim McCarthy, for believing in me (and Sarah) from day one and championing my foray into this exciting new genre.

Thank you to Leis Pederson and Cindy Hwang for giving me this wonderful opportunity to write a fun and romantic mystery (with fangs).

Thank you to my beta readers on this book, and wonderfully supportive friends, Bonnie Staring and Megan Crane. Love you guys! xoxo

And thank you to Sarah for stating very adamantly that she wanted to explore what happens next. She's very stubborn for a fictional character. I like that.

Chapter 1

The fangs don't get nearly as much attention as you'd think.

Your average, everyday person doesn't notice that they're sharper than normal human canines. If they did, they'd have to deal with the possibility that vampires really exist. It's a survival instinct on their part, culminating from centuries of living side by side with something they'd prefer to think of as a fictional predatory monster. Or, more recently, as an eternally sparkling teenager.

Real vampires make up approximately 0.001 percent of the population—that's one in a thousand. So, worldwide, there are about six million vampires.

Humans just don't see us. It does help that, despite what you might have heard, we can go outside into the sunshine on a lovely early June day like today without turning into a pile of ashes. We blend in with regular human society just fine and dandy.

It's kind of like we're invisible.

Someone bashed into me when I glanced down at the screen of my phone as I walked down the busy sidewalk.

"Hey!" the woman snarled. "Watch where you're going, you dumb bitch!"

"Bite me," I replied sweetly, then added under my breath, "or I might bite you."

She gave me the finger, stabbing it violently in my direction as if it were a tiny, flesh-colored sword.

Okay, maybe we're not *totally* invisible.

I couldn't help that I had a natural-born talent to rub people the wrong way. It had very little to do with me being a vampire and more to do with me just being . . . me. I liked to think it was simply part of my charm.

I looked bleakly at the phone again. No messages. No calls. It felt like everyone I knew had recently deserted me. It wasn't far from the truth, actually. Last month, my parents had moved to Florida to a retirement community. Two weeks ago, my best male friend, George, had headed for Hawaii to open a surf shop after he won a small fortune in a local lottery. And now, my best girlfriend and her husband were in the process of moving to British Columbia so she could take a job in cosmetics management.

"We'll totally stay in touch," Amy said to me at the airport before she got on her flight an hour ago. I'd met her there to say a last good-bye.

I hugged her fiercely. "Of course we will."

Her husband stood nearby, giving me the evil eye like he usually did. We'd never really gotten along all that well. You win some, you lose some. "Are you finished yet? We're going to miss our flight."

I forced a smile. "I'm even going to miss *you*, Barry."

He just looked at his wristwatch.

Amy smiled brightly. "This is a new beginning, Sarah. For both of us. We have to embrace change."

I hated change.

I did hope to see her again soon, not too far into the future.

The future was something I thought about a lot these days. After all, as a fledgling vampire, sired less than seven months ago, I had a lot of future to look forward to. I just hoped it wouldn't suck too much.

Yes, that was me. Sarah Dearly, immortal pessimist. I had to turn my frown upside down. Right now, I was so far down in the dumps that the raccoons had arrived and were starting to sniff around. Metaphorically speaking, of course.

It seemed as if new opportunities and new adventures had been presented to everyone but me, like they'd won the lottery—*literally* in one case—and I'd mistakenly put my ticket in the wash and now couldn't even read the numbers.

"You look sad," someone said.

I glanced over my shoulder, surprised to see a clown standing at the side of the street holding a bunch of balloons.

White makeup, poufy costume covered in colorful polka dots. Red hair. A hat with a fake flower springing out of it. Big red nose. The works.

It was like a bad omen. Clowns scared the crap out of me.

"Sad? Who, me?" I said warily, slipping my phone back in my shoulder bag. "Nah, I'm just melancholy today. There's a difference, you know. Please don't murder me."

"Somebody needs a happy happy balloon to make her happy happy." He handed me a yellow ribbon tied to a shiny red balloon. I looked up at it.

"Yes," I said. "This will make all the difference in the world. Thank you so much. Now life is happy happy for me again."

The clown glared at me. "No reason to be sarcastic, lady."

"I don't need a reason."

"The balloon's five bucks."

"Three."

"Four."

"Sold." I grinned, then fished into my purse and pulled out the money. "Thanks so much, Bozo."

"It's Mr. Chuckles."

"Whatever."

The balloon did cheer me up more than I would have guessed. It reminded me of going to the National Exhibition with my mother every fall when I was a kid. Popcorn, cotton candy, hot dogs, and balloons. High-calorie memories with a little bit of helium and latex thrown in for good measure. Those were good times.

I'd needed the walk to clear my head. My head was officially cleared, so I returned to the huge luxury townhome I shared with my fiancé and let myself in.

Immediately, I sensed there was something different there. A big clue to this was the large black suitcase placed by the front door.

I heard Thierry on the phone, speaking French to someone. He was fluent, since he was originally from France centuries ago.

Yes, my fiancé was significantly older than me—by about six hundred years or so.

Some of the words I understood:

"Aujourd'hui," which I knew meant "today."

"Seul," which meant "alone."

"D'accord," which meant "alrighty."

"Importante" . . . well, that one didn't really need a translator.

Thierry entered the front foyer with his phone pressed to his left ear. He stopped when he saw me standing there gaping at him.

"À bientôt, Bernard." He slipped the phone into the inside pocket of his black suit jacket. "Sarah, I was about to call you. I'm glad you've returned."

He didn't have an accent. His English was flawless, since he'd spoken it for at least five hundred years.

Thierry de Bennicoeur appeared to be in his mid-thirties. He was six feet tall, had black hair that was usually brushed back from his handsome face, and piercing gray eyes that felt like they could see straight through you clear to the other side. He always dressed in black Hugo Boss suits, which wasn't the most imaginative wardrobe choice, but looked consistently perfect on him anyway. He was, in a word, a total fox. Even after all the time we'd spent together, there was no doubt in my mind about that.

Some people perceived him to be cold and unemotional, but I knew the truth. That facade was for protection only. Down deep, Thierry was fire and passion. Only . . . it was *really* down deep. Most people would never see that side of him and I was okay with that. I had the rock on my finger that proved I *had* seen the fire and hadn't been burned yet.

However, I had to admit, that suitcase was causing a few painful sparks to fly up in my general direction.

"What's going on?" I asked cautiously. "What's with the luggage?"

"I have to go somewhere."

"Where? And . . . when?"

The line of his jaw tightened. "I've been called upon to meet with someone about important Ring business in Las Vegas."

The Ring was the vampire council. Thierry was the original founder of the organization that tracked any potential vampiric issues worldwide and did what they could to neutralize them. He'd left a century ago after dealing with some personal issues and he hadn't looked back since. The Ring had carried on without his input or influence.

"What business?" I asked.

"I've been offered a job with them. One I can't decline."

My eyes widened. "What kind of job?"

"Consultant."

"What do you mean, you can't decline it?"

He hesitated. "They made me an offer I couldn't refuse."

"Who were you just talking to, Don Corleone?"

He raised a dark eyebrow. "His name is Bernard DuShaw. He was the most recent of several people I've spoken with over the last couple of hours. It's his position I would be taking over now that he's retiring."

I thought of my parents settling in to Florida's sand and sunshine now that they'd reached their retirement years. "He's immortal, isn't he? He doesn't ever have to retire."

"After a contracted term with the Ring, one is permitted to leave to pursue other interests if one wishes to. He wishes to."

I tried to breathe normally. Contrary to one of many popular myths about vampires, we needed to do that regularly. "Okay. Well, the universe does work in mysterious ways. I guess this isn't a bad thing. I think you'd be a great asset for them. Keep them from making any mistakes or judging anyone too harshly without a proper assessment. So . . . you're going today to meet with Bernard about this job?"

"Yes."

"And when will you be back?"

"Perhaps you should sit down, Sarah."

"I don't want to sit down." My anxiety spiked. "You are coming back, aren't you?"

His expression tensed. "I'm sorry, but I don't believe I'll be returning to Toronto. The position calls for constant travel. I won't be able to stay in one place for very long during my term as consultant."

I tried to absorb all of this, but it was too much all at once. "How long is a term?"

He didn't speak for a moment. "Fifty years."

I just looked at him, momentarily rendered speechless by this unexpected news. Silence stretched between us.

His gaze moved to my balloon. "What's this?"

My mouth had gone dry. "My happy happy balloon. I got it from a clown named Mr. Chuckles."

His lips curved at the edges. "I thought you were going to the airport."

"I did."

"You stopped by a circus on the way home?"

"Thierry," I said sharply. "What is going on? How can you just leave? Fifty years? It sounds like a prison sentence, not a new job. Are you saying . . . are you saying that—" I didn't want to speak my thoughts aloud. After everyone else I loved put thousands of miles between me and them, perhaps I should have expected this. But I hadn't. This was a complete and total shock.

Everyone was leaving me. And now Thierry was joining the list.

"Sarah—"

"I heard you on the phone. You said *seul*, which means you're going alone."

"That's what they want. This job requires focus and twenty-four/seven availability. I assumed you wouldn't want to travel so much, never knowing where you're going next. There's a great deal of uncertainty involved with this job."

"This job that you can't say no to for some mysterious reason. A job that you're going to be doing for half a century all by yourself, with no prior warning." I crossed my arms tightly. Everything about this made me ill. "You know, maybe this job came at just the right time for you to change your mind about being with—"

"Please don't finish that sentence." He took me by my shoulders, gazing fiercely into my eyes. "All I want is for you to be happy—don't you know that by now?"

I swallowed hard. "The clown thought a balloon would make me happy."

"And did it?"

"For a couple minutes."

He looked up at it. "It is a nice balloon."

"Screw the balloon." My throat felt so tight it was difficult to speak.

Thierry's and my path hadn't been an easy one, not since the very first moment we met. It wasn't every day a twenty-eight-year-old fledgling hooked up with a six-hundred-year-old master vampire—we were so completely different in temperament and personality it was frequently glaring and often problematic. But we had and it felt right, yet somehow I knew, down deep, that it might not last forever. Forever was a very long time when you're a vampire.

Just because I knew it, didn't mean my heart didn't break into a million pieces at the thought of losing him.

I tried to compose myself as much as possible after realizing that someone else I cared about would be moving away from me. This, though . . . *this* stung even more than saying good-bye to Amy. This felt permanent. Forever.

I wanted to be cool about getting dumped for a "job he couldn't refuse," but I wasn't sure if I had it in me.

"I get it, Thierry. You don't want to be distracted by someone who has a tendency to get into trouble at the drop of a hat. I can take a hint. I'm a liability. You want me to stay here."

He let out a small, humorless laugh. "What I want is irrelevant. Can you honestly say you'd leave behind your life here in Toronto, everything you've ever known and most of your possessions, in order to accompany me on a job that will be frequently boring for you; one that will mean you'll never know where your true home is?"

I stared up at him. "Are those rhetorical questions?"

"No, they're real questions." His brows drew together. "Would you come with me if I asked you to?"

I let go of the balloon, which floated up to the high ceiling of the front foyer before catching on a sharp crystal from the chandelier. It popped on contact.

I grabbed the lapels of his black jacket. "In a heartbeat."

Something I rarely saw slid behind his gray eyes then, something warm and utterly vulnerable. "Then I suggest you pack a bag. Our flight leaves in three hours."

I looked at him, stunned. "*Our* flight?"

"I wasn't sure you'd be open to this abrupt change, but I did purchase you a ticket just in case."

My heart lifted. "You're so prepared. Just like a Boy Scout."

"I try." A smile played at his lips. "I just hope that this trip doesn't make you change your mind about me."

"Don't be ridiculous." My smile only grew wider before faltering just a little. "But I thought they wanted you to come alone. Won't they give you a hard time about this?"

"If they want me for this job, then they will get my fiancée as well. They'll just have to deal with it." He took my face between his hands. "I love you, Sarah. Never doubt it."

He kissed me and I couldn't think of any happy happy balloon that could make me this happy happy.

Change was good. I liked change.

Chapter 2

There's something important that should be known about me. Despite being an immortal vampire, I'm deathly afraid of flying. It's too bad that it's the best and quickest way to get anywhere worth going. The flight to Las Vegas was traumatic. And turbulent. And long. And I think I nearly injured Thierry's hand as I nervously clawed at it during half the flight, but we landed before too much damage occurred.

Once he'd managed to escape my death clutch as the plane taxied toward the Vegas airport terminal, he was immediately on his phone again, taking a call from someone—probably this Bernard DuShaw guy—about more details to do with this trip. I sat in my seat and relearned how to breathe before applying some lip gloss to offset the sickly green tinge my skin had taken on for the last four and a half hours.

Being on the ground was a very good thing, and I was thrilled to be in Las Vegas for this unexpected but exciting trip.

We would be staying in a suite at the Bellagio, a stunning hotel and casino right in the middle of the Vegas Strip. The one with the Italian theme and the dancing fountains out front. Our tab was being picked up by the Ring and I was more than happy to let them do the picking. It was a gorgeous hotel—the lobby took my breath away as we stepped through the entrance doors with our luggage. Marble floors, floor-to-ceiling columns, Italian archways, and a beautiful sculpture attached to the ceiling of thousands of colorful crystal flowers, which was the artistic focal point of the lobby.

I must have appeared to be a typical awestruck tourist as we walked across the floor toward the reception desks to check in. We were surrounded by scores of other people and the buzz of activity and conversation. I was having a visual overload at everything around me, and my gaze remained fixed on the flowers above my head. I really should have brought a camera.

"Stand back, Sarah." Thierry's hand tightened on my waist.

I tore my attention away from the lobby ceiling as he pulled me to my left toward a column. It was then I noticed that while we were arriving at the hotel . . . someone else was leaving.

On a stretcher.

A shiver went through me at the sight of a white sheet draped over the occupant's head, which meant he wasn't being rushed anywhere but the morgue.

As the paramedics came within a few feet of us, the top of the white sheet snagged under the front wheel of the stretcher and pulled away, revealing the face and shoulders of the man beneath.

Yes, that was a dead person, all right—and definitely not something I saw every day. On the heels of my warm and elated feeling from arriving at the beautiful hotel, this particular sight made my blood run cold in my veins. Especially when I saw something unmistakable on the dead man's throat.

This man hadn't died from having a heart attack at the roulette table; that was for sure.

The paramedic hurriedly covered up the body again and they departed through the main doors toward the waiting ambulance with its lights flashing.

"Was that a vampire attack?" I asked under my breath. "Or am I just seeing things?"

"You're not seeing things." Thierry's voice was low enough that no one else around us would overhear.

His calm tone surprised me. "You sound like you almost expected to see something like that. Did you?"

He nodded. "When we landed, Bernard called to fill me in on a new situation the Ring is dealing with here. Very recently, there have been a few incidents just like this. Humans with puncture marks on their throats, drained of blood, left in public places. I didn't think it would be quite this public, though."

My stomach lurched. "A *few* incidents?"

He took my hand in his. "It's nothing to worry about. It's part of the reason the Ring exists in the first place, to help police those who step out of line and allow their thirst to rule their behavior. But vampire-related murders like this are rarely so public."

Nothing to worry about. Sure.

You might expect that a vampire like me would relish the very thought of blood and death. Well, you would be wrong. I couldn't help but cringe at seeing a human used as an unwilling chew toy like that. Blood, in my humble opinion, should be procured at a local "blood bank"—businesses where the red stuff, courtesy of paid human donors, flowed for a set price. If that made me a fanged wimp who didn't hang with the cool kids, then so be it.

Vampires like me preferred to get their drink of choice from humane sources, rather than some random victim in an alleyway. That was messy as well as completely evil.

Vampires weren't evil.

Actually, let me rephrase that. *Most* vampires weren't evil.

Just like humans, we had some bad eggs in the basket. If you were evil as a human, then you were still evil as a vampire. No major personality change happened after a vamp acquired his or her fangs—unless there was a spell or a curse involved. At least, that had been my experience so far.

"Is that why Bernard called you? Are you supposed to investigate these murders, too?" I asked uneasily, eyeing the crowd in the lobby. Some of the people seemed disturbed by the passing stretcher a minute ago, but most were going on with their day like they hadn't even noticed.

"No, I've been given another assignment. Bernard is here to head the separate investigation personally. He has a source with the Las Vegas CSI team he's meeting with as we speak."

"I think I prefer the TV version." The whole situation had given me an incredibly uneasy feeling in the pit of my stomach, which had very little to do with the turbulent flight.

I gazed out the glass doors as the ambulance drove away. "Welcome to Las Vegas, huh? That poor guy."

"Humans are delicate creatures." Thierry squeezed my hand reassuringly. "Try to put it out of your mind,

Sarah. This unpleasantness won't come anywhere near you, I promise."

Humans *were* delicate. *I* had been delicate. There might be a lot of negative things about being a vampire, but at least I wasn't quite as breakable as I'd once been.

I decided to do exactly as Thierry suggested and try my best to put the blood-free dead body out of my head as much as possible as we checked in. The woman behind the registration desk eyed my tall, dark, and handsome fiancé appreciatively before glancing at me with some obvious disdain. I made sure to subtly flash her my engagement ring so she knew I had every right to be standing next to him—and that she should, very kindly, back off.

I never said I wasn't petty.

On the way to the elevator, we walked past a poster on an easel that caught my attention.

"Hey, check it out," I said. "They have one of those child pageants going on here. Like that reality show with the toddlers who wear tiaras."

"Does this interest you?" Thierry asked.

"Not really. It just always struck me as strange—putting lipstick, a wig, and a fake tan on a little kid. It's like they're a thirty-year-old stuck in a toddler's body."

"It's very much like that, actually." He nodded at the poster. "This is the case Bernard's officially handing off to me."

I looked at him. "Seriously? What kind of case is it?"

"One of the contestants is a vampire."

I glanced at the colorful poster with shock this time. "That is messed up."

"It's also against the Ring's rules. It's possible that

she's unaware of this, but she has to be told. It's my job to learn her history, find out when she was sired, and who exactly was responsible for turning a child. Also, she must be made aware that public spectacles involving children that never age could only draw the attention of vampire hunters."

I took this all in. "And what happens to the vamp responsible for siring her?"

"Whoever it was—if they're still alive—will be dealt with."

I grimaced. "That doesn't sound pleasant."

"It won't be. But that isn't up to me. That goes to another department." His jaw tensed. "Enforcement."

Just the sound of it chilled me. "What a fun job you've acquired, Thierry. Death, mayhem, sequins. Sign me up."

He reached down to take my hand again. "It's much better now that you're with me."

"Sweet talker." I grinned, but my smile faded as I glanced at the poster once more. "So what happens to the little vamp herself?"

"She'll be asked not to take part in these public displays in the future. Like I said, it could attract hunters. Her life, and the lives of her fellow contestants, could be in danger."

That caused a fresh churning in my gut. "That would be a very bad thing."

"Yes, it would." Thierry glanced at his watch. "There's a little time to settle in. We're meeting Bernard and his wife, Laura, for dinner at eight o'clock."

First time I'd heard about this, which wasn't a surprise to me at all. Thierry wasn't exactly what I would call the most "forthcoming with details" guy I'd ever met in my life.

"Bernard has a wife? That's interesting."

"They're a lot like us, Bernard and Laura. Bernard's a master vampire and Laura's a fledgling. She was sired only a few years ago."

"Okay, now I'm *very* interested to meet them," I said.

A "master" vampire was just another way of saying that, despite the attractive exterior, he'd been around a long, *long* time.

"I think you might get along. After all, you have a great deal in common."

I liked the sound of this a lot. It was the chance to meet someone living a life parallel to mine. Thierry and I were still engaged, not married, but I hoped to tie the proverbial knot soon. The trouble was, picking a date that would have all my loved ones—both human and vampire—in one place at the same time was proving to be a challenge now that everyone had scattered to the far corners of the earth.

I glanced down at my engagement ring, which was absolutely gorgeous. Three carats. Princess cut. Flawless in every possible way.

I wondered how big Laura DuShaw's ring was.

"*Six* carats?" I held her hand and stared at the monstrous diamond with disbelief. "Wow, it's incredible."

She smiled. "Diamonds are a girl's best friend."

Laura reminded me of myself more than I would have thought possible. She even looked like she could be my sister, with her shoulder-length dark brown hair and hazel eyes that mirrored my own. However, she wore more makeup than I did and her clothes looked a bit more designer and custom-made. I used to have a serious obsession for clothes and shoes, but had toned that down lately. I'd had to run away from a whole lot of vampire hunters and I'd come to the quick realization that this was much easier to do when not wearing four-inch stiletto heels—although I was wearing a pair right now.

I still enjoyed shopping, and being romantically involved with someone with cash to spare, I could do it every day if I wanted to, but it had lost some of its flavor for me. And now that I'd agreed to live exclusively out of a suitcase for the foreseeable future, I wasn't in much of a hurry to stock up on new threads.

But I could admire those who did. And their threads.

As for Laura's husband, Bernard . . . he was a very handsome man. Thierry told me on the plane ride here that he was a little over three hundred years old and, in his youth, had even been associated with Marie Antoinette during the French Revolution. Thierry warned me not to bring up Marie Antoinette's name in conversation since it was a touchy subject for Bernard. As if I would. My knowledge of the French queen went about as far as knowing she said something like "let them eat cake," and Kirsten Dunst had played her in the movie version.

Thierry was the history expert in our relationship, not me. Of course, he'd learned everything not from books but by living through it all firsthand—from the Black Death and beyond.

Just as Laura looked a lot like me, Bernard looked a lot like Thierry. He had dark hair, pale eyes—although Bernard's were green, not gray—and expensive suits with clean lines. Tall and lean, with an air of authority and an edge of power about him, this man wasn't a pushover.

He had a softer side, I was sure. I wondered if it had taken Laura as much digging and sheer pigheaded stubbornness to find Bernard's as it had taken me to find Thierry's.

A typical restaurant dinner for vampires included wine and coffee, which were consumed, and plates of food, which were not. I used to wait tables in university. I'd often retrieved full plates of food at the end of the meal that looked only picked at, but it never raised any red flags for me. Everyone seemed to be on a diet at any given time. It didn't necessarily mean I'd been serving a table full of vampires.

But maybe I had been.

"If you'll excuse us," Bernard said, rising from the table after the untouched dessert plates were cleared away. He, unlike Thierry, had a strong French accent. He fixed both Laura and myself with a charming smile. "Thierry and I have some business to discuss. We'll be outside by the pool to get some fresh air."

Thierry nodded. "Bernard is kind enough to give me some tips on how best to present myself tomorrow when I meet with Ms. Corday."

The miniature pageant vamp. That should be an interesting meeting.

"Take lots of notes," I suggested.

"I'll do that." He brushed his hand against mine as he got up from his seat, and then he and Bernard left Laura and me at the table.

"Bernard brought some Cuban cigars to share with Thierry," Laura told me. "He wants to celebrate."

"Nothing says congrats on your retirement like illegal tobacco."

I took a sip from my glass of red wine. As a vampire I couldn't eat anything solid, but I'd never had much of a problem with alcoholic beverages. Some vampires could still eat normal food; however, I'd noticed this was rare. They were the freaks, not me.

At least, that's how I liked to think of it.

"Have you been to Vegas before?" Laura asked.

"Never. I always wanted to, but never got around to it until now. You?" I'd butter her up with small talk before we got into the real nitty-gritty details of hers and Bernard's relationship and how that information could benefit me in the future.

"Yes. But I don't like it here very much." Laura leaned back in her seat and ran her perfectly manicured index finger along the edge of her wineglass.

"No? Why not?"

"Oh, I've been here too many times to count—many memories . . . good and bad ones. Plus, with the murders this week, it's not exactly safe for our kind to spend too much time here at the moment."

I cringed at the reminder of what I'd seen earlier in the lobby. "How many murders have there been?"

Her expression tensed and her gaze swept the crowded restaurant. "I probably shouldn't have mentioned it. Bernard didn't bring it up during dinner because he didn't want to upset anyone, but I'm sure that's one of the things he's talking to Thierry about in private right now. There have been six humans who've turned up dead in the last week here on the Strip—one a day, including the one found in the Bellagio casino today. All were drained of blood and had fang marks on their necks."

Six! That was definitely more than a few. "Thierry mentioned to me that Bernard has a source with the police?"

She nodded. "He knows it's an out-of-control vampire who's willing to expose the rest of us to get his next meal. Frankly, I think he's trying to make a statement by being so public about it."

Most vampires didn't drink blood directly from humans, so they didn't run the risk of leaving a dead body lying about. This was a huge no-no—and one enforced by the Ring. Killing humans = BAD.

Vampires were to keep low profiles and not risk exposing themselves to humans at large. It was bad enough having scores of hunters looking to put a stake through our hearts, let alone having the entire world alerted to our existence.

"Why would he do it on purpose?" I asked. "That makes zero sense."

Her red, glossy lips thinned and she counted off on her manicured fingers. "Troublemaker. Attention hound. Sociopath. You name it. He definitely came to the right town if he wants some attention. However, if Bernard finds out who it is, he has the authority to stake him on sight."

I shuddered. This would be Thierry's job as soon as Bernard officially handed it off to him—staking dangerous vampires if they needed staking. "Let's hope that happens soon."

She raised her glass. "To a job well-done."

"I'll definitely drink to that." We clinked glasses

and I took a sip. Actually, it was more like a glug as I drained my glass completely in a couple swallows.

"Now, Sarah," Laura began. "Let's talk about something more pleasant than nasty Ring business and murders. I'd love to know how you and Thierry met."

A subject that also involved violence and blood loss, so it really wasn't quite as much of a shift in conversation as she might think.

The truth was that I'd been sired against my will by a vampiric blind date, and when I tried to run away from the hunters who'd killed him shortly after—so they wouldn't do the same to me—I found Thierry standing on the edge of a bridge. Weary of his centuries of living, he'd been about to stake himself and let his remains fall into the river below. Instead, we decided to save each other.

Such a fairy tale.

I chose not to share it without excessive editing. "I was out for a jog late one night and our paths happened to cross." I shrugged. "The rest is history. How about you?"

She took a sip from her cappuccino, which the waiter had just delivered. "My original sire abandoned me and I had to find my way on my own, which was very difficult as I'm sure you know. One night, Bernard and I passed each other in Central Park and our eyes met. It sounds cliché, but it was love at first sight. Now we get to spend the rest of our lives together."

So she wasn't with her original sire, either. We had more in common than I thought. "Have you had any problems with the age difference between you two?"

Enough chitchat, already, I thought. *Let the valuable grilling commence.*

She was quiet for a moment, but a wistful smile played at her lips. "I'd be lying if I said no. Bernard has so much history behind him; he's seen and experienced so much. Sometimes I worry that I'm not enough for him, that my human ways might start to wear on his patience too much. That he won't find them as charming as he did in the beginning."

That sounded painfully familiar.

She continued. "I've said this to him, but he tells me that it's not true. That he loves me just as I am. We've been together for five years and every year is better than the last." She glanced at me. "Do you feel that way toward Thierry?"

"Well, in the beginning I felt very uncertain"—my grip tightened on my empty wineglass—"to say the least. He tried to avoid me and make me think that he didn't care about me. He was very convincing, actually."

"But you were stubborn and you let him know that you loved him."

"I was rather adamant about it. If 'adamant' is another word for *questionably intelligent*."

"And you convinced him."

"Eventually I can wear down just about anyone." I gave her a grin. "I'm tenacious like that."

"And now you've agreed to leave your home behind and join him in his travels." At my nod, she touched my hand. "It might seem like a difficult transition, but I think you'll do just fine."

That remained to be seen. "What's it like being the wife of someone who works for the Ring?"

"Honestly? It's incredibly boring. But I find ways to occupy myself."

"How? Do you help Bernard with his job?"

"Oh, no. I wouldn't want to get in his way. But I like to go shopping. Have my hair done." She slid her fingers through her beautiful blowout. "I get a manicure twice a week. Weekly massages. Pedicures. I go to the theater frequently. I attend auctions and charity events. And I have many friends in most major cities. It helps to fill my time when Bernard is too busy."

Something about her rundown didn't sit all that well with me. I'd been hoping for a life with a little more purpose to it than personal maintenance and random entertainment. "So you're saying that being the wife of someone in Bernard's position gives you the liberty to enjoy an eternal life of leisure."

Laura's smile widened. "It beats slaving away at a desk job. I did that for too many years to count."

"Yeah, me too." But at least working for a paycheck gave me a reason to get up in the morning.

"Things are better now. Much better." She squeezed my hand. "You'll get used to it. And if you really don't like traveling so much, you can always take an apartment somewhere. Then you can fly out and meet Thierry for a week or two at a time."

I pondered that. "It doesn't sound like much of a marriage."

"Which is the reason I choose to be by Bernard's side whenever he needs me. I try to support him as much as I possibly can, and the least I can do is make sure I always look as good as possible. I think he appreciates that."

I nodded, but still felt a bit queasy from the direction of this conversation. "I guess there are lots of options."

Although . . . I wasn't sure I was really totally on board with the idea of going shopping every day for the rest of forever as my main raison d'être. This was not something I would have said a year ago—nonstop shopping and beauty salons would have been right up my alley then. Funny how some things change.

We chatted for a while longer, but I wasn't getting any meaty answers to my questions like I'd wanted, which was disappointing. It was difficult to dig down through Laura's layers. That is, if she even had any beyond what was visible on the surface. I learned nothing that helped give me true insight on what my future with Thierry held, now that our relationship had taken a new, Ring-inspired direction.

But Bernard and Laura . . . well, they were *us*. Both in looks and position. Maybe I needed to accept that and be happy about it instead of always seeing the glass half-empty.

Frankly, I *could* use a manicure. My cuticles were currently a disaster.

After silence fell between us and I'd personally finished the bottle of wine right down to the very last drop, we decided to look for the men. I followed Laura out of the swanky restaurant and down marble-swathed hallways until we reached the exit to lead us to the pool and courtyard area, but objects in my peripheral vision blurred as I thought through everything she'd told me.

A life of leisure. No reason to have a job. It all replayed in my mind again and again like an iPod set on replay.

All my adult life, I'd had jobs that didn't pay much—personal assistant, waitress, bartender. I'd still been figuring out what I wanted to do with the rest of my life when that life had changed forever with one unexpected bitten neck.

Searching for meaning in my life had me constantly wandering into dead ends. Every time I thought I'd found the right thing for me, something happened to mess it up. Maybe I'd never find my perfect vocation. Maybe *this* was my destiny—to be exactly like Laura. I supposed there were worse things to aspire to. She seemed happy enough.

I never would have predicted my destiny would be to become Thierry's well-dressed, wisecracking sidekick as we traveled the world making sure vampires at large behaved themselves. If I could be useful, then that was one thing, but if he did his thing and I went off and had fake nails applied every other day like Laura—well, that was way different.

I didn't want to be just a hanger-on who didn't contribute anything to our relationship other than letting him know what designer shoes I'd bought on sale that day. I had doubts that . . .

Well, let's just say I had doubts. Big, ugly, slimy ones. I'd hoped that speaking with Laura would help alleviate them, but it had just made them that much bigger, uglier, and slimier.

It was warm outside and there was a light breeze. The stars were bright and the moon hung heavy in the clear sky. A few people lounged leisurely on the deck, soaking up the beautiful evening. The courtyard's landscaping was painstakingly manicured to a leafy and floral perfection. It felt like I was walking through the huge backyard of a well-populated Mediterranean villa. I think I could live very happily here if given the option. Plus, the poolside bar was a definite bonus—even though it was currently closed for the day.

"There they are," Laura said, after we'd walked a slow circle around the pool.

The men stood next to a stone railing near the pool on the opposite side, where I assumed they were enjoying the stinky cigars. As we drew closer, however, I realized with surprise that they weren't having a calm conversation about the toddler pageant or Thierry's assignment here.

No. There was nothing calm about the furious expression on Thierry's face.

I gasped out loud when he grabbed hold of the front of Bernard's crisp white shirt and shook him violently.

"I swear I'll kill you, you son of a bitch," Thierry snarled, loud enough to get the attention of a dozen people in the area.

I'd very rarely heard such rage in his voice before, and cold fear sliced through me. He looked like he wanted to rip Bernard's throat out. I raced up to them and grabbed his arm. "Thierry! What are you doing?"

Thierry's livid expression froze and his gaze flicked to me. He let go of Bernard as if the other vampire had suddenly burst into flames. Bernard brushed off the front of his suit.

"I'm sorry you feel that way, Thierry." He seemed calm, but his pale green eyes flashed with anger and his French accent seemed even thicker than before. "I wish we could have come to a better understanding. This, however, isn't over yet. You know that."

Laura rushed to her husband's side, her gaze now

guarded and fearful as she glanced at Thierry. She slid her arm around Bernard's and began directing him off the patio.

"Good night, Sarah," she said tightly, with a quick flick of a look toward me.

After they left, Thierry's hands curled over the railing. His shoulders looked extremely tense.

"So . . . I'd heard that there were celebration cigars being passed around out here." I tried to ignore the curious stares we received from others out by the pool. "Were they the exploding kind? I know you're not a big fan of practical jokes."

His face was rigid, but he didn't look at me. "I'm sorry you had to see that."

"What was that all about? I thought you two were friends."

He snorted softly. Whatever boiling anger had been in his expression a minute ago had settled down to a simmer. "We have some unpleasant history between us that raised its ugly head tonight, I'm afraid."

"Anything you want to share?"

His brow furrowed. "You needn't worry yourself about this."

"About my fiancé uttering random death threats? Who, me worry?"

"I lost control of myself for a moment there."

"Which doesn't ease my mind at all. Thierry, you are the poster boy for control—unless there's a serious problem. What is it? Tell me."

He reached down and took my hand in his. "There's no problem. Bernard and I won't have to see each other again after tomorrow, so any future conflict will be avoided."

"I think that's a good idea."

"I agree. How did your talk go with Laura after we left?"

I eyed him. "Changing the subject, are we?"

His lips twitched a little as if he wanted to smile. "Is it that obvious?"

"Uh-huh." He seemed to have calmed down. I had no idea what had set him off, but I probably wouldn't find out. Not from him, anyway. Thierry's secretive nature was annoying sometimes, but for now I'd let it go. "Laura gave me the details about how I will be of help to you in your new job. It involves a great deal of salon time and having perfect hair and fingernails at all times."

He raised an eyebrow. "Does that interest you?"

"Not particularly. I mean, I like to keep up a fairly shiny appearance, but I'd rather it not be my full-time job if I can help it. I'd rather . . . uh, help you. I mean, if that's even allowed."

He didn't seem surprised or disturbed to hear of Laura's intense salon commitment. "Allowed?"

I thought things through for a moment as we stood there in silence. "Can I come with you when you talk to the little pageant vamp?"

"Do you really want to?"

"We could play good cop and bad cop." I actually smiled at the picture that presented. "I'll be the bad cop."

That made him grin as well. "Sounds interesting."

I faltered a little, uncertain about the job and how it could possibly involve someone who had no experience with this sort of thing. Also, Laura specifically said she didn't get in Bernard's way. "Unless . . . I mean, unless you'd prefer I'm not involved. If it's not okay with you—"

"It's very okay with me. In fact, I think it's an excellent idea." He studied my face for a moment. "You would be a great help to me in dealing with a situation like this. You have a way about you that helps put people at ease. Alone, I might scare her."

"You, scary? Nah. Well . . . good. So we'll talk to her together—and nobody has to get scared." I felt elated that he wanted me by his side for this without it being the least bit awkward between us. Then I sobered. "You know what's scary? The vampire serial killer. Laura and I talked about it a bit. Six victims so far! Do you think it's going to be a huge problem for the Ring to handle?"

He shook his head. "Between Bernard and the local police, it'll be taken care of swiftly. The worst it will do is draw more interested hunters to the area. Just be vigilant, Sarah."

"I put the *v* into vigilant." Despite the nasty aura of danger around the city and seeing Thierry snap at Bernard, I felt pretty good about everything. "So, unless you have any other death threats to utter tonight . . . or celebration cigars to smoke . . ."

"I think I've met my quota for the day. For both."

"Then let's rest up so we can chat with Little Miss Sunshine tomorrow."

He smiled. "See? You're already an asset to this job. You're keeping me on schedule."

"I was a personal assistant in my previous life, you know."

Thierry hadn't told me what Bernard had said to upset him so much, but I didn't suppose it really mattered. When you'd lived as long as Thierry had, you ended up racking up enemies much like poker chips. When face-to-face with those enemies, you had to know when to play another hand and when to cash out.

Viva Las Vegas.

Chapter 3

Her name was Victoria Corday and she was presently wearing a little fuchsia-colored cowboy hat, a hot-pink frilly dress, and a sequined vest. With fringe. She didn't look a day over six years old as she belted out a Reba McEntire tune into the microphone in the middle of the stage during rehearsals for the Little Miss Platinum Vegas pageant that was to take place later tonight.

Thierry and I watched from backstage.

"You're *sure* that's her?" I whispered.

"Positive."

I wanted to ask him a ton of questions, but I tried to be quiet.

There was a first time for everything.

Ever since last night and his confrontation with Bernard, I'd felt that he was closed off. Whatever they'd been talking about before Laura and I interrupted had troubled him deeply, but he didn't want to discuss it with anyone. Including me.

I really wished that he would feel comfortable enough to share every last one of his secrets with me. I'd learned a bit about his past, the good and the bad—although, frankly, it was mostly bad—and all of it had shaped the man I fell in love with. But he still held back from me. I wasn't sure if this was something we'd get over eventually or if it would always be like this between us. Me, the perpetually open, pink-covered Chick Lit book, and him, the murky fog straight out of a Stephen King novel, hiding secrets with sharp teeth and claws.

I believed that he really did love me, but that didn't mean he wanted me to know everything about him.

For example, I still didn't understand why he'd take this job in the first place and every time I'd asked him what this "offer he couldn't refuse" had entailed, he changed the subject. The Ring seemed like a shadowy entity, like the mob, that did things according to their own rules, even if they didn't match up with what the world might consider proper conduct.

They scared the crap out of me, actually. In a way they were even scarier than vampire hunters. At least with hunters you knew what to expect—a stake aimed at your heart the moment they realized that you had fangs. No questions asked, no judge and jury, just an executioner. With the Ring—well, they had their own mysterious agenda. Sometimes it involved sharp stakes to take care of a problem and sometimes it involved job offers that one couldn't refuse.

And call me crazy, but I had a hard time believing they were just going to accept me joining Thierry as his official personal assistant without any argument at all, even if he seemed okay with it right now.

Thierry had to realize that him and me—well, we were a *team*. And if he started being Mr. Secretive again on a regular basis like he'd been when we first met, then it was going to quickly become a big, fat problem that no size of muumuu was going to cover.

Victoria hit the high note at the end of the song, warbling just like Reba herself. There was a scattering of applause from the few people in attendance and she sauntered off the stage, fringe swishing and her tiny cowboy boots clomping across the wooden floor.

"Well-done, Vicky!" A fat, bald man who looked around forty approached her, knelt down in front of her, and presented her with a red lollipop. "You sounded fantastic, kiddo!"

"Thanks!" When she grinned, I peered closer.

"No fangs," I whispered.

"She likely has them filed," Thierry replied.

A lot of vampires who wanted to blend just that much better into human society had their fangs filed down, which required regular maintenance, kind of like having your nails done. The only problem was, if you let yourself get too hungry and then got a whiff of the red stuff—*boom*—they were back again like tiny twin switchblades, even sharper than before.

I hadn't bothered to file mine down yet. I just tried not to smile too widely while in mixed company. I'd done that once in the presence of a hunter and the night had not gone very smoothly afterward.

We trailed after Victoria and her friend as they exited the backstage area and moved along a hallway.

"Excuse me," Thierry said after a moment.

Victoria stopped walking and turned around to look at us curiously. She'd pushed the cowboy hat back so it hung around her neck on a thin leather band, leaving her platinum blond ringlets free. Her skin was pale and perfect, her eyes the blue of violets, and she wore a bit of glossy pink lip gloss, but not enough to make her look too grown-up.

I wondered how old she really was and if she'd been turned recently or if she'd been like this for dozens, or even *hundreds*, of years. The thought made me shiver.

"Yes?" the man with her said.

Thierry approached them. He folded his arms over his chest and looked tall, strong, and suitably authoritative for a situation like this. "I'd like to talk to you. To both of you."

"About what?" the man asked cautiously.

"You're a fantastic singer." I crouched down in front of the little girl so I was eye to eye with her.

Victoria beamed. "Thank you. Who are you?"

"I'm Sarah." I nodded at my handsome, but grim and menacing-looking, fiancé. "This is Thierry."

"Victoria is late for an interview with a local paper," the man said. "But she appreciates your kind words."

"Her interview will have to wait a little longer," Thierry said firmly. "I was sent here specifically to talk to Ms. Corday. I'm in Vegas representing the Ring and need to ask a few questions about—"

"Run, Vicky!" the man yelled. "Now!"

Everything suddenly moved so quickly that I could barely register what was happening. The man shoved the little girl away from him, placing his body in front of hers like a shield. There was a flash of silver as he pulled a knife from a sheath at his belt hidden under his jacket.

He stormed at Thierry and, without any hesitation, sank the blade into his chest to the hilt. It had taken no more than a few seconds total—barely enough time to take a breath, let alone to scream, but now I let out a frightened shriek as I realized what had just happened.

Thierry had been stabbed! A silver blade to the heart

of a vampire was every bit as deadly as a wooden stake.

Thierry snarled and grabbed the man with both hands before slamming him into the wall so hard that it left a dent. The man's lips curled back from his upper teeth and I could see his fangs. Another slam—Thierry certainly didn't lack in strength; vampires only got stronger as they aged—was enough to render his attacker unconscious and he sank to the floor in a heap.

"Thierry—" I reached for him, petrified that he'd been seriously injured and I was about to lose him before my very eyes.

His brow was deeply furrowed. "No, Sarah. I'll be fine. It—it wasn't silver. Go after her. Explain that we're not here to hurt her." He gripped the hilt of the knife and pulled it out with a grunt, then braced himself against the wall. There was a thin sheen of perspiration on his forehead, and his face had paled. He was in pain, but he wasn't dead.

That was all I had time to think about—*he wasn't dead*. A sob of relief rose in my throat. The man had stabbed him in his heart, but it wasn't with a silver blade. If it had been, he'd be dead and gone. Just like that.

My head whipped to my right. Victoria ran down the hallway like a small pink streak of lightning.

I didn't question Thierry; I simply ran after the little vampire. If she escaped, I would bet we wouldn't get another chance to talk to her. I didn't think a failed first assignment would make a very good impression on the mysteriously unpleasant Ring, especially after Thierry and Bernard's violent argument last night.

I caught up with Victoria just as she was about to

enter the theater again, and I grabbed the back of her pink vest. She was about to scream, but I clamped my hand down over her mouth and dragged her around the corner into an empty meeting room with stacked chairs.

Had to say, it felt very wrong. To anyone not in the know, it would look like I was attacking a child. If her pal hadn't just tried to kill the man I loved, then I might have had second thoughts about this. I still had them, but they didn't stop me.

"Be quiet," I growled, and loosened my grip on her enough to let her talk. "I'm not going to hurt you."

"Don't hurt me!"

"Do you understand English? I just said I wouldn't. What was that back there? Do you get your buddy to stab everyone who tries to talk to you?"

"Where's my daddy?"

"He's dead," I said dryly.

Her bottom lip wobbled and tears welled in her eyes.

Guilt skittered through me. What if the Ring had been wrong? If this wasn't a vampire, if she was an actual human child, then she was going to be seriously traumatized over this. That made two of us.

"He's not dead," I amended. "I was just joking. But he tried to kill the man I was with. That's not cool."

"He was protecting me!"

"Thierry didn't even make a move on you. All he wanted to do was talk."

Her little chest moved in and out with shaky sobs. "I'm s-scared. Wh-why are you being so mean to me? Why c-can't you leave me alone? I want my daddy!"

My stomach sank.

Oh my God. We were wrong. This was a human child and she was going to be scared of fanged strangers for the rest of her life.

No . . . no. I had to stay strong. In for a penny, in for a pound, as they say. Not sure who said that, but somebody obviously did once upon a time.

"Okay, Victoria," I said firmly. "Cut the crap. I know what you are. Talk to me and I'll give you my word that nothing bad's going to happen to you. However, if you give me any more problems, then I'll have to call in . . . um, an enforcer, and I promise he won't be as friendly as I am. In fact, I bet he'll have a nice sharp stake with your name on it."

She just stared at me, her little blue eyes growing wider and wider with every word I spoke.

If I was wrong, I was *so* going to hell for this.

"But, my daddy—"

"Victoria," I said sharply, standing in front of her with my arms crossed, tapping my foot against the floor like a strict schoolmarm from *Little House on the Prairie*. "Talk to me. *Now*."

She stared up at me beseechingly through her sweet little expression—eyes glossy, blond ringlets shivering with fright—for a few more drawn-out moments while I forced myself not to back down, beg her forgiveness, and offer to take her out for ice cream.

Finally, she sighed heavily.

"Unbelievable," she muttered. "I need a damn cigarette right now or I am seriously going to freak out."

I blinked. "Excuse me?"

She patted her sides and pulled a pack of Marlboros and a Zippo lighter from the pocket of her frilly skirt. She sparked the lighter and inhaled deeply on the cigarette before blowing out a long stream of rancid-smelling smoke. Then she glared up at me.

"Okay, talk," she snarled, jabbing the cigarette in my general direction. "What's your problem?"

Maybe I wasn't going to hell. At least, not for this.

"So it's true. You really are a vampire."

She looked at me like I was stupid. "I haven't done anything wrong. Why can't the Ring leave me alone?"

"They've bothered you before?"

"Once. Thought the blissful silence was going to last. Guess not."

I spread my hands. "Look, I don't really know what this is all about. The man your friend stabbed—Thierry—he's the one who wants to talk to you."

"So who are you, his secretary?"

"I prefer the term 'personal assistant.'" My frown deepened. "No, wait. Actually, I'm his *fiancée*, if you really want to know. But, yes, I'm also assisting him."

It sounded more equal and a little less *Mad Men* that way. I held up my left hand and waggled my ring finger to prove my claim.

Victoria didn't look impressed. "Don't call in an enforcer. Just do yourself and me a favor and do not do that. Ever."

There was fear in her voice again, enough that it made goose bumps form on my arms. "Not likely to win friends and influence people?"

"You're new, aren't you?" Victoria narrowed her eyes at me and puffed on her cigarette. "I can spot the puppies from a mile away."

"Puppies?"

"How long have you been turned? A month or two?"

I bristled. "Seven months."

"Yeah. Well, you'll get the hang of it sooner or later. Or you won't. Have you met up with many hunters yet?"

"I've met my share."

"Okay, then, you might just be able to understand the words that are coming out of my mouth. Enforcers for the Ring are like vampire hunters from hell." She tugged on my hand so I could draw closer to hear her whisper. Instead, she shouted, "They're evil incarnate!"

This little girl was not going to be winning Miss Congeniality anytime soon.

"Okay," I said. "No enforcers. Sheesh. Take it easy."

She shook her head. "The last time I got involved in some bad stuff, they came for me. I barely escaped with my life. That's why I reacted like that, why Charles, my assistant, reacted like that. He wanted to give me a chance to escape."

The genuine fear in her eyes made me uneasy. "Thierry wouldn't just kill someone who didn't deserve it. Doesn't matter who he works for. He's one of the good guys."

She exhaled shakily. "Fine. I'll meet with your boss for fifteen minutes. That's it. He can have his say and then I want to be left alone. I don't cause trouble. I do my very best to fit in. And I need time to mentally prepare for the pageant tonight." She dropped the cigarette butt onto the carpeted floor and ground it out with the toe of her pink cowboy boot.

I nodded. "Fifteen minutes sounds reasonable. And like I said before, he's not my boss. He's my fiancé."

"Whatever." She shrugged. "Let's go see him, whoever he is. And if there's any funny business, then I can't be responsible for how many pieces I'm going to tear you both into."

I feared this tiny vampire. And now my clothes stank from cigarette smoke.

"Talk," Victoria snapped.

We'd gone up to my and Thierry's suite on the thirty-second floor with Victoria and her assistant, Charles. While recovering from being knocked unconscious, he scurried to the honor bar when Thierry gave him the nod to help himself. Victoria had a scotch on the rocks and another cigarette.

It was extremely disconcerting to see her smoke and drink like a sailor on leave in the big city. I felt the urge to get her a glass of milk and a chocolate-chip cookie instead.

Thierry sat next to me on the sofa in our large suite. I sensed he wasn't feeling very well after being stabbed through the heart. I didn't really blame him. If it had been a shallower wound, he would already be healed. Since Charles got his heart—the bastard—it would take more time and energy before he was good as new.

He put up a very good front. If I hadn't seen what happened with my own eyes, I would never guess he was seriously injured. Plus, his regular black suit didn't show the blood very much. Maybe that was why he'd settled on that color scheme for his wardrobe in the first place—to hide bloodstains.

Gee, that was a rather morbid thought.

"When were you sired, Victoria?" Thierry asked evenly.

She downed the rest of her drink and eyed him as if

deciding whether she wanted to be truthful or not. "Ninety-six years ago."

I gaped at her. The child with the taste for booze and nicotine was old enough to be my great-grandmother.

"Who sired you?"

Another pause. "A vampire named Madeline Halward. She lived in the small English village where I was being raised in an orphanage. My parents died in the war. She promised that she'd take care of me, that she would be my new mother. She waited until I agreed to stay with her and . . . well, it happened. She wanted to have a child forever—one who'd never grow up and leave her—and she chose me."

"The Ring has rules about this," Thierry said. "To protect children from this fate even if the child is originally given the choice to change."

Victoria paced to the floor-to-ceiling windows that had a great view of the fountains and clear across Las Vegas Boulevard to the Paris Hotel. "Do you honestly think I would have chosen this for myself?"

My chest tightened. "I'm so sorry. It must be horrible for you."

She spun around, eyes flashing. "Don't feel sorry for me, puppy. I haven't regretted what happened to me a single day of my life. Do you know how much I can get away with by looking like this? People love me the moment they see me. I can use that to my advantage."

I stared at her. "You don't feel trapped in the body of a child?"

"Trapped? Hell no. This is awesome. I'm just a kid—I'll always just be a kid. I can get away with murder."

Thierry stiffened next to me. "Funny you should say that. You wouldn't happen to have anything to do with the recent string of vampire-related serial killings in Vegas, would you?"

Her cherublike face fell. "It's just an expression, sourpuss. I don't murder people. Charles brings me my blood. It's one of his duties."

"And where does Charles get this blood?"

Thierry was a natural at this interrogation stuff. Had to say it was sort of turning me on. I'd always had a secret crush on Columbo.

Charles moved into my view. "There's a blood bank here in Vegas called Blood Bath and Beyond. Its front is a vampire novelty shop."

This was the first I'd heard of a local blood bank. "Where are they?"

"Right here on the Strip, down by the MGM Hotel. You can't miss it."

"Do you need to visit there soon, Sarah?" Thierry asked.

I placed a hand over my empty stomach. "I am getting a bit hungry. I think I'll check it out after we're finished here."

He shook his head. "I'm sorry. I keep forgetting that you should drink something every day to keep up your strength."

"Luckily, I don't forget. I have a nice little built-in reminder when random necks start to look appetizing to me."

Yes, vampires and blood. One of the myths that *was* very true, no matter how much I wished I could have a normal diet. The need for blood was like a dull ache inside me, a lot like hunger pains, a craving for food when you were otherwise on a diet, but . . . different. It was best to pay very close attention to those pains and do what you could to satisfy them. If they were ignored for too long, then . . . well, it would become increasingly difficult to be around humans.

He turned back to Victoria. "So, this . . . Madeline. Do you know where she is now? Does she stay in touch with you?"

The little vampire shook her head. "I haven't seen her in more than fifty years. I don't even know if she's still alive."

"You parted ways?"

"I ran away from her. She was a kook. Completely insane. She sired me—even though it works for me, she didn't do it with a clear head. She'd lost three children and she wanted a child who'd never age, never die. She treated me like a china doll, dressing me up and showing me off to her friends."

"You didn't like that?" I asked. "I mean, you seem to like to dress up."

Victoria looked at me sharply. "Do you think I do this for fun, puppy?"

I wasn't thrilled with the nickname she'd chosen for me. "You don't?"

"The Little Miss Platinum Vegas pageant is the top pageant in the country. It has a ten-thousand-dollar grand prize. This is how I make my living. It's not like I have a whole lot of options. Not many Wall Street brokerages want to hire a six-year-old. No, instead I strut my stuff and sing my songs and I have a fifty percent success rate with being named Ultimate Grand Supreme. Other contestants shrivel with fear and awe when they see the name Victoria Corday on the contestant list."

"We have so many sashes and trophies, we have no idea what to do with them all," Charles said proudly.

"Congrats." My stomach rumbled. I was getting hungrier by the minute.

"You can't continue on in this vein, Victoria," Thierry said bluntly.

"No pun intended," I added.

She looked distressed. "Are you telling me I can't compete in pageants anymore?"

"That is exactly what I'm saying. I know it's difficult, but you must be able to see how dangerous it is. If a hunter got wind of what you're doing—and if they assumed that other children around you are also vampires—"

"It would be a massacre," Charles finished, stunned by this possibility as if he'd never considered it before.

The glass in Victoria's hand shattered when she squeezed it too hard, betraying her nerves. "So what am I supposed to do? How is a hundred-and-two-year-old vampire who looks like a little kid supposed to support herself?" She paced to the window and stared at the view outside before turning to look at us, her expression already brightening. "Well . . . I guess I could go to Hollywood and become an actress."

Thierry crossed his arms gingerly over his injured chest. "Excuse me?"

She beamed, clearly pleased by her new idea. "Kids can't act worth crap. I could be the ultimate child actor. I'd take direction well, deliver my lines perfectly. I could win an Oscar! I'd considered it before, but—"

"But you don't age," I reminded her. "So they'd probably figure out there's a problem in a few years."

She swore under her breath and glared at me.
"You're annoying, puppy."

"Sorry. Just telling it like it is." Was I supposed to be
the good cop or the bad cop? At the moment, I was the
tired and hungry cop.

Victoria looked at Thierry. "You're a master vampire—one who works for the Ring."

"Yes."

"And you're engaged to this fledgling?"

"I am."

"I find that difficult to understand. She seems dumb
as a rock to me. Why would you bother with someone
like her?"

I pressed my lips together. I wasn't sure how pointing out the obvious about her potential acting career
made me dumber than anyone else. "Well, forgive me
for trying to be helpful."

"Why would I bother with someone like her?" Thierry repeated, without an ounce of friendliness in his
tone directed at the girl. "I'll have you know that Sarah
is the most genuine woman I've ever met in my entire
existence—and trust me when I say that's a very long
time. She is warm, funny, caring; beautiful both inside
and out. That you don't see this as clearly as I do is
entirely your loss." He was silent for a moment as his
words settled over everyone present. "I think we're
done here for now. If I have more questions, I'll contact
you. Please leave."

Victoria placed her hands on her hips and pouted. "I
want to compete tonight. One last show. That's it."

"That's not a good idea."

"I'm not asking your permission, sourpuss. I'm
doing it. It will be my swan song. If you feel like you

need to call in an enforcer because of that, you can feel free to do so. You can also feel free to kiss my sequined butt. Come on, Charles. We're out of here."

She stalked to the door with her assistant right behind her. Charles looked over his shoulder. "Sorry for stabbing you earlier, Thierry. It's been a pleasure meeting you both."

They left.

Thierry finally looked at me to see I was staring at him.

"Warm, funny, caring, and beautiful?" My heart had swelled with every compliment he paid me in front of the nasty little vampire.

He nodded. "Did I forget anything?"

"Nothing comes to mind." I smiled as I drew closer to him on the sofa. "You know, if you hadn't just barely escaped death, I would be crawling onto your lap right now."

"Promises, promises," he whispered against my lips just before I kissed him. The kiss deepened quickly, but I was careful not to jostle him too much. I knew the wound would still hurt him for another hour or two as it healed. After a moment, he groaned. "Sarah . . . there's a problem. . . ."

As I pulled back from him, I drew in a sharp breath when I saw that his eyes had darkened from gray to black. Black eyes signified that a vampire was hungry to the point of losing reason. Thierry was injured and his body instinctively wanted blood to help speed along his recovery.

At this moment, his body wanted *my* blood.

As a master vampire, Thierry didn't need to drink blood regularly to survive. In fact, he really shouldn't drink blood at all anymore if he could help it, since he was a bit of an alcoholic when it came to the red stuff. When he got started, it was very difficult for him to stop. It was like a darkness descended over him and changed him into somebody else: somebody scary as hell. I'd experienced this up close and personal a couple of times when he'd drunk my blood and nearly lost his mind completely.

He'd worked very hard on his control since I'd first met him, but it was still shaky. Better for me to be safe than sorry. Or dead. Death-by-fiancé would be a very bad way to go.

"What should I do?" I asked tentatively.

He swept my hair back and traced his fingertips along my jugular before sliding the strap of my dress off my shoulder to bare it, his gaze locked on the pulse at my throat. "I suggest you leave. Now. Before I can't control myself any longer."

My breath caught. "Will you be all right?"

"I will. But I won't be all right if you stay here for much longer. My head feels cloudy and . . . you smell so good, Sarah." His eyes moved to mine and I could see the dark hunger there. "I'll need at least an hour to recover before you can return . . . before you're safe this close to me again."

A shiver went through me. It was a strange dichotomy when Thierry got hungry. While I knew that it was dangerous and I was putting myself at risk the longer I stayed near him, the way he looked at me was just so . . . exciting. So primal. Like he wanted to devour me. Which, really, wasn't far from the truth.

It was a moth-and-flame thing. Thierry was the fire and I was the hapless insect that wanted to feel a little heat. I just didn't want to get completely incinerated in the process.

He slid his hand over my bare shoulder and curled his other hand around to the small of my back and pulled me closer to him so his lips could brush against my throat and up to my ear.

"Why are you still here?" he asked, his voice raspy. "Go while you still can. I'll be better soon, I promise."

"Okay." I stroked the dark hair off his forehead, desire and concern teeter-tottering inside me the longer I stayed on this particular playground.

Then I struggled to escape from his tightening grip. It was a halfhearted struggle at best. Hungry Thierry was extremely appealing to me, despite what I already knew he was capable of in this state.

"I'll be back soon." I forced myself not to look over my shoulder at him. I grabbed my purse and went to the door, let myself out, and moved down the hallway. I leaned against the wall as I waited for the elevator to arrive and tried to breathe normally.

The moth had escaped the flame once again. But she'd be back after a quick bite.

Chapter 4

Blood Bath & Beyond was a vampire-lover's paradise. The three-level store was laid out like a wax museum with Madame Tussauds–like statues of every famous vampire and vampire hunter you could think of, from Dracula to Edward Cullen; Lestat to the Count from *Sesame Street*; Buffy to Van Helsing. They were set up so customers could have their pictures taken with them as they browsed the ten thousand square feet of retail space.

There were T-shirts of all sizes and colors sporting various vampire movie-poster or book-cover images; DVDs of past movies and TV shows; Goth jewelry; joke jewelry with huge silver crosses; blatantly fake fangs and legitimate-looking porcelain ones that could be cemented onto normal teeth if someone was so inclined.

The carpet throughout the store was red and black. The red part looked like spilled blood. The walls were red and plastered with huge movie posters. Realistic-looking bats hung from the ceiling, some automated so they swooped overhead, low enough to make me want to duck when they catapulted toward my head. The scary swell of organ music filled my ears as I browsed the shop, feeling equal parts stunned and amused by everything I saw.

However, there was no indication that this was anything but a tourist trap. There was even a flank of six vampire-themed slot machines at the front of the store near the cash registers. I slid a quarter into the first one I passed and pulled the handle. Two bats and a wooden stake came up. No jackpot for me today.

I ventured farther into the store. Charles had said this was the go-to place for a little vampiric sustenance, but now that I was here, I wasn't sure who to talk to about that. The three employees I'd seen so far—one dressed as Elvira with enough cleavage to merit an R rating, and the other two generic Draculas—were busy with other customers.

Finally, I spotted someone who might be helpful. He had a feather duster in hand and was cleaning a wax statue of David from *The Lost Boys*. Quite honestly, Kiefer had never looked so good as when he'd done that movie. The platinum blond mullet totally suited him.

"Excuse me," I said.

His shoulders tensed and he glanced at me. He had red hair, freckles, and a college-guy air about him. I'd guess his age at about twenty-four. "Hi there."

"Hi. Can you help me?"

He turned to face me and I saw that he was wearing a T-shirt that read: "I Bite on the First Date."

"Of course. Are you looking for something specific?"

"Yes." I smiled at him enough to show my sharper-than-normal teeth.

He cocked his head a little. "Are those our new porcelain fangs?"

"No."

"They're real?"

I hesitated only a moment before I answered. "They are."

"They look good. Very petite. I'm sure you fit in just fine out in the real world, don't you?"

"I try my best. So I'm asking again . . . can you help me?" I refrained from giving him an obvious "get my meaning?" wink.

"Come with me." He walked away without another word. I followed him, feeling wary, but my hunger pressed me onward. It was getting worse with every passing minute and giving me a headache and stomach cramps that made it hard to think straight.

"What's your name?" I asked as I followed him.

"Vladimir." He grinned over his shoulder at me and I noticed that he had very natural-looking fangs, too, which helped ease my mind a little. "Vladimir Nosferatu."

I stared at him. "You have got to be kidding me."

"That's just my stage name. I have a magic show at a little club four blocks from here called Club Noir. Real name's Josh Sanders. And you are?"

"Sarah Dearly."

"Nice to meet you, Sarah. Glad you found Blood Bath and Beyond. We're here to serve."

We'd reached the very back of the store on the main level and passed through a red beaded curtain into a small circular room. I eyed the unusual merchandise back here, all upright and leaning against the wall.

"You sell coffins?" I asked with surprise.

"Yup." He glanced around. "Five thousand dollars for this one." He touched a mahogany coffin with a rose carved into the lid. He opened it up to show me the padded red satin lining. "It's very comfortable if you're not too claustrophobic. This one has a lock on the inside, an MP3 stereo system built into the lid, and a recharge jack for your cell phone."

"Fancy."

"It is. But this is the one I think you're looking for." He stood in front of a very large coffin, shiny black, with a cross set into the lid that looked like it was made from mother-of-pearl. Crosses didn't actually bother vampires at all. Since we weren't necessarily evil or fearful of the Great Almighty, or, for that matter, possessed by a demon, that myth-buster was just common sense.

"Maybe you didn't understand me properly." I tried to find some patience, but my tank was nearly empty. "I'm not looking for anything like this—cool though it is. Maybe I'm in the wrong place. Somebody told me I should come here, that you might be able to help me." I eyed him, trying to judge whether I was making a mistake. It wouldn't be the first time. "Maybe I should leave."

"Trust me, Sarah. You want this. I know you do."

I opened my mouth to argue, but then turned to look at the coffin again. He slid his hand around the side of it and flicked a switch, then gestured for me to open the lid. I finally reached forward and grasped the side of it. I noticed a sign taped to the coffin that read NOT FOR SALE.

I opened it up to find that it wasn't a coffin after all. It was a door.

"After you," Josh said with a wave of his hand. "For new customers, the first drink is on the house."

Charles had been absolutely right. Blood Bath & Beyond was a very large and impressive front for a small Vegas blood bank—kind of a speakeasy for fanged citizens. I'd been in my share of vampire night-clubs before, most of which had innocent fronts to throw off any curious hunters, like a used bookstore or a tanning salon. This one wasn't a nightclub, though; it was more like a café. Brightly lit, small, maybe six hundred square feet in total, and with a counter rather than a bar. Padded stools. Tables with brightly colored tablecloths. A mural painted on the far wall of the Vegas skyline on a bright and sunny day.

In a nightclub you could get alcoholic beverages along with your blood. Here you could get coffee. There was a familiar logo on the sign behind the counter.

Along with being a blood bank, this was a Starbucks franchise.

I honestly couldn't think of anything better than that.

There were a half dozen other vampires in here, reading newspapers and magazines as they casually sipped on their drinks. A couple of them also had cookies or muffins, marking them as solid-food eaters. I glared at them with envy. Sometimes I just missed the act of chewing. I'd done a liquid protein diet in my teens and felt the same thing then. But that had only been for a week. This was forever.

"Are you in Vegas for a vacation?" Josh asked.

"Business trip with my fiancé."

"Where you staying?"

"The Bellagio. We arrived yesterday." My gaze swept the area. "Have you owned this place long?"

He raised an eyebrow. "How did you know I'm the owner?"

I grinned. "I didn't, but you just told me."

"Tricky girl." He snorted. "Yeah, I've been in business a little over a year. It's going pretty well. There's a lot of competition here on the Strip. My money mostly comes from the store out front, of course, but I've always tried to have a safe place for vamps to come to. Just doing my part to keep humans safe from us."

I must have looked at him funny because he continued.

"If there weren't places like this in every city, then where would you go for your blood?" He shrugged.

My stomach grumbled. It was a good question and one I'd never really given much thought to. If there was nowhere to go where we could humanely get our blood . . . and the hunger swept over us little by little, removing our self-control a fraction at a time . . .

I guess it would be like an animal lover who was stranded on a deserted island. It wouldn't take too many days of starving before he or she started whittling a sharp spear and wandered farther inland to go hunting. Survival instincts are a powerful thing.

"Give Sarah whatever she likes, on the house," Josh said to the barista who stood waiting for my order before he returned his attention to me. "Hopefully you'll come back again while you're in town and spread the word, confidentially, to anyone else you know who might like to stop by."

"Thank you," I said, feeling a swell of gratitude toward him.

"Anytime." He gave me a nod, then walked away.

"So what'll it be?" the girl asked. She was a short,

gum-chewing blonde wearing a Starbucks smock over her street clothes.

I felt utterly gleeful all of a sudden. Coffee and blood. In the same place. This was so awesome. "I'll take a . . . an espresso and . . . a double shot of B-positive, please."

It was my favorite blood type for obvious reasons. I liked to think it helped me to be more positive. It rarely worked, but it wasn't for lack of trying.

She nodded. "Coming right up."

I moved to the far end of the counter to pick up my order. I didn't bother to get a seat first before I tipped back the small plastic cup of blood right where I stood and swallowed it down.

Sounds gross, I know. But it really wasn't.

For a vampire, drinking blood when you were extraordinarily hungry was sort of like drinking a cold bottle of water after wandering through the Sahara desert in the heat of high noon. It was the best thing in the world. It didn't even taste like what you might think, coppery and thick and warm. Because . . . yuck.

No, blood to a vampire's palate was mouthwateringly delicious, essential, energy giving, quenching, hunger abating, and a full and total relief.

Blood was necessary for me to keep on living now that I was different from human. Fighting that fact never led directly to a happy ending.

I immediately felt my hunger cramps subside, my headache ease. We didn't really need that much of it to make a difference. The human body held five quarts of blood. That would be impossible to drink all at once, so total exsanguination was never caused by a solo vampire in one fell swoop. Most humans who were unfortunate enough to become the victims of a vampire, like those of the serial killer here in Vegas, might die *after* they'd been fed upon—two gaping fang wounds in their neck didn't just heal up automatically, which meant they'd continue to bleed out.

It was possible for an older vampire to enchant his or her prey during the feeding to make it more pleasant or to make them forget the act, but if they didn't or couldn't, the humans might be so afraid that they'd have a heart attack. But a true draining like in horror movies was very rare. It would be like drinking a keg of beer all at once. Like a boa constrictor trying to swallow a small goat. Not pretty.

Which made me wonder about the local vampire attacks. I didn't know if the bodies had been drained or if they were just dead bodies that happened to have fang marks on their necks. I had to admit, I was curious.

Humans didn't have to be fully drained to die from blood loss. Losing more than forty or fifty percent of their total blood supply could do the trick if they weren't very strong. Still a lot to consume, but not quite as impossible.

Yes, I'd been doing my homework lately. I found the best way to deal with what I'd become was to find out absolutely everything I could about it. Thierry was helpful in filling in some of the blanks, but there was still a lot for me to learn.

I glanced around at the other people in the blood bank with me as if they were a lineup of suspects. Any one of them could have done it. However, a vampire who wanted to go directly to the human source for a meal likely wouldn't bother coming to a place like this. Wouldn't want to spoil his or her appetite.

A moment later, the coffin-shaped door swung open again and a familiar person walked though. It was Bernard. He scanned the café, his gaze coming to rest on me, and then his eyes widened a little as if he was surprised to see me here.

A smile stretched his cheeks as he approached me. "Sarah, it's good to see you again."

"You too." I felt a little awkward after witnessing the bitter end of his argument last night with Thierry, but that was no reason for me not to be polite.

"I'm glad you found this place. I was going to send word to you today that this was a reputable location."

"I got the tip from someone an hour ago." I sipped my espresso, which was rapidly cooling off.

"Is Thierry here?" He glanced around the small café.

"No. He's back at the hotel."

"Will you be here long? I'd like to speak to you for a minute."

I watched him a bit warily. "I'll be here for a little longer."

He nodded, then went to the counter to order his drink. He returned a couple minutes later to find me at a table in the corner. I eyed a discarded copy of the newspaper with today's date on it. There was no mention made on the front page about the murders, nor in the first few pages I flipped through.

He sat down across from me on a padded black leather chair. He also had two cups, one with what looked like a regular brewed coffee, and the other that had been filled with blood but was now empty.

"Laura raved about you last night," he said. "She likes you a lot."

beth and Jane Austen—the version without the zombies."

"Yes." He smiled wistfully. "Laura loves to read Jane Austen as well as modern-day historical romances, so I don't like to tell her that it wasn't all parties and courting, dukes and duchesses. For those not part of the upper crust of society, it was a very bleak and miserable time."

"Glad I missed it. I much prefer cell phones and flush toilets. So these hunters that stole from vampires— what happened to them?"

"Thierry and I decided to show them that they couldn't walk over us anymore." He shook his head. "Funny, we were so similar back then—so different than now. That he has agreed to take over my job as consultant amazes me. He never struck me as someone who was interested in the welfare and safety of others."

I gave him a sour look at the passive-aggressive insult toward Thierry. "He says they made him an offer he couldn't refuse."

He cocked his head. "I wonder what it was. Money?"

"I doubt it." Thierry would never take this job for a basic paycheck. That much I knew for sure.

"I know that he has assets tucked away in many hidden places—apart from the diamonds. Even if on paper he appears bankrupt, there is a great deal of money he has stored away for a rainy day. Does that make you happy, Sarah?"

I shifted in my seat and tried to hold back my glare at what he was implying. "Do you think I'm a gold digger?"

"Are you?"

"No. Money's nice, but I know it doesn't buy happiness. Thierry's money isn't the reason I'm with him. I'm with him because I love him."

"That's good to hear. As much as I have my differences with him, I don't like to think that he'd let himself be taken in by someone who doesn't really care about him."

"What did you do to the hunters?" I asked, feeling a bit of anxiety creep in at the sides. I wanted to keep this conversation on track so it could be over with quickly. Out of the corner of my eye I saw the coffin open up, and two new people entered and headed to the counter. "I'm hoping it was a strict talking down to, explaining the situation and telling them to stop being stake-flinging jerks."

Bernard took a sip of his coffee before putting the cup down on the table between us. "We planned to kidnap the leader so we could talk to him and rationally explain the situation, but it didn't turn out that way. He fought us, his friends joined in, blood was spilled. And Thierry . . ." He trailed off.

I watched him tensely. "Thierry what?"

His gaze flicked to mine. "I'm sure you know by now that he has difficulties with his thirst."

"He's a master vampire. I heard you all have issues in that department."

"That's not true." He nodded at his empty glass. "As you can see, I can drink whenever I like—although I don't need it nearly as much as a fledgling would."

I glanced around the café. Nobody seemed particularly interested in listening in on our conversation at the moment. The gathered vampires were all minding their own business, which was a good thing. "So the hunters were bleeding and you're saying that Thierry lost control of himself because of that." I said it simply. I could put two and two together and come up with something vaguely close to four.

He nodded. "There were ten hunters in that house and when we were done, none were left alive."

A wave of nausea swept over me at that carnage-filled mental image. "That was a long time ago."

"Yes, it was. And to be quite honest with you, Sarah, I never felt a great deal of guilt over it. They were horrible men who'd done horrible things. That I was partially the cause of their deaths did not keep me awake that night or any night afterward."

I swallowed hard. "And Thierry? How did he feel about it?"

Bernard smiled, but it lacked any trace of humor. "He didn't want to talk about it, but he never showed any regret. I think for the first time in a very long time his thirst had been totally satisfied. I don't know for sure, but I think he might have even enjoyed himself."

I struggled to keep my expression as blank as possible. "You think he enjoyed helping to massacre ten humans trapped in a house with two bloodthirsty vampires?"

He noted my look of disgust and had the grace to look ashamed. "That is a question only he could answer. But it wasn't the cause of our argument last night. After the hunters were dead, we found the stash of diamonds that the hunters had stolen from their previous victims. We hid them away and agreed to meet again in the future to decide what to do with them. We eventually placed them in a safety-deposit box to which we both hold a key. The box can't be opened without both parties present—or, as far as the bank is concerned, their descendants."

I looked at him with disbelief. "So you're telling me that these diamonds are the reason for your argument."

"I asked Thierry to come with me to get the diamonds and to donate them to a good cause rather than let them sit in a box where no one can benefit from them."

My mouth was dry. The last cold sip of the bitter espresso didn't exactly help matters. "I find it hard to believe that Thierry would have a problem with that."

"I guess you don't know him as well as you think you do. He erupted when I even made mention of it. He now denies that anything ever happened with that group of hunters." His tone shifted to one of bemusement. "Although I wonder how many times that happened— that uncontrollable bloodlust—and how many have died horribly because of it."

It was something I rarely thought about, but it did exist in the back of my mind. Thierry had been a vampire for six centuries. How many humans, or even vampires, had come across my fiancé when he was feeling less than his perfectly controlled self?

Or, in other words, just how many people had Thierry killed?

Normally, I didn't like to think about how many women he might have been with over the centuries, but this was disturbing on a whole other level.

I exhaled shakily. "So I guess now is when I ask you why you wanted to tell me this, Bernard. Because none of what you've said changes how I feel about Thierry. Everyone has skeletons in their closet—some just rattle a little louder than others. I forgive him for his past mistakes, even the more unpleasant ones."

He scanned my face with his pale green eyes. "You can accept a man that is so completely different from yourself and expect to have a long and healthy relationship with him?"

"You're with Laura and you two seem to be doing all right."

"I'm a very lucky man."

I forced a smile. "So is Thierry."

He mirrored my expression. "I'll admit, I did follow you here, because I wanted a chance to talk to you alone. I didn't want you to have the wrong impression about me after last night."

"Why do you care what I think?"

"Just the kind of man I am. As a consultant it's my duty to get to know those around me, those who hold influence over others."

Did he think that I had some sort of sway over Thierry's decisions or actions? "You're not a consultant anymore."

"Thierry hasn't signed the papers yet. Once he does, my job is at an end."

That surprised me. I thought this was a done deal. "There are papers?"

He nodded. "He'll have to sign them today or tomorrow. The Ring will be very unhappy if I let them know he hasn't."

I tensed at the unspoken threat. "Wouldn't want to make the Ring unhappy, would we?"

"No, trust me. You definitely wouldn't want to do that." His smile became strained. "Please let Thierry know that they've decided to intervene when it comes to the local murders. I won't be their main representative in this matter any longer."

I pushed the newspaper forward. "You mean the murders that nobody seems to know about?"

He glanced down at the front page. "The police are keeping the details secret so there isn't a lot of fuss made about a potential killer vampire in town. It would make national headlines and cause things to become . . . complicated. The Ring wants to avoid that at all costs."

My heart pounded faster than normal. The Ring seriously freaked me out. "What do you mean they've intervened?"

His knuckles whitened on the arms of his chair. "They've sent an enforcer to investigate."

"An enforcer." I'd only heard the term a couple of times and it already made a shiver of fear race down my spine.

"I told them it wasn't necessary, but they disagreed. He'll be arriving later today."

"So what does that mean?"

"Nothing to you, but it would probably be a good idea if both you and Thierry stay out of his way. Enforcers can be very particular when it comes to their investigations."

I shuddered. "So an enforcer is basically a vampire with a license to kill . . . vampires."

"Exactly."

"Sounds charming."

"I'd tell Thierry myself, but I have the feeling he doesn't want to speak with me again if he can help it."

"I'll tell him. But what about the diamonds you

mentioned? Do you think I can help you with that? Is that why you told me all of this?"

"I'd appreciate it if you tell Thierry that handing over his key to me would do more good than bad in the world."

I stood up and my legs felt shaky. I was dealing with a case of information overload. "I'll think about it."

"Thank you." Bernard stood as well. "Have a good day, Sarah."

I watched as he left the blood bank, leaving through the coffin-shaped door that led back into Blood Bath & Beyond.

I looked over at the listing behind the counter. I really wished they served something a bit more potent than lattes and Frappuccinos.

After everything I'd just heard, another shot of B-positive sure wasn't going to do the trick.

Chapter 5

When I returned to the suite, Thierry had recovered from his black-eyed state and even changed his shirt to an identical but stab-free one. He hadn't buttoned it up, so I could see that his chest wound had healed to become pink scar tissue. In a day or two it would vanish completely. It was one of the perks of being a vampire.

I didn't say much to him, since I was still absorbing everything I'd learned today, but I was relieved that he was feeling better. Laura called after I'd been back only a couple of minutes and I made plans to go shopping with her for the rest of the afternoon.

It would be a good opportunity to think about what Bernard had told me—as well as learn how to spend money like the wife of a wealthy master vampire. It involved a platinum American Express card and sales-girls who fell over themselves to get the commission. If I hadn't been so distracted by tales of diamonds, dead hunters from days of yore, and lethal enforcers, I would have been mightily impressed.

When I finally returned to the suite at six o'clock, Thierry was seated at the large black desk studying the screen of a new laptop computer.

"Watching YouTube?" I asked.

He frowned at me. "YouTube?"

"It's a Web site where you can watch videos of people and animals doing stupid things."

"I'm aware of what YouTube is, Sarah. Actually, I'm researching the woman Victoria told us about to see if I can find any clues pointing to her current whereabouts."

"I was just kidding, anyway. You're not a stupid-pet-tricks kind of guy." I approached the desk slowly. "Any luck?"

"I've found some information, but it all stops around forty years ago. It's very likely she's dead, which is why Victoria hasn't heard from her in so many years."

My heels clicked against the marble floor as I made my way over to the window and pulled back the curtain to look outside. The view of the fountains from the thirty-second floor was absolutely stunning. The suite was gorgeous—I'd never stayed anywhere so luxurious. It was bigger than some of the places I'd lived. Scratch that, the *bathroom* was bigger than some of the places I'd lived.

"Everything all right?" Thierry asked after a stretch of silence. "You're much quieter than normal."

That could have been an observation or a compliment. I wasn't sure which.

I crossed my arms, turned around, and regarded him. "I want to know what you and Bernard were arguing about last night."

He leaned back in his chair and closed the lid of the computer. "It's not important."

"Whatever he said upset you. So that makes it important to me."

"It was a disagreement, that's all."

"What was the disagreement about?"

He watched me carefully. "Why do you suddenly want to know this?"

"Why are you suddenly evading my questions?"

"I didn't realize I was stepping foot onto such dangerous ground when I asked why you were being quiet."

I hissed out a breath. "It's not dangerous ground. No land mines, promise. I just . . . I—I guess I just thought we'd gotten over this."

"Over what?"

"You holding back from me. You keeping things secret." I swallowed past the thick lump in my throat that had been growing ever since I'd left the blood bank earlier.

"Sarah." He drew closer and pulled my hands out from their crossed position and held them in his. "Please don't be angry with me."

"I'm not angry, I'm just . . . ." I sighed. "I don't know. It's more evidence that you've lived more than a dozen lifetimes to my single one."

"Which means what?"

"There's no possible way I could ever wrap my head around everything you've been through. I know a lot of it has been lousy and I get that you want to keep that to yourself. But I want to know more about you, and when there's the opportunity to share . . . I can handle it, Thierry. Even the really bad stuff."

His grip on me tightened. "Who have you been speaking with?"

I chewed my bottom lip. "Who do you think?"

"Bernard." It wasn't a question.

I looked up into his gray eyes. "The one and only."

"What did he tell you our argument was about?" His expression was unreadable. He had his poker face perfectly in place. Maybe he should head down to the tables later and try it out for real.

I inhaled deeply and let it out slowly. "That the both of you massacred a houseful of hunters once upon a time, stole diamonds from them, and put the diamonds in a safe place. Now he wants your key so he can donate them to charity to make the world a happier place and you're being Mr. Anger Mismanagement about everything."

Surprise flickered in his gaze before Thierry finally let go of me and stepped backward. He crossed his arms over his chest. "What a pleasant conversation that must have been."

"It was fairly vivid."

"And what did you think of what he told you?"

I glared at him. "Just be straight with me, Thierry. Is that possible for you? Was what he told me true or not?"

"Did you believe him?"

My glare intensified. "Can't you just answer a question when I ask it of you? God, you're so unbelievably infuriating sometimes."

His lips twitched almost imperceptibly. He sometimes found it amusing when I lost my temper with him. "I apologize."

"Don't apologize. Just answer my question."

He walked to the other side of the suite before turning around to face me. His poker face had slipped just a little and he now wore a pensive expression—as if he was gauging how I'd react to every word he spoke.

"You want to know if it's true that I once helped murder a group of hunters with Bernard and then stole from them." He was silent for a moment, but his gaze didn't waver from mine. "Yes, it's true."

"Oh." My stomach sank. A large part of me had really hoped it had all been a lie.

"I'd like very much to tell you that I've always done the right thing, that I've always tried my best to protect humans from any threat. But that would be a lie. I've killed—and more than just the men Bernard told you about. I've given hunters full reason to try to end my life over the years, and I've simply been lucky enough to avoid them long enough as I sought redemption for the sins of my past."

I drew closer to him. "They were hunters. They weren't nice, innocent people."

His jaw tightened and his gaze had a faraway look to it. "It doesn't matter who they were; I know it was excessive. I knew things had to change. I eventually went about organizing those who would govern the Ring and bring some sort of regulation to vampire behavior so there would be penalties for stepping too far outside the boundaries of acceptable behavior. At the time, I thought it was an excellent idea."

"It *is* an excellent idea."

"Debatable. But when I finally distanced myself from the Ring, I never would have guessed a hundred years later I'd be working with them again."

"And yet here we are."

"*We*," he repeated.

My hands were on my hips. "What?"

He searched my face. "You said 'here *we* are.' Is it still we?"

I frowned. "Do you think that just because I find out without any doubt that you're a mass murderer, I'm calling off our engagement? I knew you weren't an angel from the very beginning, Thierry."

He managed a genuine smile at that. "I'm definitely not that."

I moved closer so I stood right in front of him and pressed my hands up against his chest. "If there's enough good in someone, it helps to balance the bad. And there's heaps of good in you. I know that without any doubt. But can you please, *please* do me a favor?"

He was quiet for a moment. "What?"

"Be straight with me. Tell me what's going on. Don't think that just because it's something bad that I won't be able to handle it. Because I *can* handle it. And when you decide to threaten an old buddy's life in public because he wants to get his hands on some stolen gems . . ." I frowned. "What's the deal with the diamonds, anyway? Why won't you get rid of them?"

"Because they're cursed," he said simply. "And they need to stay right where they are or any human who touches them again will die a horrible death—something a couple of those hunters found out the hard way when they stole them from their original victims. Bernard doesn't understand that. He only understands cold, hard currency. By opening that Pandora's box he'd be putting the lives of many people at risk."

I just stared at him. "Well, that makes perfect sense to me. Death curses are definitely something to avoid at all costs."

His brows drew together. "No one must ever find those diamonds again. And Bernard and I are the only ones who know where they are."

I blew out a long breath. "Don't you feel much better about getting all of this off your chest?"

He laughed then, low in his throat. "So much."

"I'm here to help. And, quite honestly, the 'greedy jerk' accusation bothered me more than the 'death to nasty hunters' one."

"It was two centuries ago. The past is best left in the past."

"Agreed." I tried to put my thoughts in order again. That had been a lot to take in all at once, but I did feel a bit better, all things considered. "Bernard wanted me to tell you something. . . . Maybe I should have said it after I came back from the blood bank earlier, but I was mad at you."

He raised an eyebrow. "You're not mad any longer?"

I shrugged. "It's still simmering, but I'm getting over it."

"What did he want you to tell me?"

"The Ring has sent an enforcer to investigate the murders here. He says if we just steer clear of him, we shouldn't have a problem."

His expression turned grim again. "When does this enforcer arrive?"

"Bernard said today. He might already be here." I looked around nervously as if the Ring's assassin might be hiding under the king-sized bed in the other room.

"For once I'll have to agree with Bernard. We'll avoid the enforcer to the best of our ability. I'd rather you never have to meet one face-to-face. They look at everyone with suspicion and the only friend they trust is the silver stake the Ring assigns them when they sign on to the job. Quite frankly, they make me look like the life of the party."

I raised my eyebrows. "Wow. Scary."

He smiled. "Since we weren't in Vegas when the murders began, at least we won't be included on the list of potential suspects."

My stomach twisted into knots again. "A bright side. Good stuff."

"So, if we can leave any misunderstandings behind us, I'd like to take you out for dinner—or, rather, drinks. Then we're going to have to attend the Little Miss Platinum Vegas pageant to make sure Ms. Corday behaves herself."

"And then?"

"And then I want to have another talk with her about not doing any more of these pageants in the future. She shouldn't even be doing this one. Once she learns there is an enforcer in the general vicinity, I feel she will be much more receptive to my suggestion tonight."

"Sounds like a plan." I glanced off in the direction of the closet, where I'd neatly hung everything I'd hastily thrown into my suitcase yesterday. "So should I wear something frilly or sexy for such an occasion?"

He leaned closer, then hesitated for a second as if he half expected me to pull away from him. When I didn't, he brushed his lips against mine. "I'm very confident that you managed to pack something that is both frilly *and* sexy."

I couldn't help but smile. "You know me so well."

"I think I do."

That made one of us who knew the other extremely

well. But I figured a little progress on that front was better than none at all.

After dinner, we took a walk though the casino on our way to the theater where the pageant was going to be held. A tall man walked toward us, his attention fixed on Thierry. He looked to be in his early fifties. He wore a black leather jacket, black pants, and a gray T-shirt. His dark hair was silver at the temples and cropped short. Dark stubble speckled his jawline.

Thierry stopped walking, and his hand curled around my left wrist to have me do the same.

This could be the enforcer we were supposed to avoid speaking to. Cold fear slithered through me at the thought. The heels I'd chosen to wear tonight were way too high to run in without twisting an ankle.

The man smiled then, an expression I wouldn't have expected an assassin to wear. I didn't see fangs, which also surprised me.

"Good evening, Thierry," he said.

"Duncan. Is there a problem?"

"No problem. What we spoke about earlier is still a work in progress."

Thierry's gray eyes scanned the casino floor. "Is there a reason you're telling me this in public? You could have called me with any updates."

Duncan's smile held. "I saw you and thought I'd simply speak to you personally. Hope that isn't a problem for you."

"No, it's fine."

The man's gaze moved to me. "And who is this lovely lady?"

Thierry's grip on my wrist grew tighter. It was the

only way I could tell that he was anything but calm and collected. "Sarah, this is Duncan Keller, a local hunter."

My right hand, which I'd begun to stretch out for a handshake, fell slackly back to my side as my eyes bugged. "Do you mean a hunter that likes to shoot innocent little furry animals and call it a sport? I'm hoping?"

Duncan laughed and the sharp staccato sound made me tense. It reminded me of a gunshot. "Some are a bit furry. But, no, I think you know what I really hunt."

He was a vampire hunter, right here in the center of the Bellagio casino floor. And he was speaking with two vampires as if he and Thierry were old friends.

"Thierry," I said under my breath. "What is this?"

He looked at me. "Nothing to concern yourself with. Duncan has been one of my paid informants in the past. He means us no harm."

"It's true," Duncan replied. "Money talks."

"So you're not a real hunter?" I asked.

"Oh, I'm as real as it gets, sweetheart." His gaze raked me in a predatory manner that made me regret the short, tight dress I'd chosen to wear tonight. "But I can be bought for the right price whether or not you have fangs."

"This is not a discussion to have in such a public place," Thierry said calmly, although his tight grip on my wrist might succeed in separating my hand from the rest of my arm if this conversation went on for much longer.

"I totally agree," I managed.

"Anyway—" Duncan slicked a hand through his

salt-and-pepper hair. "I have nothing yet to report, Thierry. But I'm on it. You can expect a genuine result very soon."

"Glad to hear it."

"Thierry, Sarah." He nodded toward each of us. "Have a lovely evening."

He walked away, leaving us standing there, surrounded by hundreds of gamblers at roulette and blackjack tables.

I looked at Thierry. "What was that all about?"

His grip on me finally loosened. "I'm sorry that he was so bold to approach us like that with no warning. I took the liberty of contacting him earlier today to see if he could be of any assistance in trying to find the local serial killer. He has some important connections both in the hunter and the vampire communities and he has been a valuable contact in the past."

I glanced uneasily in the direction in which Duncan had departed. "Seems like a real sweet guy."

"He's an opportunistic bastard with a true love of the hunt. But sometimes qualities like that can be an asset." Thierry exhaled slowly. "Let's try our best to forget about him and go to the show."

I nodded. "Consider him forgotten."

I really did wish it were that simple, but Duncan's introduction to yours truly had definitely left me with a bad taste in my mouth.

Mercenary hunters and beauty pageants starring tiny vampires who didn't take direction well. It didn't sound like a very good combination to me at all.

Victoria easily won the title of Ultimate Grand Supreme in the Little Miss Platinum Vegas pageant and the ten-thousand-dollar prize. I couldn't say I was that shocked by the outcome. She displayed a maturity and level of talent that far surpassed what any of the other kids possessed. Since she wasn't actually a kid, this wasn't all that surprising.

She sang; she danced; she charmed the judges with her innocent yet eloquent answers to their standard beauty-pageant questions.

"How do you think we can all help to achieve world peace?" a judge had asked.

"By loving each other," she chirped in reply. "And singing songs!"

"Who is the most important person in your life?"

"My daddy," her little voice sang out proudly. "And my teddy bear. His name's Gummi-Boo!"

The audience aahed at her answers as if they were the most adorable thing ever. I just rolled my eyes.

At the end, she wore her sparkling sash proudly as she waved and took her victory walk across the stage while the audience cheered for her and her fellow contestants looked on with envy.

There was a reception afterward outside on the *Terrazza di Sogno,* a terrace used for special events and weddings with a balcony flanked by two staircases that looked out over *Lago di Como*—the man-made lake out front that held the dancing fountains—and Thierry and I milled about, glasses of red wine in hand, as we waited for the chance to speak with the tiny, glowing champion, who looked as if she really wanted a cigarette.

"It would have been better for her not to place at all, let alone win," Thierry said, his gaze fixed on her as she posed for photos. "She's drawn too much attention to herself."

"Like she said before, it's her swan song."

"I hope it is. I worry that her choosing to ignore my warnings will come back to haunt her. With the enforcer in town—" He stopped talking and swore under his breath.

The uncharacteristic reaction surprised me. "What is it?"

"The man over there, the one with the pale blond hair and long black jacket. Do you see him?"

I followed the direction of his gaze to see the man he referred to steadily making his way down the left side of the staircase to the main terrace. He was hard to miss. He was pale—hair, eyes, and skin. He wore a long black coat. He was handsome, but not in a perfect male-model way. More like in a good-looking grim reaper way.

"I see him. Who is he?"

"His name is Markus Reed. He was an acquaintance of mine, a good man who worked in law enforcement before he was sired a hundred years ago. He had a wife whom he adored, and three children, all of whom were murdered by hunters in their attempt to get to him. That tragedy changed him, hardened him, and he was never the same afterward."

My stomach twisted with everything he said. "How horrible."

"It was. But it turned Markus into the perfect candidate for the Ring to recruit to become their lead enforcer, a position he's held for well over fifty years now. When it came time for his contract to expire, I was told he signed on for another fifty-year commitment. He has nothing else to fill his life other than his work."

"*He's* the enforcer," I said quietly, tearing my gaze

away from the man now standing on the opposite side of the terrace.

"He is."

"Why is he at the after-party for the Little Miss Platinum Vegas pageant?"

"I have no idea."

"Do you think Victoria's in any danger?"

Thierry cast a glance in the little girl's direction. "No. A low-level case like Ms. Corday's would hold no interest for Markus."

"Good to know."

I glanced in the enforcer's direction again and managed to lock eyes with him for a moment before I looked away, feeling suddenly chilled.

"Perhaps we should return later." Thierry directed me up the right-hand side of the staircase to the balcony, which had doors leading back into the hotel. There weren't as many people up here; most were on the main terrace with the contestants and their parents or guardians.

Bernard stood at the opposite end of the large balcony, gazing up at the starry sky. Thierry and I exchanged a wary glance.

"Is Bernard here checking up on your progress with Victoria?" I whispered.

"I wouldn't be surprised."

"Can he make your life difficult with the Ring now that Mr. Enforcer is on the scene?"

Thierry's lips thinned, his attention fixed on the other man, who currently stood ten feet away from us. "He can make things unpleasant if he chooses to, but that's all. What's done is done. I now work for the Ring and I can't renege after I sign the papers."

"Why haven't you signed them yet?"

"I don't want to seem too eager to do what they want me to do. But I can't delay much longer before there will be no turning back."

"So you can still walk away from this if you want to?" The thought made me hopeful that there were alternate endings to this Choose Your Own Adventure novel. If Thierry was that interested in this job, I figured he already would have signed the next fifty years of his life away. "You don't have to do this job at all if you really don't want to."

He turned to face me to show his expression was tense, his forehead furrowed. "I can't walk away from this. It's much more complicated than that."

I shook my head, confused. "But why do you—?"

"Thierry . . . Sarah . . ." Bernard approached us. "Here you are."

"Here we are," Thierry agreed thinly. "And where is your lovely wife?"

"She went up to our room for a while after spilling a glass of red wine on her white skirt, but will be joining me shortly for drinks once she changes. Despite our differences, Thierry, we'd be happy for the company."

Thierry's eyes narrowed. "So kind of you, but I think we'll pass. Unless you feel differently, Sarah?"

"No, passing is a good idea. So, *so* tired." I stretched my arms in a mock yawn. "Got to get my eight solid hours a night or I get seriously cranky."

Bernard smiled, but it looked forced. "Sarah and I ran across each other at a local blood bank earlier today."

"Yes," Thierry said without a sliver of affability. "She told me."

"And did she also tell you what we spoke about?"

"She did." His jaw tensed. "And I would appreciate that any further conversations of that nature be held in my presence."

"I had the impression that you didn't wish to be around me anymore," Bernard said.

"And yet here you are standing directly in front me."

I curled my arm tightly around Thierry's as if to remind him not to let this jerk get to him again. For some reason, Bernard was able to push Thierry's buttons like nothing I'd ever witnessed before.

Bernard's smile shifted into something much less pleasant. "It sickens me to see what you've become, Thierry. I once looked up to you as a leader, a rebel, a man who would push forward and make things happen no matter how difficult it might be. It's different now. That you would allow yourself to become a pawn for the Ring—"

"A position that you've held for five decades."

Bernard gave a small shrug. "Some are born to be pawns. Some are born to be kings. I'm now free to be whichever I choose. And I mean to get my hands on those diamonds no matter what I must do to facilitate that. I don't think you doubt the lengths to which I will go."

Thierry's arm felt like solid marble. "I'm finished with this subject, Bernard. And I'm finished with you."

"Is that another threat?"

"Take it however you wish."

Bernard glared at him. "You'll regret this, Thierry. You have no idea how much."

"Come on, Thierry, let's go back to our suite," I urged, feeling more and more uncomfortable with this standoff the longer it went on. "We'll catch up with Victoria tomorrow morning."

"That's an excellent idea. *Bonne nuit*, Bernard." Thierry and I turned away from Bernard and headed toward the entrance back into the hotel. Out of the corner of my eye, I saw a familiar face emerge onto the balcony and a small gasp escaped my throat.

"Thierry," I whispered. "It's the vampire hunter."

It was Duncan, the man we'd seen earlier in the casino: Thierry's informant. He moved past the gathered pageant organizers, contestants, parents, and others who'd stayed for the after-party of photo ops, drinks, and food. He glanced at us, but kept walking without saying a word. There was a small smile on his lips as he nodded in Thierry's direction, before fixing his full attention on Bernard, who stood at the railing of the balcony overlooking the crowded terrace below.

Bernard watched his approach cautiously, a glass of red wine held tightly in his right hand.

"Bernard DuShaw?" Duncan asked.

"Yes, that's my name. What do you want?"

Duncan reached into the inside of his jacket, pulled out a sharp wooden stake, and sank it into Bernard's chest. Bernard dropped his glass of wine and it shattered the moment it hit the floor. He stared down at the stake sticking out of his heart, his pale green eyes wide with pain and shock.

He turned toward us, gasping for breath. "Thierry—"

And then he disintegrated right before our eyes as

vampires over a century old do. Their bodies made like a water balloon that had just hit the ground. *Splat*. All that was left of Bernard was a pool of black slime that spread like thick blood on the floor next to his broken wineglass, the black and red liquids mixing together to form a gory puddle.

Shock rocketed through me. I couldn't believe what had just happened in a matter of seconds. Bernard was dead—killed by a vampire hunter. And at least a dozen humans had witnessed it firsthand.

A dozen humans who all began to scream in terror at the exact same time.

Chapter 6

Immortality sounded really good on paper, but it was also a bit of a lie. Vampires had many enemies that could snatch that promise of eternal life right out from under our noses. While we were stronger than humans, we were far from invincible—what just happened was proof positive of that.

Bernard was dead. Nothing remained of him but a stain and a memory.

A memory of Thierry threatening his life last night.

A memory of Thierry speaking to his murderer only three hours ago.

Thierry, who gripped me by my arm and directed me away from what remained of Bernard and out of the Little Miss Platinum Vegas after party. We took the elevator up to our floor in stunned silence. When we arrived and hurried down the hallway to our suite, he slid the key card into the door and swung it open.

"Thierry, what are we doing?" My voice shook. "Did that really happen?"

He pressed his hand against the small of my back and guided me into the room. "Yes, it happened. Bernard is dead. And we need to leave immediately."

"Why are we leaving?"

"Because it's not safe for you to be here right now." His voice was as strained as his expression.

"For *me* to be here? What are you talking about?" I grabbed my suitcase and began to throw my clothes into it without bothering to fold anything first. "We need to find Laura. We need to—"

I couldn't finish the sentence. I'd never before told anyone that her husband had been murdered. They'd been so happy together and now it was over. I looked at Thierry, imagining the horror of someone telling me that he was gone, killed by a hunter, and that I'd never see him again.

Thierry came to stand in front of me and he took hold of my upper arms. "It's going to be all right."

"Is it?"

"Yes, I promise you that. I'm putting you on a flight back to Toronto and then I'll deal with the aftermath of what's happened here tonight."

"What really happened? I'm still trying to figure that out. He was standing there, talking to us, pushing your angry buttons again like he seems to be able to do. Then suddenly the hunter you were talking to earlier was there and he—he *killed* him. Why would he do that?"

"He's a vampire hunter."

"But . . . right in front of everyone?"

"Vampire hunters are unpredictable, even if we're lulled into thinking otherwise." He gently held my face between his hands. "This is not something that happens every day and there will be harsh ramifications. But first I must make sure that you're safe."

I wanted to argue, but he snapped my suitcase shut and took it in hand. I grabbed my purse and we moved to the door. When Thierry swung it open, someone stood on the other side.

It was the man he'd pointed out to me at the party, the pale one.

The enforcer.

"That was quite a party, wasn't it?" he said. "It ended with a bit of a bang."

"Markus." There was nothing in Thierry's voice to indicate how he felt about finding the Ring's personal assassin blocking our way. As for me, I was about ready to pass out.

"Saw you downstairs, Thierry. I won't take it personally that you chose not to say hello to me."

"I know you're not here to socialize."

"No, I'm not." The enforcer's gaze moved to me. "This must be the infamous Sarah Dearly."

Infamous, huh?

I swallowed, but fixed a pleasant yet neutral expression on my face. "That's my name."

He glanced at the suitcase. "Going somewhere?"

The way he was scanning the suite, my suitcase, and us was more than a little bit intimidating. More than a little bit threatening. Even I couldn't find a suitable, lighthearted quip to help balance things out.

"I had nothing to do with this, Markus," Thierry said evenly. "You must realize that."

Markus cocked his head. "Nothing to do with what? With the murder of Bernard DuShaw not ten minutes ago? A man with whom you've had a history of unpleasantness and shared violence? A man whom you were overheard threatening only last night? No, Thierry, I'd say I'm not entirely convinced of your innocence in this unfortunate matter."

"You've got to be kidding me," I managed, my heart thudding in my chest. "He was killed by a *hunter*, not by Thierry."

"A hunter that Thierry is very familiar with and could easily have hired for this purpose. I was sent to this city to investigate the other local killings, but now it's also my duty to take care of this new one as well."

Thierry remained silent for a very long, tense moment. I wanted him to immediately jump to his defense, to argue with this jerk about how he couldn't have had anything to do with Bernard's death.

"So I am to be detained while you investigate?" he asked.

"Yes. And I will personally appreciate your cooperation in this. I'll have men stationed outside this suite while I look into matters over the next day or two." He shook his head, his expression neutral. "Got to say, though, it's not looking good for you right now."

"Thierry . . . ," I began.

Thierry held up his hand to stop me from saying anything else and turned to look me in my eyes, full on; he'd fixed a blank look on his face so I couldn't read him at all. His talent for that was as frustrating to me as it might have been useful to him right now.

He said nothing to me before glancing again at Duncan. "I do have one request and it's nonnegotiable."

Markus raised his eyebrows. "What's that?"

"I'll remain here without argument while you investigate Bernard's murder, but I insist that Sarah is safely escorted to the airport so she can go back to Toronto. I don't want her to be any part of this."

I felt sick inside with every second that ticked by.

I wanted to wake up and find out this was just a really horrible dream, but I was out of luck. I was wide-awake.

Markus regarded me with a cold, appraising gaze—so cold I could have sworn I felt ice crystals form on my bare arms. "Request granted." He smiled at me, but there was nothing nice about the expression. "Sarah, it was a pleasure to meet you. My men will accompany you to the airport. Your fiancé is smart to give you the opportunity to remove yourself from this situation. It's not going to be a very pleasant couple of days."

I ignored him and instead clutched Thierry's arm. "You can't just send me away and—and then what happens to you?"

Thierry remained silent, but his gaze was fixed on Markus.

"I'm an enforcer," Markus said simply. "I enforce."

Which meant he had full authority to decide for himself if Thierry was guilty of hiring Duncan to kill Bernard in full view of other humans because of a public disagreement they'd had over a stash of diamonds. The motive was clear and the opportunity was there. Thierry looked guilty as sin right now—even I could see that.

If Markus decided that Thierry was guilty, then he was going to kill him with full permission of the Ring.

Thierry touched my face and I tensed. "Please, Sarah, don't argue this. Just go. It will be fine—*I'll* be fine."

I shook my head. "No, you won't. I feel it, Thierry. This is bad."

"If so, then I definitely don't want you here." The cool facade slipped and I could see raw concern slide behind his gray eyes. "Please, Sarah, go back home. Forget about this as much as you can. Do it for me."

I clutched his arm and looked up at him, but then he crushed me against his chest.

"Are you guilty?" I whispered. "Did you do it?"

"No," he replied. "But I've been set up. I'll have to figure out who did it and why."

"How are you supposed to figure that out while sequestered in this suite?"

"I'll find a way." He pulled back from me, then glanced at the men standing by the door, whom I hadn't even noticed until this moment. He nodded at them before returning his gaze to me. "Please try not to worry about me."

One of the men, a big brute with a crew cut and a tattoo on his biceps of a skull and crossbones, took me by my arm. The other one, bald with a thick black mustache, circa 1978, grabbed my suitcase. They directed me out of the room so fast that I didn't have a chance to say another word. I didn't have a chance to kiss Thierry one last time or even to say good-bye.

Stunned and shaken, I sat in the back of a black sedan as Markus's thugs drove me to the airport. They took me to the counter so I could buy a ticket. They accompanied me to security clearance. Then when they were certain they'd done their job, they left me there in the line that moved slowly toward the scanners and the boarding gates beyond.

My head swam with everything that had happened. Bernard had been murdered and it looked as if Thierry had set up the hit.

Despite all evidence to the contrary, I knew he was innocent. But if he couldn't prove that—and how could he prove something like that while he was stuck in a guarded hotel suite?—he was going to meet his own death at the end of Markus's Ring-appointed silver stake.

He wanted me to go back to Toronto so I'd be safe. For me to say good-bye to him and try to put everything out of my mind.

You'd really think he'd know me better than that by now.

I waited five more minutes, making sure that the men didn't return, before I slipped out of the line and exited the airport. I flagged down a cab to take me and my suitcase back to the Strip.

The man I loved—the man I fully planned to marry one day very soon—was in mortal danger. The least I could do was save him.

Chapter 7

Even though Las Vegas was a 24-7 kind of town, I knew I wouldn't get very far tonight in figuring out who framed Thierry for Bernard's murder. Plus, I was worried I'd be spotted by Mr. Enforcer and sent back to Toronto in pieces instead of in coach.

That guy scared the crap out of me. And after some of the things I'd faced since becoming a vampire, I didn't say that lightly.

I needed to find a motel and get an early start tomorrow. Nothing else would happen tonight. Nothing except me reliving Bernard's murder and the look in Thierry's eyes as I was pulled away from him by Markus's men—again and again and again.

It was just after midnight, and I was all alone in Vegas with only a shiny pink, slightly beaten-up suitcase as my companion. Even though I was surrounded by the bright lights of the Vegas Strip and the hum of tourists out living the nightlife, I'd never felt so lost and alone.

I desperately needed to confide in somebody I trusted and hopefully get some sort of advice to help guide me from here.

I decided on my best friend. She picked up after three rings.

"Sarah?" Amy exclaimed. "Oh my God! It's so great to hear from you!"

She sounded as if it had been months, not a day and a half, since we'd last seen each other. I was happy to hear her familiar voice. "Amy, I really need to talk to you."

"Thanks for checking in! You know it's after midnight here in Vancouver, right? That's okay, though. Call me anytime. Yeah, we totally settled in here fantastically. I love this city. There are mountains here, Sarah. Big, tall, majestic mountains. It's like a freaking postcard."

"I'm glad to hear it. Listen, I really need—"

"I'm almost finished unpacking. Everything arrived perfect, although that lamp that I love didn't do so well. It's got this big chunk missing from it and I have no idea where it went. So now my cool lamp is a cool lamp missing a big chunk. I've faced it to the wall. I don't think anyone will notice."

I gritted my teeth. "I called for a reason, Amy. Can you just let me talk for a second?"

There was a pause. "Somebody sounds grumpy tonight."

"I'm not grumpy."

"Everything going okay with Thierry?" She hesitated. "There are no . . . *problems* . . . are there?"

It had taken Amy a while to warm up to my fiancé and I knew she still had difficulties now and then with the idea of me wanting to marry him, even though she kept these opinions mostly to herself now that I had the ring on my finger. "Well, there are problems, but not what you might think."

"I'm here for you, Sarah. Anytime, any way. Seriously. If you ever, I don't know, change your mind about anything, you should feel free to come out here. A couple days, a week, whatever you need. Barry won't mind if you take the guest room. Well, he'll mind a little, but he'll get over it."

My grip tightened on my phone. "That's probably not going to happen."

"Not surprised. But consider the offer out there, anyway." She yawned loudly. "Sorry. Wow, I'm so tired. Today's been jam-packed and I have to get up super early tomorrow. But it's been really great talking to you. Thanks for calling, I really appreciate it."

"Yeah, no problem. But—"

"E-mail me! Bye!"

And then the line went dead.

I scratched Amy—who admittedly hadn't been the most reliable person I'd ever known—off my list of people who could potentially help me. It only reminded me that I needed to deal with this alone. The last thing I needed, even if she'd been willing to fly down here and help me, was to draw someone else I cared about into trouble with the Ring. My blatantly going against their orders by not getting on that plane was bad enough.

Amy had improved a lot when it came to accepting Thierry as a major part of my life, but I knew he didn't make a fabulous first impression on a lot of people. Two months ago I'd taken him with me to announce our engagement to my parents—who'd been anticipating their only child having a wonderful, flashy wedding one day, since as a kid it was one of my favorite subjects. I even tore pictures out of wedding magazines of the dresses I liked best and tacked them to my bedroom wall.

"Engaged," my father had said with surprise when I showed him my diamond ring. "To *him*? Sarah, honey, what are you thinking?"

I'd really thought this would go over better. Sure, the first time my parents met Thierry, the fact that *technically* he was married to someone else was a bit of a fly in the ointment, but things had changed. A lot.

"I love him," I'd said simply, as if that would smooth everything over.

"But he's so completely different from you. You are lightness and joy and humor and he's . . . well, he's none of those things." My father had glanced over at Thierry sitting stiffly with my mother as she showed him some photo albums from when I was a kid. "I get a bad vibe from him."

"You get a *bad vibe* from him?" I repeated. "What is this, the seventies?"

"Does he ever smile?"

I felt defensive. "Sure he does."

"I mean, he's handsome. And I know he has money. I can see why women might be attracted to him. But, Sarah . . . you need a man who will truly love you, not just provide for you. You need a partner in life, an equal, not one who will treat you like a possession." He shot another glance in Thierry's direction. "I'm sorry, but I just don't see the two of you together forever."

There wasn't much more to say after that. I could argue until I was blue in the face, but it was clear that my father—and my mother, although she'd never state it so bluntly—didn't approve of my fiancé.

But I was twenty-eight, not eighteen. If my father told me not to date somebody because he got a "bad vibe," I couldn't really be expected to toe the line and go up to my room and behave myself. Could I?

I mean, I hadn't even told my parents I was a vampire yet, so they had no idea how deep the waters ran with me these days. I was putting that little conversation off. Indefinitely, if I could manage it.

Later, in the car, things were quiet until Thierry finally spoke.

"Your father despises me."

"I don't know if I'd use the word *despises*."

"What word would you use?"

"Um . . . dislikes? Intensely?"

Thierry's hands tightened on the steering wheel. "I don't know what I could have done differently."

I hissed out a breath. "Well, maybe *smiling* might have helped. You looked like you were doing an impression of the angel of death tonight. And when you're around recent retirees who are packing up their things to head to Florida, I don't think that's appreciated very much."

"I smiled."

"You briefly bared your teeth. Most living creatures consider that a threatening gesture." I pressed back in the passenger seat. "Whatever. I don't care."

"You don't care that I am inept at smiling or that your father hates the sight of me?"

"Actually, he thinks you're handsome. And wealthy."

"But not good enough for his daughter."

"He thinks you'll treat me as a possession, not as an equal."

"I see."

"If it's any consolation, I'm sure he wouldn't think anyone's good enough."

Thierry kept his eyes on the road ahead as he merged onto the highway heading back toward the city. "I'm not used to . . . family situations. I regret that I was unable to make a better impression on your father. I don't know how to make amends for this."

A little of the tightness in my chest lifted and I turned my face to look at Thierry's profile in the darkness of the car. "You don't have to make amends."

"I don't?"

"People don't cozy up to you easily. My parents included. I'm not surprised."

"Old habits. I naturally try to keep people at a distance."

"You do, no question about it. You did the same with me too many times to count, remember? You have a very prickly exterior that needs to be navigated very carefully. Kind of like a really sexy cactus."

His lips curved a little at that. "A cactus."

"Cactus, porcupine, thorny lizard. Pick one."

"If I'm so prickly, then how do you let yourself get so close to me?"

"Simple." I slid over a little so I could place my hand on his chest, over the left side of his jacket. "I know what's in here."

"My cell phone?"

"Oh my God. A joke. No, Mr. de Bennicoeur, I know your heart. And there's nothing prickly or cactusy about it. I mean, sure, it's a little blackened and singed at the edges—"

He raised an eyebrow. "Really."

"And a bit shriveled."

"Sounds unpleasant."

"Nope. It's beautiful, actually. Best heart I've ever met."

"That's good to hear."

"Oh yeah? Why's that?"

His gray eyes flicked to mine. "Because every last shriveled and blackened piece of it is yours."

His shields were down—his prickly protection he'd built up toward the world all around him. In his eyes I could see his worry about disappointing me when it came to my parents' approval, and his uncertainty—even after all the time we'd spent together—about whether I'd change my mind about him.

He knew as well as I did that we were opposites in so, so many ways—from age, to experience, to demeanor, to outlook on life. Opposites might attract, but did they have any real chance to stay together?

My own heart warmed up so much by what he'd said that it spilled over like a tiny volcano in my chest. My hand slipped beneath his jacket to feel the slow but steady beat of his heart beneath my touch. "I promise to take very good care of it."

He brought my hand up to his lips. "I appreciate it."

When people ask me how I could love a man like Thierry, I think of moments like that—moments that make me realize I'd do anything for him because I know he'd do the same for me. And that we have something very special between us, something private, something not everyone in the world is lucky enough to have.

And that? That's worth fighting for.

I got a room at a crappy little motel off the Strip, one that didn't have a flashy interior or fantastic stage show. It was called Glitter, and much like the Mariah Carey movie by the same name, it made me want to curl up in a ball and rock myself to sleep. Luckily, there were no cockroaches hiding under the stiff cotton sheets, or at least none that wanted to come out and say hello while the lights were on. However, I knew they were in here somewhere. I sensed their curiosity about the fanged brunette sitting on the edge of the bed try-ing not to lose hope.

I stared up at the stained ceiling just before I shut off the light and thought about Thierry. I missed him so much. My heart ached that he thought I was back home by now, back to my normal life without him. He might be staring at the ceiling of the beautiful Bellagio suite that was now serving as his temporary prison before he was found guilty of murder and immediately put to death by a cold-blooded assassin.

Still, that was a five-star hotel and this was . . . not. At least he could get room service if he wanted.

I tossed and turned for an hour before, finally, a chorus of cockroaches sang me to sleep. Or maybe it was just the TV left on in a neighboring room.

I really hoped it was.

The next morning, I'd escaped the mildew-scented clutches of Glitter. I honestly didn't know how long I'd be staying in such absolute nonluxury, but I didn't think I'd get away with only one night.

The tight black dress I'd worn last night had been shoved unceremoniously into my suitcase and replaced with much more practical black jeans, a plain white tank top, and a pair of red Keds.

I'd hoped I would wake up with the answer to what

had happened and who was to blame, but I utterly had no idea. Why would that hunter kill Bernard in public? Even hunters had a code they operated by. In their own misguided way, they were trying to protect humans from your average fanged threat. Protecting humans didn't include traumatizing them in large numbers.

It made no sense to me.

"Money talks." Duncan said that. He was a hired mercenary, informant, whatever. Much like a stripper, he moved in the direction of dollar bills, wherever they waved.

"Somebody must have hired him," I mumbled to myself.

Yeah, well, it looked like *Thierry* had done just that, didn't it? He'd threatened Bernard in public. But if Thierry wanted Bernard dead, Bernard would have simply disappeared without a sound, without a trace, never to be seen or heard from again.

He'd be able to have someone killed and the body hidden—easy as pie. The chilling thought was strangely reassuring. It only reminded me that Thierry was one hundred percent innocent here. He'd never be this sloppy.

So who else would do this and try to point the finger at Thierry?

As I walked quickly along the sidewalk and past the shiny black pyramid of the Luxor Hotel, although I wasn't exactly sure where I was headed yet, I turned my attention to my phone to check messages— presently, zero. I'd thought I might hear from Thierry by text or e-mail, checking that I arrived home safely. Since there was nothing here, I decided his laptop and phone must have been taken away from him.

Bastards. They weren't giving him any chance to prove himself innocent, locking him up in that room without any way to contact the outside world. It was all up to me—and, given my worm's-belly level of confidence this morning, that really didn't ease my mind at all.

Again, I wasn't watching the sidewalk and I did what I normally did in a case like that and slammed right into someone.

"Sorry," I blurted out before I even saw who it was.

Jesus Christ stared back at me. Long white robes. Long hair, full beard, kind brown eyes.

"Are you all right, my child?" he asked.

Talk about a sign from God. "I—I'm fine. Thank you."

He smiled as he rubbed the shoulder that I'd come close to dislocating. "You're troubled, aren't you?"

"Yes, I am. Very troubled." I cocked my head to the side, surprised by what I thought I'd just seen. "Are those—do you have fangs?"

His smile widened to show off his sharp canines. "I do indeed."

Jesus Christ was a vampire. At least—*this* one was.

Now that I thought about it, it wasn't totally out of the realm of possibility. Immortal, forever young, rising again after death, et cetera.

I peered closer at his pointy pearly whites. "Are they real?"

"What is real, my child, is what we *believe* to be real. Are you aware of the apocalypse? It is coming very soon. The signs are all around us."

"The apocalypse?"

"Yes. Armageddon. The end of the world as we know it."

I blinked. "Given the week I've had, that sounds about right, actually."

"Take this." He thrust a flyer at me that was printed on neon green paper. "Memorize it. The vampires are coming to kill us all and turn us into creatures of the night. All humans will be destroyed. But don't be afraid, my child. It's the next stage of our evolution. We must embrace it."

"Okay, if you say so." I stared blankly at the flyer, which was printed with type so tiny that it made even my supernaturally perfect eyesight go a bit squinty at the edges.

"They're here in Las Vegas as we speak," he continued, although he'd lowered his voice as he warily looked around the busy sidewalk. "Gaining strength and draining specially chosen victims. There have been six so far. The seventh will be today. Onward to thirteen, the original number of my disciples. Every one is important to lead us to the glorious future." He clutched the stack of flyers to his chest. "I am here to personally witness the future of mankind forming in the shadows of the night."

I stared at him. "I'm guessing that those fangs in your mouth are the stick-on kind, right?"

He nodded. "For now. But you must have faith that I am here to lead us all forward toward the vampire apocalypse. I do this purely out of love to help humans evolve to their next level of existence."

I nodded. "So I'm going to . . . uh, leave now. I have other things to do. Great talking to you, though."

"Go with God, my child. Go with God. I will next see you when we all rise again."

I went. Whether it was with God or not, I couldn't

say for sure. Talking to Vampire Jesus did help give me some new information, after I sorted through the crazy parts. It told me that the serial killings weren't totally off the grid. People did know about them, even if it hadn't been confirmed in the newspaper or anywhere else.

I hated to say it, but I honestly didn't care about the serial killer. It had nothing to do with Bernard's murder, so I couldn't waste time worrying about it.

Maybe Thierry could talk to Markus one-on-one and work this out. It seemed as if they had some sort of history together, since Thierry knew all about what happened to his wife and kids that had helped to turn the enforcer cold as ice. Then again, when you had been around as long as Thierry, there probably weren't all that many people you *didn't* have some kind of history with.

I knew I was fooling myself. Markus was a black-and-white kind of guy—he wouldn't see any shades of gray here. All logical signs pointed to Thierry being responsible for killing Bernard—he had the motive, he had the means, he had the opportunity. Now Bernard was dead and somebody had to pay for that.

Markus was going to kill Thierry.

I *had* to figure this out before that happened.

You're going to fail.

No, I'm not.

Yes, you are. You're going to let Thierry down when he needs you the most.

My inner voice had never been my biggest cheerleader, but today she was louder than ever before. I leaned against a wall and squeezed my eyes shut.

"Breathe," I told myself. "Just breathe. It's going to be okay."

I couldn't lose him. We'd only just begun.

Great. To make matters even worse, I now had the Carpenters song stuck in my head.

"Who could have done it?" I murmured. "Come on, Sarah. Think. Who could have hired that hunter to kill Bernard?"

"I have an idea or two about that," a dry and familiar voice said.

I opened my eyes and hitched my purse up higher on my shoulder. Out of all the people on the sidewalk who were walking past me without a second glance, only one had stopped. And it was a very short one.

Victoria Corday looked brightly up at me, a sweet smile on her adorable face. Today she wore a fuchsia sundress and her sunlight-blond hair was straight instead of the ringlets she'd worn last night.

"What did you just say?" I managed.

"Let's make a deal, puppy. You help me and I'll help you." She glanced nervously behind her. "And I'm going to need some of that help in about three . . . two . . . one . . ."

A man in a security uniform thundered up beside her, his face red and sweaty. "Thought you could get away from me, did you?"

"Mommy, help!" Victoria ducked behind me and put her hand on my leg as she peered out at the man. "This bad man is chasing me!"

"Darn right I'm chasing you, kid. That's what I do with thieves." The security guard glared at me. "Is she yours?"

Oh, hell. I really didn't need this right now.

In that split second, I had to decide what to do next—not that I had a whole lot of choice here. I looked down at Victoria, who had that "I'm an innocent child!" look—she did come by it honestly—painted on her face. And the security guard . . . he looked furious. It wasn't hard to piece together what had just happened.

Victoria had handed in her beauty pageant sash for a license to steal. Well, Thierry *had* told her to find other ways of making money. I guess she'd started immediately.

"You help me and I'll help you."

Sadly, I knew I needed help today. A lot of it. And whatever bizarre form it came in, I wasn't crazy enough to say no.

I fixed a serious and hopefully maternal look on my face. "What has my little Vicky done now?"

"Your little Vicky stole a necklace." The guard glared at both of us. "A *sapphire* necklace. The salesgirl thought your daughter was so adorable that it would be fun to let her try it on for a second. And then she just took off. I've been chasing her for five minutes. Where were you? Don't you keep an eye on your child? What kind of a mother are you?"

A lousy one, apparently.

When I was younger, I'd been an aspiring actress. While it hadn't worked out so well, apart from a local maxi-pad commercial and a fleeting chance at a soap opera job via the casting couch—which I'd strongly declined—I still liked to think I had enough skill left to weave a bit of dramatic magic from time to time.

"I'll have you know," I said sternly, "that I've been looking all over for Vicky. I've been worried sick about her. I turn my back for one moment—and she's gone! Do you know what that does to a mother? Thank you for returning her safely to me, sir. You're a true hero."

The guard faltered just a little. "I'm sorry you were so upset, but that doesn't change anything here."

"You're right." I put my hands on my hips and looked down at the tiny blond vampire, who fixed me with an innocent look. "Where is it, Vicky?"

"Where's what?"

"You know what. That necklace you took. You can't do that, honey. Stealing is wrong." I shook my head and glanced again at the guard. "I swear, she's like a magpie. You know how they're attracted to shiny things? My little Vicky is just the same. She sees something glitter"—I cringed at the reminder of the cockroach motel—"and she can't resist."

"I'm sorry, Mommy." She didn't sound all that sorry. In fact, she sounded annoyed. She didn't want to give back the necklace. I could see it in her little beady blue eyes.

"Ever since her father died tragically in that deep-sea fishing accident"—I sniffed dramatically—"and left us with nothing, she's had this idea in her head that she should help me out with the bills. But this isn't the way, baby. Now give this nice man back the pretty necklace and I'm sure he'll forgive you. Won't you, sir?"

The guard's expression tensed, as if he was fighting his better judgment as he listened to my sob story. I never said I was a great actress, but I hoped I was good enough.

Finally, he nodded. "I'll forgive you, Vicky. Promise. Now, hand it over."

It took a minute. I waited there tensely until Victoria begrudgingly pulled the necklace out of her pocket and thrust it at the security guard.

"Fine," she said sullenly. "Here."

"Thank you." Only a small tug-of-war ensued before she finally let it go. He glanced at me. "Keep a close eye on her from now on, you hear? She's a trouble-maker."

"No kidding."

When he finally left, Victoria looked mad enough to spit.

"Yeah, thanks so much for the help just now," she grumbled.

"You're welcome."

"I was being sarcastic."

"Oh, I know. I'm fluent in that dialect. You know you can't steal things like that, right?"

"Says the woman whose sourpuss fiancé is up for first-degree murder."

I flinched. "He's innocent."

She grinned maliciously. "Uh-huh. If you say so."

I gave her a withering look. "I do."

"Not something you'll be saying if you don't clear his name, is it? Dead master vampires don't recite their wedding vows so well."

"I really don't like you." If there was one thing this pip-squeak was doing, it was helping to raise my level of anger to match my anxiety.

"Feeling's mutual, puppy. But you know who I did like?"

"Who?"

"Bernard DuShaw." She wasn't smiling anymore.

That took me a second to process. "You knew him?"

"Long time ago. Remember I said I got in trouble with the Ring once upon a time? Bernard was the consultant assigned to my case. He helped me when no one else did. I owe him for that."

I had no idea they'd met before. "Why wouldn't he handle your case this time, then? If you had history with Bernard, then why would Thierry be the one told to contact you?"

She shrugged a tiny shoulder. "The Ring does what it wants even if it doesn't make any sense. Bernard trashed some of my files last time to protect me, so our contact might have been swept under the proverbial rug. I'm not saying I was his biggest fan or anything, but he did me a favor once. The least I can do is lend a hand to help find out who hit his delete key."

"You're handling this all very matter-of-factly. Do you get emotional over anything?"

"Emotions are for chumps, puppy. I only cry onstage if it's going to get me more votes."

"Charming."

"So you don't think sourpuss hired the hunter."

My glare returned. "His name is Thierry, not 'sourpuss.' Just like my name is Sarah, not 'puppy.' And, no, he didn't do it."

"I think you're right. But I think I know who did."

Derogatory nicknames forgotten, my glare turned into a gape. "You do?"

"Sure. It's not too difficult to figure out."

"It isn't?"

"Not when you've been around as long as I have. I've seen it before. It's so common that cops will always pinpoint a certain suspect in almost any murder."

"Who?"

"The spouse, of course. Duh."

I frowned. "Laura? But she adores him. She says

their marriage is like something out of a fairy tale. She would never want to hurt him."

"Bingo. Isn't that the best fake-out ever? I saw her a couple of times at the hotel over the last few days. She's even shinier than you, puppy. It can't be real—it's just an act. She's a black widow spider underneath it all."

I considered this possibility. Wives *did* kill their husbands. Crime of passion, crime of wanting to get her hands on his money. You name it. Laura DuShaw—someone who'd reminded me so much of myself, a fledgling involved with a master vampire—*could* have hired Duncan Keller to kill the man she'd told me she was madly in love with.

And she also could have neatly pinned it on Thierry.

My anger immediately flared, but then reduced to a sick-feeling and uncertain simmer. "I don't know about this. I really thought she was genuine, but if she isn't . . . how would I even begin to prove she had anything to do with it?"

"You get her to admit it. For starters."

Victoria was right about one thing—as his wife, Laura was definitely a suspect. But, still, I needed to find out much more before I'd totally believe she was guilty.

This little vampire, annoying as she was, might turn out to be the help I needed to prove Thierry's innocence.

In fact, I was putting all my chips on it and rolling the dice.

Chapter 8

I'd been outside long enough that I was really starting to notice how blazingly bright it was today. Sunlight tended to exhaust me easily when I was out in it for too long—I'd recently turned into an indoor girl whenever possible. I pushed my dark sunglasses higher up on the bridge of my nose and tried to ignore it.

Something occurred to me as I followed Victoria down the busy sidewalk headed toward the Bellagio.

"Where's Charles?" I asked.

She glanced over her shoulder at me. "He's around. Sometimes he disappears to take care of personal business."

"Shouldn't he stay with you? For, you know, supervision?"

"I don't need supervision."

That was debatable, given what just happened. Could they send children to jail? "Then the *illusion* of supervision. Whatever. Call me crazy, but most people would think it's weird to see a six-year-old wandering around Las Vegas all by her lonesome."

"Well, now I'm with my mommy, aren't I? And everything's just fine with the world."

A swell of sympathy for her filled me. It must have shown on my face.

"What?" she asked.

"It must be horrible—having a child's body all this time."

She looked at me curiously. "You just don't get it, do you?"

"Get what?"

"You think I'm a hundred-and-two-year-old woman trapped inside a little kid."

I frowned. "Well . . . yeah. Aren't you?"

She shook her head. "Doesn't work that way. I'm six. I'm six with experience and an expanded vocabulary, but I'm still six. I see the world like a six-year-old would, if a bit jaded. I like puppies and kittens and waterslides and picture books. And Jell-O. I love Jell-O. Lime's my favorite. And if sleeping with a pink teddy bear named Gummi-Boo every night is wrong, I don't want to be right."

My frown deepened. "So you're . . . just a kid. Permanently."

"Exactly. If you're a cute kid when you're turned, you'll always be a cute kid. If you're a surly, angsty teenager, you'll always be a surly, angsty teen. If you're whatever age *you* are—"

"Twenty-eight," I offered.

"—you'll always be twenty-eight. Just with a few modifications and world experience. Frozen in time, like a snapshot."

I had a hard time grasping that, but I think I got the gist of it. It made me feel a bit better, actually. Better, but still confused. "Then . . . why do you smoke and drink?"

"Mostly because I like seeing the look on other people's faces when I do it. It freaks them out. It's hilarious." She blinked. "Also, smoking is relaxing and it won't ever give me lung cancer. One of the perks."

"But what about—?"

"Hush, puppy." Then she giggled. *"Hush puppy!* But seriously, shut up and let me figure out how we're going to get you back in that hotel without the enforcer seeing you. I don't think he'll believe you're my mommy. He'll probably kill us both on sight just to make a point."

I shuddered at the thought.

I was allowing the derogatory nickname only because I needed her help. For now. If this didn't work out, I wouldn't spend too much more time humoring the eternal six-year-old. We'd arrived outside the hotel and I could now see the front entrance.

I grabbed Victoria's arm to bring her to a stop. "Wait. . . . There she is."

Laura DuShaw had just exited the hotel. Today she wore all white—stylish and elegant white shirt and white linen pants. Considering her husband had died horribly only last night, she didn't exactly look the part of a grieving widow.

An attendant hailed a taxi and held the back door open for her. She got in and just before the cab drove past us, I jumped behind a cart piled with suitcases to hide.

"I guess we'll have to talk to her later," Victoria said.

"No, this can't wait. We need to follow her. Now." I waved my arms and another taxi pulled up next to us. I climbed in the backseat, half-surprised that Victoria joined me without further argument. I pointed toward the windshield. "Uh . . . follow that taxi!"

Just like in the movies or reality-TV races, the cab-driver did just that without asking any questions. Cool.

I tensely kept my attention on Laura's car, not letting it out of my sight. I wanted to look up at the hotel, to the floor and window where I knew Thierry would be, but I couldn't risk it.

Hang on, Thierry, I thought. *Just a little while longer.*

Telepathy would be a really nice perk right about now. I'd send him that very message.

And he'd probably reply with: *What are you still doing in Las Vegas, getting yourself in more trouble than you were to begin with?*

And then I'd say: *Trying to save your butt, mister.*

My butt doesn't need saving.

You could have fooled me, what with you being stuck up in that hotel room.

I'm exactly where I need to be right now. I'm biding my time.

Well, you can bide your time while I figure out who set you up.

And how do you intend to do that?

Any way I can.

And he'd just sigh in that way he did when I was being particularly stubborn.

But no telepathy. Too bad.

I wondered what he'd think about Laura being a suspect. It troubled me deeply to think she could be the mastermind behind this horrible crime. It would mean she'd been completely lying to me about how madly in love with Bernard she was. But maybe, now that he was retiring and would be around more, she couldn't handle it.

But if it turned out to be true . . . if she'd hired that hunter to turn her "beloved" husband into a stain on the expensive marble floor—and made sure she wasn't there when it happened—then that was cold as ice. It would prove that there was way more to Laura DuShaw than the polished, manicured fashionista than met the eye.

Laura's cab let her off at a smaller hotel/casino in Old Las Vegas. She moved quickly, but so did I. Victoria's little legs worked hard to keep up.

Frankly, I was surprised Laura hadn't noticed us yet. We weren't being all that subtle. I caught a glimpse of her face as she moved down a long hall and then went through a black door with a silver handle. She looked worried.

"Why are you worried, Laura?" I said under my breath, my throat tight. "Feeling guilty about something?"

"Ooh!" Victoria said, halting in front of a glassed-in room. "That looks like fun! Can I play?"

My attention snapped to Victoria, who was ogling the day care the hotel had set up for its guests' children: the "Funtime Zone." Inside were about a dozen kids, supervised by three gray-haired women. There were storybooks, toys, and a winding slide that dropped into a container full of red foam balls.

I blinked. "I thought you were going to help me question Laura."

"I was, but . . ." She looked up at me beseechingly. "Please? Please, can I? Pleeeeaase?"

She wasn't kidding. Well, she *had* said that despite the snark and the nicotine she was only six years old. I'd have to deal with Laura by myself and I didn't have time to debate this with Victoria if I wanted to catch up to her. "Fine. Go and, uh, play. I'll be back as soon as I can—well, unless Laura kills me."

"Okay, bye!" She smiled brightly and ducked inside the room. Without a moment's hesitation, she leaped into the vat of foam balls.

Kids.

Immediately, I hurried toward that black door behind which Laura had disappeared. My hand was shaking as I twisted the handle. It was unlocked and it led into a narrow hallway. I followed it, pressing on despite my reservations. Of course I had so many reservations by now that I was practically a restaurant waiting list.

Despite my nagging doubts about her guilt, I was about to boldly confront a potential murderess about her crimes.

This could go very, very badly indeed.

Maybe it was a good idea not to have Victoria along for the rest of this ride. This could get even more turbulent than the plane had been.

The hall led past a couple more closed doors and then, suddenly, it opened into a darkened theater. Smaller than the one in which the toddler pageant had taken place, but still large and cavernous. This was a dinner theater, with tables strewn around the floor on two levels.

About a hundred feet in front of me, a few women were onstage in leotards, stretching and practicing dance steps. The only lights in the theater shone up there and the rest of the area was in shadows. I didn't care about the dancers and they paid no attention to anything that wasn't onstage. I only cared about the brunette twenty feet to my left talking to a big man with a shaved head and broad shoulders, his back to me. She didn't look in my direction and seemed oblivious to anything except for the man.

Laura's face was strained and she had her hand on his muscled arm. "Please, Joe. For old times' sake."

"Laura, you're the last person I ever thought I'd see again—let alone come here to ask me for a favor."

"I know, but I'm desperate. I don't have anywhere else to go."

He shook his head. "Sorry. I can't help you."

"But last time—"

"That was a long time ago. A lot's changed since then. You picked up and left me for that other guy—broke my heart. You think I can just forgive and forget?"

Tears were now streaming down her cheeks. "I'll beg for that forgiveness if I have to."

"Don't demean yourself." There was a harsh tone to his voice that told me even if she continued to beg, it would only harden his resolve.

Laura's tears only became more sloppy and messy, smearing her perfectly applied makeup. "Joe, please!"

"I'm done with this, Laura. I have enough problems to deal with on my own. Don't come back here if you know what's good for you." He yanked his arm away from her and walked across the dark dinner theater up to the bright stage without a backward glance.

She was about to take a step toward the stage, maybe to keep begging—which I was finding all kinds of pathetic—when I finally caught her eye.

Her face paled. "Sarah . . ."

"Laura," I replied. My heart pounded hard. "I want to talk to you."

She took a step back and seemed to hesitate for a moment, as if she didn't know what to do. Then she turned and bolted away from me like—and I don't use this cliché lightly—a bat out of hell.

I didn't have time to be surprised that she was fleeing the scene, because I was too busy racing after her. It was the second time in two days I'd had to chase somebody down and it wasn't something I enjoyed. But I'd do it if I had to. And at the moment, it looked as if I had to.

On the far side of the theater was a hallway parallel to the one I'd used to enter the place and another black door at the end of it. But there was a big difference, and one that worked in my favor. This one was locked.

Laura pulled on the door and I was pretty sure that with vampire strength she might be able to pry it open if she had enough time. But she didn't.

She froze before slowly turning around to face me, pressing backward against the door. Her eyes were very wide.

"Sarah, please," she began.

The fear on her face confused me deeply. "What's going on, Laura? Why did you come here?"

She blinked, then rubbed at her eyes. Her black mascara had run from her tears. "Please, Sarah. Please—don't kill me."

Um . . . what?

It really didn't sound like a "Please don't kill me for framing your fiancé for murder." It sounded more like a "Please don't kill me. Period."

"I'm not going to kill you," I assured her, uncertain now.

She frowned. "You're not? But I thought that you . . . that you and Thierry . . ."

"That me and Thierry what?"

"When he had Bernard killed, I figured that I became a loose end—that I knew too much, or something. If he was willing to do that to my husband, then it meant that I really didn't know you like I thought I did. That you were capable of anything. I know what it's like to be involved with such a powerful man, Sarah. They can make you do bad things. Things you might not normally do."

Confusion rained down over me. "So you're trying to tell me that you thought Thierry sent me after you to . . . kill you."

"I'll scream." Her voice shook. "I swear I will."

My first suspect in the murder of Bernard DuShaw had all but convinced me in record time that not only was she pathetic and weak and needy, but she was also totally innocent of her husband's murder.

Now what?

Chapter 9

"I'm *not* going to kill you." I said it again. "Seriously, I'm not."

That something like this had to be stated so bluntly was disturbing.

Laura began to calm down. Slowly. Agonizingly slowly. If she really was innocent in all of this, I felt bad that I'd upset her so much.

"Then why did you follow me here?" she asked, her voice trembling.

I nodded at a small table to our left. "Give me five minutes."

"For what?"

"I need to talk to you."

Her breathing slowed to a normal rate and her eyes narrowed to tiny slits. "Why should I talk to you? Your fiancé murdered my husband."

My fading antagonism toward her flared inside me like a tiny pissed-off demon. "He was set up."

She gave me a look then—one of pity. "Oh, Sarah. You poor dear."

I glared at her. "I'm not deluded. He didn't do it."

She opened her mouth as if to argue with me, but closed it. Her entire body sagged in defeat before she finally moved toward the table and sat down heavily. "I don't even care who did it. It's done. And now I don't know what I'm going to do without him."

My emotions were seriously on a roller-coaster ride today. Anger, to confusion, and right into sympathy. It was dizzying. "I'm so sorry. I know how much you loved him. This must be absolutely horrible for you."

She looked older now than she had before. Drained and weary. "Loved him? Maybe once."

I sat down across from her at the small round table. "What are you talking about?"

She exhaled shakily. "What I felt for Bernard . . . it had faded. A lot."

"But the other night at dinner you said that everything was wonderful."

"I know what I said. What else was I supposed to say? I'd only just met you—and you and Thierry seemed so happy together. Was I supposed to admit that my relationship was only a shadow of what it once was?"

I shook my head. "I'm surprised you're admitting this to me."

"What difference does it make anymore?" She glanced over toward the stage. "That man up there—Joe—he's the one I really loved. *Still* love. But I left him for Bernard."

I glanced over at the muscular man directing things onstage. "Who is he?"

"A nobody. Or, at least, he used to be. I worked as a dancer five years ago. He was a bouncer then. We were lovers—*more* than that."

"So what happened?"

"Bernard happened. He came and saw one of the

shows, and then made it known afterward that he wanted me."

"Wait a minute. I thought you said you met in Central Park."

"I lied. It sounded prettier than the truth—that he was a rich customer at a strip club."

More surprise flooded through me. "You were a . . . stripper?"

Laura shrugged a shoulder. "Despite what you might think, it's an honest living. I'm not ashamed of it—but Bernard insisted I change my ways. I quit and broke up with Joe, all for the chance to be with Bernard."

"Because you fell in love with him?"

"The thickness of his wallet helped a lot." Her bleak expression told me she took no pleasure in sharing this, but had some inner drive to get it out as if I were a priest in a confessional booth who might absolve her of all sins. "Joe had sired me, but Bernard provided for me—money, jewelry, things I'd never had before. But he wasn't faithful—and neither was I, to be honest, after a while. I took it as an even trade. I spent his money and he got to fool around without any complaints from me while he went on his assignments."

I repressed a shudder at hearing that Laura had sold out true love for a rich husband. "That's horrible."

She looked at me sharply. "Get used to it, Sarah. That's how it is with a master vampire—especially one that works for the Ring who must deal with certain stresses related to the job. Thierry's no different."

I bristled. "Wrong. He is."

"Sure." There was more bitterness in that one word than I'd ever heard before. "It would have been worth it for you, though. If he hadn't killed Bernard, he would have provided for you, protected you, taken care of whatever you needed . . . and the world would have felt like it was yours for the asking. But when he's gone"—she swallowed hard—"you find that you have nothing left and no one to look after you."

I just stared at her. "So that's why you came here— to see if Joe would take you back? So he could take care of you?"

Her expression was pale and hopeless. "I'm desperate, Sarah. Bernard's will didn't include me. I know it. And we had an airtight prenup. He was fond of me, but he never really loved me. Vampires who've lived as long as he had—they don't trust anyone. They're secretive about everything."

The last part wasn't exactly news to me, at least where Thierry was concerned. But this didn't jibe with what I thought I knew about her husband.

"Bernard told me he that he was an open book with you about his past—that he'd told you almost everything about him."

Laura shook her head. "More like an open checkbook. That's all. I had no idea what he did during his days, past or present. I didn't want to know. The Ring—" She grimaced. "They're horrible, shadowy, scary. It's best to stay out of their business as much as possible. Now that Bernard's gone, I want to get as far away from anything to do with that organization as I can, but how am I supposed to do that without any money or protection?" She glanced at the stage again. "Joe will take me back. It's only been five years. He'll remember how good we were together. He produces shows now—it was always a dream of his. The one they're rehearsing today—it's a vampire show called *Fang* that he's producing with a partner. An all-vampire topless revue. I could do that—I'd be great at it. I just need to figure out how to get Joe to give me another chance."

An all-vampire topless revue? A worrying thought occurred to me. "They're not promoting it as having real vampires in it, are they?"

"Of course not. The Ring would have a meltdown if they did. But there's that air of mystery about it *maybe* having real vampires. Rumors are okay. Hopefully, it'll sell tickets—although I know interest in vampires is waning. To think that vampires are practically mainstream now." She gazed up at the stage, worry creasing her forehead. "Hard to believe. I hope the show finds its audience—for Joe's sake."

I fixed her with a questioning look as I tried to figure her out. Was there more to Laura than met the eye? Was she holding something back from me right now? Or was this exactly who she was? A recently widowed woman in dire need of a powerful and influential man to protect her from the big, scary, expensive world?

As if she felt my stare, she glanced at me again. "Why did you follow me here, Sarah?"

"Because I thought you had Bernard killed and pinned it on Thierry," I said bluntly.

Her eyes widened. "Why on earth would I do something like that?"

"That's exactly what I was wondering."

"I didn't love him—and I knew he didn't love me, not really—but I never wanted him to die. Without him, I have nothing." A tear slipped down her cheek. "I *am* nothing."

Her pain was so palpable it made me wince. "Don't say that."

"But it's true." Her gaze grew more intense and she surprised me by reaching across the table to clutch my hand. "Learn from this, Sarah. It doesn't have to happen to you, too. Put money aside for a rainy day. Steal, if you have to. And don't trust Thierry, ever. He'll lie, he'll cheat. Those who've lived that long will do whatever they have to do to continue existing. You're just a plaything to him—something he finds interesting now. Soon you'll be exactly where I am."

Her harsh and cold words hit me one by one like sharp icicles. However, there was a difference that I'd heard in her story that helped deflect them. Bernard didn't love her, but I knew Thierry loved me. I *knew* it—not just because he told me so, but because I felt it deep in my gut. I clung to that knowledge like a life preserver.

I shook my head. "Bernard and Thierry are different."

"You're right. Thierry's twice as old, so he might be even worse. Be very careful with him. Bernard didn't tell me much, Sarah, but he did tell me how much he hated your fiancé. How much he feared for his life knowing he'd be near him again after all these years."

This entire conversation was making me nauseous. "Feared? Seriously?"

She nodded gravely. "And believe me, Bernard wasn't afraid of much, not after being the Ring's errand boy for fifty years. Be on your guard at all times, Sarah. Plan ahead. Be wary of the man you've given your heart to. Take it away while you still have the chance before he tears it apart." She nodded as if agreeing with everything she was saying. "It's for the best that he was caught for this crime. He'll be executed by the enforcer soon and you'll be free to start your life somewhere else. Find yourself another man who will cherish you and provide for you. Don't be like me."

That she was offering this advice as if she was doing me some sort of favor put a rancid taste in my mouth. Everything she said or intimated, from Thierry being a hateful and violent murderer, to me needing a man to take care of me in order to survive—it all turned my stomach.

"I need to go." I pushed back from the table. I didn't have too many amusing wisecracks or clever remarks to offer at the moment that might help to lighten the mood. There was absolutely nothing funny about any of this. What I really wanted to do was go back to my room at the Glitter motel, curl into a tight ball, and fall asleep, hoping that when I woke everything would be better.

"You should take this." She reached into her purse and put something small and metallic on the table. "I don't want it. Bernard always carried it with him—it was found among his . . . remains. I know it has something to do with Thierry and that just makes my skin crawl."

It was a small silver key—a safety-deposit box key, maybe? Was this the one that Bernard had to the safe filled with cursed diamonds? The reason for his and Thierry's violent argument the night before he was murdered?

"Who did this, Laura?" I asked, forcing myself to sound strong. "Who killed Bernard?"

Her lips thinned. "A hunter who was associated with your fiancé killed him. A hunter known to take money for doing the dirty work of vampires and humans alike."

I already knew that. Laura couldn't be any more help to me. In fact, I think she'd succeeded in making everything much worse.

I snatched the key off the table and slid it into my pocket. Then as I looked at Laura, some remaining concern for her well-being sneaked past my distaste for everything she'd shared with me. "Is there anything I can do to help you?"

She looked up at me, her eyes glossy. "Find me a time travel machine so I can go back five years and not marry a master vampire who sold his soul to work for the Ring. My life would have gone in a much different direction if I hadn't."

My throat felt thick. "Sorry. I'm all out of time travel machines this week."

She offered me a weak smile. "Then there's nothing you can do. Good luck, Sarah."

"You too."

After everything she'd said, my belief in Thierry's innocence and general awesomeness hadn't budged. But my belief in myself? Budge city.

I turned away from the broken (and broke) vampire in the Chanel blouse, Louboutin heels, and smeared makeup, feeling uneasily like I was walking away from my future self.

"Oh my gosh! That was so much fun!" Victoria exclaimed as I retrieved her from the Funtime Zone.

"Hooray for you," I said dryly. "You done?"

"I could stay here all day. And I made friends—ones

who aren't envious of my wicked pageant skills. That's Eddie there, and Britney. Hey guys!"

The other children waved at her.

"Excuse me." One of the gray-haired women approached with a pursed and sour look on her face. "If you're going to leave your daughter here, you need to fill out a form first. And you need to be a hotel guest. Are you a hotel guest?"

I stared at her. My brain wasn't working at full capacity at the moment after my nausea-inducing discussion with Laura. "Hotel guest . . . yes, I sure am. And sorry about this. My little Vicky, she loves . . . rubber balls. They're a magnet for her. Thanks so much for looking after her."

She glared at me. "You're not a very attentive mother, are you?"

"No. No, I'm not."

"Your daughter deserves better."

"Trust me, she really doesn't."

"Where's her father?"

"Deep-sea diving accident. Let's just say that he found Nemo the hard way. Bye, now."

Taking Victoria by her arm, I directed her out of the day care and back to the lobby of the hotel. She was pouting.

"Stop pouting," I said. "I'm the one who should be pouting right now."

"Oh, right." She looked up at me curiously. "How did things go with the black widow?"

"She said she didn't do it."

"Lies!" she cried.

"No, she wasn't lying. She really didn't do it." I raked a hand through my hair, getting caught on a tangle I'd developed. "She's pitiful and needy and I can't help but feel sorry for her, even though I wouldn't exactly say she's grieving Bernard for the right reasons. She wasn't any help."

Victoria crossed her arms over the embroidered sunflower on the front of her pink dress. "Well, damn."

"Exactly."

"Any clues at all?"

"No. She thinks Thierry did it."

"Maybe he did."

I glowered at her as we exited the hotel and started walking along the sidewalk. I'd get us another taxi, but I currently had no idea whatsoever about where we should go next. "I thought we'd settled that."

"Well, *somebody* hired that hunter." Victoria paused. "I guess you could find him and ask him who."

A chill went down my spine. "Ask the hunter who hired him?"

"That's exactly what I'm—Ooh, look over there! Pretty balloons! Can I have one? Can I?" She scampered off toward a group of street performers, all dressed as clowns that reminded me of Mr. Chuckles from the other day. There were many happy happy balloons here and the bright colors had caught Victoria's eye.

A crowd of fifteen watched the clowns perform their impromptu street show of magic and juggling. One balanced on a unicycle while juggling five eggs. But I was too tense to enjoy it. I thought through everything I'd learned—or not learned—from Laura DuShaw, former stripper-with-fangs.

I scanned the street, looking for anyone associated with Markus who might be looking for me. Call me paranoid. I didn't see his henchmen in the general area, which was a relief. However, I did see a familiar face heading our way. It was Charles.

All I saw when I looked at him was the moment he'd sliced that knife into Thierry's chest. I knew he'd done it to protect Victoria, but it didn't leave me feeling all that friendly toward him . . . What was he, anyway? Her personal assistant? Her pageant coach? Her hired daddy? All of the above?

I didn't like him at all.

A big smile grew on Victoria's face when she spotted him. "Charles!"

She ran toward him and gave him a big hug. Despite myself, my heart warmed up at the sight of it. Victoria was a strange creature—just when I thought she was a no-nonsense she-devil in a pint-sized body, she kept having these very childlike moments that reminded me what she'd said was absolutely true—she was still just a six-year-old with a bit more world experience.

"Victoria, I'm glad you're okay," he said, patting her head affectionately before he looked at me. "Thanks for looking after her."

"You're welcome. Where have you been?"

"Around." He glanced over his shoulder. "Do you mind watching over Victoria for a bit longer? I need an hour to take care of some business."

"She doesn't mind." Victoria did the honors of answering for me. "Hey, do you know where we might be able to find that hunter from last night? The one who killed the guy from the Ring?"

Charles blanched a little. "You don't want to find him, kiddo. He's a bad man."

"I know, but hypothetically. Where do hunters hang in Vegas?"

"There's a bar near Fremont and Fourth where I've heard they congregate—everyone says to steer clear of it. And there's a reason there are rumors like that, Victoria. It's dangerous. You hear me?"

She waved a hand flippantly. "Yes, I hear you."

I frowned at Charles. "You have a little something . . ." I pointed at the corner of my mouth. "Right about there."

"Thanks." His eyes flicked to me and he wiped the drop of blood away. "I'll meet up with you soon, Victoria. Promise."

And then he was gone. He hadn't even glanced at the juggling clowns only a dozen feet away from us.

I looked down at Victoria. "What's his problem? And why was he walking around in public with blood on his lips?"

She shrugged. "He has issues."

"What kind of issues?"

"Addiction issues. He doesn't like to talk about it."

That was troubling. "What's he addicted to?"

"Charles, well, he gets a little crazy when it comes to blood."

I cast a surprised glance in the direction Charles had departed. I thought Thierry was the only one—the only one I'd met so far, anyway. To think that Charles had the same kind of struggles as—

Somebody slammed into me. And this time it definitely wasn't my fault.

I turned and pushed the guy away. "Hey, watch where you're going, buddy."

He staggered back a couple of feet. He smelled human—but he also smelled of something else, something very familiar that immediately made my saliva glands kick into action.

He held his hand to the side of his neck and it was covered in blood. His face was pale, his eyes glossy. His shirt was soaked red all down one side.

"Oh, my God!" I exclaimed. The violent sight doused my knee-jerk reaction of hunger. "Are you okay?"

His lips moved, but no sound came out. I drew closer, my hands shaking when I grabbed hold of his shoulder. He didn't have to answer me. He couldn't be less okay if he tried.

"Somebody call an ambulance!" I yelled.

Finally, the rest of the crowd looked our way. When a woman near me registered that the man was covered in blood, she let out a high-pitched shriek.

"Please . . ." The man's voice was barely audible. "Help me. . . ."

"Who did this to you?"

With his free hand, he pulled me closer so he could gasp into my ear: "Vampire."

He fell to the ground, his hand dropping from the side of his neck to show the two gory puncture wounds. Blood continued to ooze out onto the sidewalk. He let out a hiss of breath as his eyes closed.

"Did—did he say *vampire*?" the shrieking woman shrieked.

I clamped my hand to my mouth with shock. I'd just discovered a brand-new skill I had—one I didn't even know I possessed until now. I didn't have to get down on my knees next to this man to check his pulse. I could just sense it as his heart stopped beating. His blood stopped flowing. The life had left him in a matter of seconds.

He was dead.

Chapter 10

"Uh," one of the juggling clowns said, "is this some sort of street performance? Because, hello? This is our corner."

I reared back from the dead body, grabbing hold of Victoria to pull her back as well. She looked just as shocked as I was.

Victim number seven of the vampire serial killer just walked right up to me and practically introduced himself.

Some of the scared and confused witnesses moved closer to the body, some moved farther away. Cell phones moved to ears—and some of the people started to take pictures and video of the dead man.

I caught a bit of the conversation one man had on his phone.

"Yeah, another one. Get Markus here as soon as possible to contain this. There are witnesses, lots of them."

I didn't look at him or try to hear anything else. I pulled Victoria along with me as we fled the scene. The last thing I needed right now was to be found present at a murder scene with the Ring's enforcer showing up at any moment.

"That was bad," Victoria said, stating the obvious.

"No kidding."

"So are you like a magnet for trouble, or what?"

I cringed. "It's a natural talent of mine."

"I need a cigarette." She frantically patted her pockets. "Damn it. They must have fallen out in the Funtime Zone."

I tried to slow my racing thoughts and make sense of what had happened. Charles had just been here—a known bloodaholic, according to Victoria—and he'd had blood on his lips mere moments before the most recent serial killer's victim had moseyed along the exact same route he'd taken.

Was that only a coincidence?

"Victoria, how long have you and Charles been in Vegas preparing for the pageant?" I asked slowly.

"A week," she replied.

A shiver went through me. A victim a day, seven victims, seven days. Last time I checked, that counted as a week.

Was Charles the serial killer?

"How long have you known him?" I asked carefully.

"Who, Charles? I don't know—forever. I found him shortly after I ran away from my crazy sire."

"How did you find him?"

"Believe it or not, he's an ex-hunter. Got turned one night by a vampire he tried to slay. Changed his ways soon after. But he still had the urge to protect—and he's been protecting me ever since."

An ex-hunter. *Oh boy.*

Hunters hated vampires. It was ingrained in them—a way to take their frustrations in life and channel them into something they felt was the right thing to do. You could literally stand in front of a hunter calmly explaining that their worldview was wrong—that all vampires weren't evil or in need of slaying—and he'd just smile and nod his head before he sank his stake straight through your heart anyway. It was like talking to a big, ugly (and often *smelly*) brick wall. On average, they weren't the most open-minded people in the world.

If Charles hated vampires—even if it was a long time ago—maybe there was a part of him that still did. Enough to try to expose the existence of them for all to know.

No. What was I thinking? Was I trying to point the finger at him after only seeing a red smudge on his lips? I was totally jumping to conclusions.

I eyed Victoria. "So what do *you* think we should do now?"

"I think we should give up."

"Give up?"

She shrugged. "The widow was a dead end, pardon the pun. And if you're a trouble magnet, who knows what else we'll run into if we keep going? Personally, I think you should kiss sourpuss good-bye and start your life somewhere much safer."

I crossed my arms, fighting the annoyance rising inside me at her suggestion. "Well, that's not going to happen. Another suggestion, pretty please?"

She shrugged. "Well, there's always that hunter bar Charles mentioned. You want answers? You can ask the murderer yourself. But that would probably be a stupid move."

Marching into a bar full of hunters would be an extremely bad move. I might have tried something like that a few months ago when I didn't fully comprehend how risky it was. But now?

Not so much.

Still, I had to admit that Victoria was right. Getting the answers from the hunter himself was very likely the only way I could clear Thierry's name at this point. This day wasn't getting any younger.

"Charles said it was near Fremont and Fourth, right?" I asked.

"Didn't you hear my 'stupid move' comment?"

"We're not going in. I want to lurk outside and wait for him to come out. It's worth a shot."

She appeared to ponder this. "We'll have to stick to the shadows, which will be difficult." She looked up at the bright, sunny, midafternoon sky with not a cloud currently visible. It was easily over a hundred degrees today. "But this is it. If we don't find any answers soon, I need to scram. I have a hair appointment later."

"It's all about priorities," I replied dryly. "Murder investigations, hair appointments. Whatever works."

"My hair is my crowning glory, puppy." She eyed me. "Yours looks like a brown tumbleweed right now."

I touched my dark, tangled mop. "It's been a rough day."

"For both of us. But you can easily see that my hair is still a blond halo of fabulousness."

Priorities. Victoria's was bouncin' and behavin' hair. Mine was saving Thierry.

But a brush might come in handy right about now, too.

There really was no question which was the hunters' bar. It was the one that looked the most dangerous. Hunters, on average, were big burly dudes who pumped iron, wore leather, and rode hogs. And by hogs, I obviously mean Harley-Davidsons, not large pigs. There were other hunters who didn't look so tough, but they were usually just the amateurs. The tough guys? They were the pros.

My original plan was to follow Duncan when he left, but that could take forever—and despite my current potential for immortality, I didn't have that kind of time. Besides, I didn't know if he was even here in the first place.

"How do you know he's still in the city?" Victoria echoed my circling worries after we'd waited for over an hour in the blazing heat and bright sun.

"I don't."

"I mean, if I just killed somebody in public, I probably wouldn't stick around. I'd leave so I wouldn't be caught. He killed Bernard last night in public, right?"

"Right." I kept my eyes glued on the front door.

"He's probably long gone by now." She yawned. "Oh my God, I'm so bored."

The sun was making me tired and woozy the longer I stood outside. Just because the sun didn't kill me, it was still . . . draining. I had just never realized how draining it could be, with or without the dark shades covering my eyes.

We'd taken refuge behind a rusty green Dumpster, but it wasn't exactly shady. Plus, it smelled like Satan's sweaty armpit.

Victoria was right. I had no idea if Duncan was still in town. If I'd been him, I would have taken off last night. Frankly, I didn't know how he got away, or even if he did, considering that Markus the enforcer had been present at the murder.

A tiny sound piped up then. I think it was a Miley Cyrus song.

"What is that?" I asked.

"My cell phone." She dug into her pocket and pulled out the pink phone to look at the screen. There was a sparkly Hello Kitty sticker on the back of it. "Oh, it's Charles. He says for me to meet him back at the hotel and he'll take me to the salon."

I wanted to bite my tongue to stop from saying anything, but that just wasn't me. "Victoria . . . you might think this is crazy, but I'm worried that he might be dangerous."

"Who, Charles?"

"He tried to kill Thierry yesterday—no questions, nothing. He just attacked."

"He was trying to protect me."

"I know. But it was still more violent than it needed to be. He could have talked to us. Thierry wasn't threatening anybody."

"Sourpuss looks mean. There's just something about him that's off-putting. Well, except for the way he looked at you."

"How was that?"

She shrugged a tiny shoulder. "Whenever you say anything, the rest of the world seems to disappear for him—like you're the feature act of his sourpuss theater. Just a random observation."

A random observation that only made me miss him more and harden my resolve to get him out of that hotel suite as soon as I possibly could.

"Pretty dangerous, though," she continued.

I frowned. "What is?"

"Most master vampires are sourpusses, not just yours. It comes with the territory. But the kind of affection I saw on his face—it could be used against him if he's not careful."

I didn't like the sound of that at all. A line of perspiration slid down my spine. "We were talking about Charles, remember?"

Victoria twisted a finger through her flaxen hair. "If I hired a Rottweiler to protect me, I'd expect him to bite someone who wanted to hurt me. Ditto Charles. I have no problem with what he did."

"And the fact that he's a vampire who's addicted to blood . . ."

She waved a hand. "Not a big deal."

"*And* the fact you've been in Las Vegas for the same amount of time that the serial killer's been murdering humans."

That earned me a sharp look. "That's the stupidest thing I've ever heard. Charles wouldn't hurt anybody— not unless they were threatening me. He's not a hunter any . . ." She trailed off.

"Not a hunter any . . . *what*?" I prompted after a moment.

The color drained from her little cherublike face and her attention was no longer on me but on something behind me. A shiver went through me, despite the heat of the day, and I turned very slowly to see a young, dark-haired man smiling at us.

"Hi," he said. "Couldn't help but overhear your conversation."

I pasted a smile on my face. "Me and my darling daughter love to make up stories together."

"You're both vampires."

"No, we're not. But we do think they're kind of cool. Right, honey?"

"Very cool," Victoria confirmed in a nervous, squeaky voice.

He held up his hand. "No need to deny it. Haven't seen one in weeks, actually. You all have been keeping a seriously low profile. But look at you two, just strolling right up and practically introducing yourselves. Helpful."

"We're not what you think," I managed. Denial was always the best option for starters. It might buy me enough time to figure out how we could slip away from this guy before he alerted his buddies.

"It's okay," he said. "I love vampires."

"You do?"

"Yeah. They're lots of fun to play with." He raised his other hand, which held a dart gun. He squeezed off two rounds, the first hitting Victoria, the second hitting me, its sting similar to that of a large, angry bee. I pulled the small dart out of my shoulder and looked at it bleakly.

"Garlic darts," he explained, but he didn't have to. I already knew what they were.

Funny thing about garlic. While myth says that it repels vampires, the truth is that it knocks us out cold.

I had enough time to glance at Victoria. Her eyes were filled more with annoyance than fear.

Well, she'd said herself that I was a magnet for trouble. She was absolutely right.

The next moment, the world all around me faded to black.

I would have bet cold hard cash on waking up in the middle of that hunter bar. Or, even worse, not waking up at all.

But neither happened.

When I finally pried my eyes open, I was somewhere pitch-black. The thick air smelled stale. It was slightly cooler than before. I had no idea how long I'd been unconscious. It didn't feel like outside, since I sensed walls all around. I was indoors somewhere.

Pitch-black for humans, but my vampire senses kicked in and my eyes slowly adjusted to the lack of light. I couldn't see more than shapes, no real details, but it was better than nothing.

"H-hello?" I managed, my mouth and throat dry as sandpaper. Fear fluttered in my chest.

Oddly, I sat in a dirty but padded easy chair and it didn't take more than a second to realize that I was tied to it with ropes that were infused with silver. I felt the burn warning me not to struggle any harder against them. Silver: not my favorite precious metal.

I frantically scanned the darkness, pinpointing shapes and forms until I found Victoria. She was on an old, dirty sofa to my left, also restrained and currently unconscious. I was incredibly relieved she seemed otherwise unharmed.

Where were we? My head still felt like it had gone out partying last night and was dealing with the early stirrings of a hangover. I was only half-awake. The effects of a garlic dart didn't wear off all at once.

I squeezed my eyes shut.

"Sarah?" It was a familiar voice . . . so familiar. "Are you there?"

My eyes snapped open again and my heart picked up its pace. "Thierry? I'm here!"

His tall form appeared from around a corner and he came directly to my side. I could barely make out his handsome features in the darkness.

I let out a long, shaky sigh. "You don't know how happy I am to see you."

He gently touched my face, his expression tense. "I'm happy to see you, too."

"I don't know how you're here, but I'm totally okay with any miracles today. How about untying me?"

His lips thinned. "That will be a problem, I'm afraid."

"What? Why?"

"Because this is only a dream."

I blinked. "No, it's not a dream. I just woke up."

"Yes, but then you closed your eyes again and went back to sleep. However, I am heartened to know that you dream of me as your rescuer."

"Wait a minute—you're not really here?"

He shook his head gravely. "I'm still imprisoned in our hotel suite under house arrest. Should I step one foot outside, Markus's men would stake me immediately. It's quite inconvenient."

I was confused. "And this . . . is this one of those cool shared dreams? Are we here together all psychically?"

"Sorry, no. This is one hundred percent your dream. For all I know, you're safely back home and have left me far behind both in distance and in memory."

Disappointment crashed through me. "You know I'd never do that."

"Do I?" His eyes searched for mine. His touch felt so warm, so genuine, but my heart was breaking that this wasn't actually happening.

"I'd never leave you, Thierry. I'm trying to find the real killer."

His gaze swept the darkness. "So I'm assuming that you're having a few problems with that?"

"To put it mildly."

"How will you free yourself if you don't even know where you are?"

"I'm working on that."

His brows drew together. "You should have left this city. You know I wanted you to be safe—it's why I made Markus promise that you'd be unharmed. Why would you stay and put yourself in danger like this?"

"You know why."

"Why?"

I let out a frustrated groan. "You're really annoying sometimes, even in my dreams. You know that?"

His lips quirked. "If I am, then you must cherish my annoying ways. I could be anything you want me to be here, but you choose to make me just as I am when you're awake."

He was right. My throat tightened. "I miss you."

Dream-Thierry was about to kiss me, but before his lips touched mine, he faded away just like a ghost before my eyes.

My eyes popped open. I was awake. For real this time.

Same place, same darkness, but definitely awake and the wooziness was finally disappearing. I sucked in the stale air and craned my neck to look around, finding nothing helpful. "What is this place?"

"Tunnels," a voice—unfamiliar and female this time—replied. "Storm drains, to be precise. It's one of the City of Sin's many secrets. There's three hundred miles of these crisscrossing beneath the city. Fun, right?"

Every muscle in my body tensed at her conversational tone. "Who are you?"

"I'd say I'm a friend, but that would be a lie."

I saw her outline but not much else as she swept past me. I cast another glance toward Victoria, but she was still out cold. Same garlic dart, but she was much smaller than me, so it would take that much longer for her to recover. Poor kid. She was going to have one hell of a headache when she woke up.

"Are you a hunter?" I demanded, forcing myself to sound strong and in control when, given my current tied-up position, I was anything but.

She snorted. "Hardly."

"But the hunter who darted us—"

"Oh, yeah. He brought you down here and tied you up. Murmured something about getting his friend. Probably thinks this is an abandoned spot he magically discovered where he can torture his victims in peace and quiet. Wrong."

Fear snaked through me at the thought that the hunter would be back with reinforcements, and I was at a distinct disadvantage at the moment thanks to these ropes. Victoria, even though she was old enough to be my great-grandmother, was still just a six-year-old kid I'd promised to look after. If something happened to her, it would be completely my fault.

Charles would kill me. And from what I'd been guessing, he'd been practicing.

Actually, he wouldn't get the chance to kill me. I'm sure the hunter would check that off his to-do list right when he got back. And bringing me somewhere like this made me think he wanted to take a long time doing it.

I shuddered at the thought.

I needed to protect both myself and Victoria and get us out of here before those hunters returned.

"Okay," I forced out. "So you're not a hunter. But you're not a friend, either. However, you have come across two people in major need of help. Are you going to do something about that?"

"Haven't decided yet."

I pushed back against my frustration and circling panic. "Again, I'm going to go ahead and ask: Who are you?"

"My name's Charlotte. Nice to meet you." Her form moved closer to me and she reached up toward a dangling bare lightbulb to switch it on. Light bled into the dark area, helping me to see much better than before.

I blinked a couple of times as my eyes got used to the new amount of light and then looked toward Charlotte.

Death itself looked back at me.

Chapter 11

Okay, maybe I was being overly dramatic. But not by much.

At first glance, she looked like a bone-thin Goth teenager. Maybe seventeen or eighteen at the most, dressed in black, her bare arms covered in tattoos. Apart from the ink, her skin was smooth and unblemished, but pale. Inhumanly pale. Her long, pin-straight hair was platinum blond with black and purple streaks. And her eyes were black. Those black eyes glittered at me in the semidarkness.

"You're a vampire," I said. One who, by the looks of it, didn't do much work to fit in with regular human society.

"Yup." She drew closer so I could see the look of contempt she was giving me.

"Are you hungry?" Her eyes were the same black as a vampire who'd pushed him- or herself past the point of normal hunger pains. "Your eyes . . ."

"I'm always hungry. But my eyes are like this since I live underground. Sustained darkness makes them go like this all the time." She reached forward and pushed at my upper lip to show my fangs. "I thought so. You're a vampire, too."

I wrenched away from her curious touch. "You live down here? Are there more of you?"

"Sure. Some vampires. Some humans. Lots of rats. Home sweet home."

She was a subterranean vampire street kid. With a bad attitude. And she was currently my only hope of getting me and Victoria out of here in one piece.

"You said your eyes are like that all the time. How long have you been down here?"

"Long enough." Her lips stretched into an unpleasant smile. "You must be new if you don't know this little fact. If a vamp stays out of the sun for a few months it's nearly impossible to go back outside during the day. It's killer on the eyeballs, and our skin gets really sensitive—burns with any exposure to sunlight . . . hurts like hell. Would take a long, painful time to get used to it again. It's easier to stay hidden during the day and come out at night."

I'd honestly never heard of this before. I loved sunlight, even if I found it draining. I couldn't imagine staying away from it for months. Not voluntarily, anyway.

I inhaled some of that stale air. "Can I do anything to help you?"

She blinked those big black eyes with surprise and cocked her head to the side. "Help me?"

"I mean . . . yeah. If I can do anything, I will." Even with the bad attitude, I felt the loneliness emanating off her in waves. There might be other vampires who chose to live under the city in the darkness, but I wondered how many she considered friends.

"You mean that, don't you?"

"I don't usually say things I don't mean."

"I don't want your help. You're obviously help*less*, given your situation." Her gaze moved over the ropes and flicked to Victoria. "Honestly, do you have absolutely no survival instincts at all?"

"I've been working on it." But her words did make me flinch. Ever since my conversation with Laura I'd been worried that I was like her—helpless and vulnerable if I didn't have someone around to protect me. My current situation hadn't exactly set my mind at ease about that.

"I bet you don't even know how lucky you are, do you?"

I snorted at that. Couldn't help it. "Lucky? Trust me, Charlotte, I'm one of the least lucky people I know."

"Oh, I don't know about that. I mean, you obviously have had some hard knocks. You getting dragged down here and tied up proves that. But otherwise . . ." Another sweeping appraisal. "You're well dressed, well groomed, and that rock on your finger means somebody up there cares about you." Her black eyes snapped to mine and I saw endless depths of envy there. "Like I said, you're lucky."

She was right, I was lucky in so many ways. Sometimes I forgot to be grateful for what I had. This—well, this would work as a nice reminder. If I survived it.

"I need your help, Charlotte," I said evenly, holding her gaze. "Help me get out of here and I will do whatever I can to help you in return. If you want me to."

She eyed me. "I don't know if I care one way or the other about what happens to you."

My throat tightened. "If that was true, you'd already have walked away from me. But you haven't. You're a good person—I know you are. You won't leave us here to die."

"I won't?"

"No, you won't."

She smiled and it looked really genuine this time. Then the pleasant expression on her pale face fell. "Wrong."

She flicked off the light and walked away.

Damn.

I never said I was the best judge of character.

Silence and the bitter taste of disappointment reigned for what felt like an eternity, but was probably only twenty minutes or so. My thoughts raced and the darkness felt like a living thing pressing in on every side of me. Finally, I heard a rustle next to me as Victoria woke up.

"Urrum mphhh," her little voice squeaked out.

I sighed. "You took the words right out of my mouth."

"Wha—? What's happening? Where are we? Ohhh, my head!"

Concern twisted inside me. It was bad enough for me to take that garlic dart, let alone this little girl. "It gets better. Just give it a minute."

"I'm going to kill you," she growled.

"I thought you might say something like that."

"Where's the hunter?"

"I don't know." I was trying really, really hard not to panic, but with every passing moment it grew more difficult to stay calm.

Charlotte was long gone. She'd stayed just long enough to make me believe she might help, and then disappeared into the darkness.

I bit back my fear and disappointment, and tried to figure out a plan B.

"These ropes are made with silver," Victoria commented after a moment.

"Yup."

"So what you're basically saying is that we're sitting ducks."

"Quack." I refused to let my voice tremble. I had to be strong.

"I'm going to miss my hair appointment." She sounded mad, but I now heard an edge of panic there as well.

"I think you already did. I have a feeling we've been down here for a while."

"Did I mention that I'm going to kill you?"

"Yes, you said that already."

"Wonderful," she said dryly. "And just for the record while we're waiting to die, puppy, Charles is not a serial killer."

I pressed my lips together. "If you say so."

"Charles has looked after me for forty years—he's like a real father to me after all this time. I trust him with my life. If I'd been with him today, this wouldn't have happened."

I tugged on my restraints, but the silver burned too much. How was I going to get us out of here before the hunters got back?

"Right. If he wasn't off doing his mysterious errands around Las Vegas. I mean, seriously. What kind of errands does someone need to do in Vegas? Someone with a blood addiction and a penchant for violence?"

"It's not him." Even so, the tiniest edge of doubt had crept into her voice as if she'd been thinking over my admittedly shaky evidence.

"But you think it might be," I pressed. "Just a little."

"I don't know. Do you think that sourpuss could have had Bernard killed?"

I hissed out a sigh. "No."

"Just no? Not . . . maybe?"

"He didn't. I know Thierry." Not nearly as much as I wanted to, but enough. "It wasn't him."

"Then it's too bad he's going to die for it anyway, isn't it?"

Before I could reply to that tactless statement, I heard the vampire hunters approaching and every muscle in my body tensed. Their telltale heavy boots gave them away. You'd think they'd walk quietly so they could sneak up on their prey, but since their prey were already trussed up like a couple of fanged turkeys, I guess they decided that stealth was not necessary.

Flashlights shone on my face and I winced at the sudden light, trying not to let any fear show in my eyes.

"Oh, man, you're right. She's a looker." The flashlight then moved toward Victoria. "A kid? That's going to be weird, man. I've never slayed a kid before."

"It's a vampire, not a kid," the hunter who'd darted us replied.

"Still. It gives me the creeps."

The flashlight returned to my face and I'd plastered a fake but confident smile on my lips, avoiding baring my fangs, small though they were. "So, let's talk about this, boys."

"What do you want to talk about?"

I commanded myself to be brave. "Oh, I don't know. Stuff. Like how awesome you two are. You totally win."

"Win what?"

"The prize," I said as if it should be obvious. "You know how they have secret shoppers in department stores who report on how the salesclerks do with customers? Well, we're a team of secret vampires who test the skills of fantastic hunters. All you need to do is let us go and we'll report to your superiors about how amazing you are."

"That sounds great," the new hunter said.

"Don't be an idiot," the first hunter snapped. "She's trying to fool you. There are no secret vampires."

"How do you know, Shane? I mean, if everybody knew about them, they wouldn't be secret, would they?"

I liked slow-witted hunters. Too bad I didn't have two of them to work with today.

The flashlight shone on the sharp silver blade one of these guys held. I suddenly couldn't look anywhere else.

"Her fiancé has money," Victoria offered shakily. "He'll pay big bucks if you let us go."

"The kid speaks," the dim hunter said with a smile. "She's so adorable. She looks like that—what's her name?—Shirley Temple. From the old movies. Hey, is that you, Shirley? You stayed the same age all these years?"

"Sure, that's me," Victoria chirped immediately, not missing a beat. "Adorable, right? I can sing a song for you if you'd like. 'Good Ship Lollipop'? Remember that one?"

"That would be delightful!"

The flashlight shone on the stupid hunter's face. "Seriously, Dan. Shut up."

The second flashlight shone on the other's face. "Why do you always have to ruin my fun?"

"Fun is what I brought you down here for, dumbass. Singing isn't a part of it." Shane moved toward me, shining his flashlight right on my face. "So here we are, pretty little vampire."

"What do you want?" I asked without humor. My throat was tight. "Money?"

"Money's never really held much appeal for me."

"Spoken like someone who comes from it."

"Good guess." He stroked the hair off my forehead. His touch made me shudder with disgust. Quite honestly, he wasn't a bad-looking guy. My guess was that this was a rich kid who'd picked up a hobby that filled his boring days—someone who liked to kill just for the sport of it. From my brief experience as one of the hunted, those were the absolute worst kind.

His friend I might be able to manipulate. Shane, the vampire hunter whose trust fund helped buy his wooden stakes, was another story.

This wasn't going well at all. "I've never hurt anyone. I know you see the fangs and you think I'm a threat, but you're wrong."

"Sure. And what about the trail of dead bodies left around the city this week with fang marks in their necks? That's the doing of just another nice, nonthreatening gal like you, right?"

So news of the serial killer's victims had reached the hunters. I wasn't too surprised by that. Hunters were hateful, but resourceful. And they loved to gossip as much as blue-haired grannies. "Are you looking for whoever did it?"

"As far as I'm concerned, the one who did it is tied

up right here in front of me." He cupped my cheek and dragged his thumb across my bottom lip. "Looking all cute and innocent."

"You're right," Victoria growled, sounding as dangerous as a fierce kitten. "Sarah plays innocent, but she's a beast. Better watch out. You're close enough that she could tear off your hand with her teeth if she wanted to."

Shane yanked his hand away from me a split second later. Victoria's threat proved that this hunter could be intimidated by a vampire he'd tied up.

I couldn't do anything about it since I couldn't freaking move, but it was still interesting. Extra speed and strength, or even the ability to see in the dark, did me absolutely no good right now, not until these ropes came off. My only weapon was my words. I had to choose them very wisely.

"There's more like me," I said evenly, channeling what little confidence I had left into my voice. If Shane was legitimately afraid of vampires, I might be able to work with that. "I'm in constant contact with them thanks to my . . . vampire telepathy. I've waited until you got back to call them in. They're almost here and they're going to hurt you very badly. And maybe, eventually, if you're really lucky, we'll let you die."

Both hunters shuddered at the threat. Then they cast their flashlights off to the left and I followed the track of the beams to an opening that led to a set of stairs.

Exit stage left. Noted for future reference.

"Not long at all," I said again, trying my hardest to keep my voice steady. "I think I can hear them coming through the darkness. You'll never see them until it's too late."

"Shane . . ."

"Just relax. She's bluffing."

"I don't want my throat torn out by a vampire." There was genuine fear in Dan's voice.

Even though I was absolutely, positively not any more evil than I was when I was human, there was something exciting about eliciting the fear of an enemy. I could taste it, smell it, feel it. And somehow, on some deep level, I liked it. Especially when it came to these two.

The bright flashlight shone on my face again and I winced. Shane didn't look the least bit afraid anymore. He looked like a rich kid ready to unwrap his latest expensive toy. But now he'd just be extra careful not to get a paper cut while he did it.

"So, vampire," he began, drawing closer. Confidence had filled his hateful expression again and a cold line of perspiration slid between my shoulder blades. "I think you're all talk. You're not telepathic. And I know that silver keeps you pinned like a butterfly on a board. You're bluffing. And it's not working." He twisted a piece of my hair around his finger and tugged on it painfully. His flashlight shone down onto my hand. "Engaged, are you? Do you think he'll miss you when you're gone?"

"Any second now," I said, struggling not give in to despair as my heart thundered in my chest. "Vampirepalooza. All over you."

He slid his fingers over my ring. It felt like more of a violation than if he'd grabbed my butt. "Will he seek vengeance for what I'm going to do to you, do you think? Can monsters really fall in love?"

"I don't know," I bit out through clenched teeth. "Why don't you tell me?"

That earned me a grin just before he put the tip of his knife to my throat and then slid it slowly down to my chest right over my heart. "I was going to take my time, but you're a bit of a wild card, I think. Best to get this over with."

"Do it!" Dan urged him on.

I wouldn't scream. I wouldn't beg. I knew neither would do me any good. Fury rose up level with my terror and I kept my eyes open, blazing into those of the hunter—the one who would finally manage to kill me in the dark storm drains underneath Las Vegas. But first he'd had to tie me up to do it so I wouldn't be able to fight back.

Some hunter.

I'm so sorry, Thierry, I thought. *I'm sorry I wasn't strong enough to save you . . . or Victoria.*

I braced myself for what he was about to do.

And then, with a loud crash, all the lights went out.

Chapter 12

Luckily, finding myself in pitch-black surroundings again didn't mean I was dead.

It meant the flashlights had been smashed. I saw a shape move in the darkness, which would have been completely indiscernible to a human eye. Shane flew backward and away from me. Then there was the sound of the hunters' heads smacking together and their bodies hitting the ground.

Total silence hung in the inky blackness for a good ten seconds while I tried to find my voice.

"See?" I said shakily. "I knew you wouldn't abandon us."

A low chuckle. "You didn't really know that for sure."

"No, you're right. I didn't."

Charlotte flicked the light back on, but I figured she did it for my benefit, not hers.

"Holy cow!" Victoria exclaimed. "Who the hell are you?"

Six years old or 102, Victoria Corday was not the most tactful creature on the planet.

Charlotte's black eyes tracked to her and her lips curved back into a chilling smile, showing off her sharp fangs. "A nightmare you'll be having for weeks to come, little girl."

"Stop messing around and untie us," I snapped.

"I took out the hunters—you can untie yourselves."

"Charlotte," I snarled.

"Nice tone. Maybe you've learned something down here. Being pretty and polite will only get you so far." She came toward me and crouched down. "There's just one thing."

"What's that?"

"I didn't do this because I like you. I did it for payment."

"I would be happy to pay you for saving us in the nick of time. How much money do you want?"

"No, I'm thinking of something else." Her black eyes moved to my left hand.

I tensed. "Don't even think about it."

Her grin widened. "Too late." She yanked my engagement ring off me so hard it nearly broke my finger before she slid it onto her own. She admired it. "Pretty."

There weren't too many things I owned anymore that I really cherished. I'd found that possessions could be destroyed or taken away in a second, and the more you cared about them, the more it hurt to see them vanish.

My ring from Thierry was one of the few things I never wanted to lose. Ever. It wasn't just a ring—it was a promise.

A promise that I was going to kick this chick's butt as soon as I got loose.

"Untie me," I said through clenched teeth.

"You betcha." She reached around me and fiddled with the knots. "The silver burns a bit, doesn't it?"

The moment I felt the tight ropes slacken, I burst forward and grabbed Charlotte by her shirt, slamming her against the concrete wall to our right.

"Thank you for saving my life," I said as sweetly as possible. "I'd be happy to offer payment to you in another agreeable way. But give me my ring back. Now."

She had the audacity to look amused. "Didn't know you were a fighter."

"I'm usually not."

"Maybe that's changing."

"Maybe it is." Maybe I was evolving and changing with the times. Becoming less of a potential victim and way more kick-ass.

It was a lovely thought.

"It's good. The world is a tough one. Maybe you've been stuck in your bubble for a while wherever you came from, dealing with a couple hunters here and there. But out here in the real world things are way tougher than that. And when you're faced with your darkest fear, you have to decide right then and there if you're going to fight it or if you're going to run away. You looked more like a runner to me."

"I do like to jog a little. Burns calories."

"I'm not giving the ring back."

"Oh, believe me. You are."

She shook her head. "Finders, keepers—"

Just as I was maneuvering to hold her in place with one hand and grab the ring back off her finger with the other, she managed to twist around so she had *me* pinned against the wall instead. She was strong—stronger than she looked. By a whole lot.

"—losers, weepers," she finished, and then launched me over her shoulder like a discarded banana peel. I landed hard on my back fifteen feet away, the wind knocked out of me. I gasped for breath while I stared up at the dark ceiling. As soon as I could, I scrambled to my feet and spun around, searching for her.

She was gone.

And so was my ring.

I let out a strangled scream and fought the tears of frustration stinging my eyes.

"Nice try," Victoria said.

I stared off into the blackness. I had no idea what direction she'd gone or how fast she could run. "Yeah, if nice means pathetic."

"Sometimes it does, puppy."

"Don't call me that anymore," I growled.

That shut her up for a moment. "Um . . . are you going to untie me before these two hunters wake up? Please?"

That much I could accomplish successfully. First I grabbed the garlic dart gun lying on the ground and tossed it into my gaping open purse next to where I'd been tied up. I had no idea what I might need it for, but one less dart gun in a hunter's hands was a good thing. Then I stepped over the unconscious hunters like human-sized land mines and as I did, I searched for that special sense of mine that had told me the guy on the street was dead. These guys weren't. They were still breathing. It half surprised me that Charlotte didn't want to add murder to her list today as well as theft. As far as I was concerned, that vampire's morals weren't much better than the serial killer's.

I would have paid her. I would have paid her *lots* for her help. I knew I would have died if she hadn't come back. But she didn't have to steal my damn ring. I ran my hand under my nose as I sniffed while forcing myself to work on Victoria's ropes. The silver in them burned my fingers as I loosened them enough for her to slip out. I rubbed my hands together and tried not to look down at my naked finger. I hadn't taken the ring off once since Thierry had first given it to me three months ago. I'd grown very accustomed to the comforting weight of it.

"You okay?" Victoria asked quietly. It surprised me that there was no sarcasm or edge to her words this time.

"I'm alive," I replied as I zipped up my purse and threw it over my shoulder. "And so are you. Now let's get the hell out of here."

She surprised me again as she reached for my hand. I let her take it, reminding myself that she was just a kid. And, despite her semitough exterior, this might have been the closest brush with death she'd ever had.

Damn, there it was. My instinctive need to protect things that were smaller and weaker and more scared than me. At the moment, that was Victoria.

I think we both could have used a shot of whiskey at this point. I'd pass on any cigarettes.

Hand in hand, we moved toward the stairs, going up them until they changed, turned into rickety wooden ones that led to a door about four stories up. I turned the handle and pushed it open.

Surprisingly, it was some sort of public place. Being around a group of people after spending who knew how much time down in that dark storm drain felt like a huge relief. The door closed and clicked shut behind us.

Which was around the moment I realized exactly where we were.

The storm drain stairs had led up into the hunter bar. And we were currently surrounded by about fifty hunters of varying shapes and sizes.

Crap.

"You were right." Victoria squeezed my hand so tightly that it actually hurt. "You *are* a magnet for trouble. I think you're a whole fridge door full of them."

I reached for the door again only to find it had locked behind us.

I braced myself for the attack . . . any second now. . . .

But no attack came.

Nobody even paid any attention to us, other than a random surprised glance here and there to find a bedraggled brunette and a cute blond kid suddenly in their midst.

They hadn't guessed what we were. Not yet, anyway. I mean, what sane vampire would ever knowingly stroll right through the middle of a hunter bar?

Well, me. My common sense had improved some over the months, but my sanity had always been a bit of a question mark.

"Just passing through," I said casually as we started walking toward the exit. I didn't dare show even a glimpse of fang. No smiling allowed—which wasn't all that difficult to manage at the moment.

The door wasn't far away, really. And the two hunters downstairs were still unconscious. For now.

One foot in front of the other. Had to keep walking. Sunlight was ahead. Freedom was beyond. We'd recharge and reassess; then I'd figure out what my next move would be.

But then someone stepped out in front of me, blocking my path. I stared directly into his black T-shirt-clad chest.

"Sarah?" he said with surprise. "I don't really think this is the right place for you, sweetheart."

My eyes widened and I looked up at his face to see the very hunter I'd put my neck on the line to find today.

"Duncan," I managed.

He was grinning, but I couldn't say it was all that friendly. Looked more like the smile of an amused predator. "How on earth did you even get in here?"

He wasn't immediately sounding the alarms. I hoped that was a good sign. "Magical powers."

"You're funny. No idea what a cute little thing like you is doing with Thierry, but maybe he has a side he doesn't show anyone else. Am I right? Does he have a soft underbelly I just don't know about?"

Letting on that Thierry was anything but the stone-cold, emotionless master vampire he appeared to be to most people was not in his best interest. Or mine, for that matter. "Nope. He's a total hard-ass, through and through. He'll kill you as soon as look at you. He just tolerates me because he lost a bet."

Victoria had my hand clutched in hers so tightly I was certain it was literally changing the shape of it.

Soon I would have one good hand and one bloody stump. She tugged on my arm. "Sarah?"

Well, if nothing else, severe stress and trauma had made her use my real name for a change. Miracles do happen.

And I wasn't letting any other miracles like the one right in front of me escape just because I was freaking out inside. "I need to talk to you, Duncan. Um, away from here would be a good start."

"Oh yeah?"

"I'll pay."

"This must be my lucky day."

Mine too, maybe. In more ways than one.

He kept that grin on his face, and it filled me with more hope. While Duncan's expression was filled with greed, it was a greed that would lead me to the answers I needed to help Thierry. I knew it.

"I want to know who hired you to kill Bernard," I asked him, point-blank. I flicked a look at the door, wishing I was on the other side of it right now. "Somebody did, didn't they?"

"They sure did," he confirmed. "Went down a bit differently than planned, though. One of my best kills ever, I think. Did you see the look on everybody's face before that enforcer started wiping their memories? If he hadn't been so damn busy, I might not have been able to slip out of there."

Markus was able to wipe the witnesses' memories? How could he do something like that?

No time to ask right now, so I filed that away for later.

"How did it go differently than planned?" I pressed. "And who hired you? I need answers."

"To save that hard-ass who tolerates you because of a bet?"

"Maybe I'm the one with the soft spot, not him."

He leered at me. "You and Thierry, huh? I guess *you're* his soft spot now, aren't you? Interesting."

I really didn't like this guy, but I needed him. "Talk to me, Duncan. Please. I said I'd pay."

"Oh, you bet your sweet little ass you will. You pay me enough and I'd be happy to tell you every last detail you need to save your fiancé's life."

I hated hoping. A lot of the time, hope was a big, shiny, colorful bow that did its best to hide nothing but an empty box underneath. Duncan was saying everything I wanted to hear right now. Everything except the real answers I desperately needed.

It seemed as if I now required a bank machine. Stat.

"Okay, then let's go," I said firmly. "I'll get you the money and you can get me my answers."

"Lead the way, sweetheart."

Money talks.

I was counting on that being Duncan's rather nasty personal philosophy. He hadn't raised the alarm that two vampires were smack-dab in the middle of this Vegas hunter bar. He just grinned at the thought of money, ready to sell out whoever hired him at the first flash of green.

I could totally work with that.

This was going to happen. This was what I'd been looking for all day and it had practically fallen into my lap. I was going to prove Thierry's innocence and make Mr. Enforcer leave him alone. For once, something was easy. For once, I wasn't a magnet for trouble. I'd walked right through the lions' den and found that one of the lions was willing to help me get out of here in one hopeful piece. For a price.

I should have known it wouldn't last.

A shadow loomed at the entrance just as we'd reached it. A large, fierce-looking man in leather and chains whose dark eyes flashed with anger. For a split second, I froze because I thought he was looking at me and Victoria. But he wasn't. He was looking just past us at the hunter standing behind us.

"Duncan Keller!" he bellowed. "You son of a bitch!"

"Uh-oh," Duncan said.

I turned to face him. "Who is that?"

His attention wasn't on me. "Just the husband of a woman I've been sleeping with. This shouldn't take long. Just give me a minute to deal with this."

Victoria's grip on my hand increased, if that was even possible, as the other man stormed toward Duncan and grabbed him by the front of his shirt.

"Attila," Duncan began, "I can explain."

The guy's name was Attila?

That did not bode well.

"Couldn't keep your hands to yourself, could you, Keller?" Attila growled. "You should have. I've forgiven her indiscretions too many times, but not this time. I thought we were friends, and you'd do this behind my back? It's over!"

The entire bar had turned to watch the confrontation with varying degrees of interest and amusement. No one seemed the least bit concerned, even when Attila shoved Duncan back. The other hunter slammed into a table, sending beer glasses and plates crashing to the ground.

"Duncan!" I yelled as he got to his feet. But instead

of backing away and apologizing profusely for what he'd done, he attacked. Fists flew and in a few moments those witnessing the fight were placing bets and cheering their choices on as if this had suddenly turned into a steel cage match.

Victoria tugged on my hand as a beer bottle smashed on the wall dangerously close to where we were standing. "We should leave."

"Not yet. I can't leave—he's going to help me!"

Attila's face was bleeding from being repeatedly smashed with Duncan's fist, but he wasn't backing down, either. He finally got the upper hand, grabbing hold of Duncan and raising him up above his head, wrestler-style, and then slamming him down hard on top of the ratty-looking pool table in the far corner. Duncan scrambled for his wooden stake—a decent weapon when fighting vampire *or* human—but he didn't have a chance to use it to defend himself. Attila had snatched the pool cue from another hunter's grip and—

"Just remember, Keller," he bellowed. "You brought this on yourself!"

I covered Victoria's eyes as he brought the pool cue down, pointy end first, at Duncan's chest.

Duncan's attention flicked to me before his eyes glazed over.

I sensed the moment his heart stopped beating and his life left the building.

My hope hitched a ride right along with it.

Chapter 13

We didn't stick around. The damage had been done.

My mind reeled from what just happened. All so fast. We'd been close—*I'd* been close. Duncan was going to talk to me, with a little monetary coaxing. He would have told me who hired him to kill Bernard. Thierry would have been proven innocent—I mean, as soon as I got Markus to believe it. The point was, it would have been a step in the right direction instead of scrambling to keep my footing on this slippery slope.

I hated this. Every direction I turned just led to more failure and the day was fading fast. It was late afternoon by now—almost five o'clock. We'd been unconscious in the tunnels longer than I thought we were. That garlic dart had been extremely potent.

I sighed shakily. "I don't know what to do now."

"Give up," Victoria said.

"Excuse me?"

"Sometimes you need to know when to quit. I wanted to figure it out, too, but it's not looking like that's possible." She had her hand on her hip and was looking at her little pink cell phone. "The hunter's dead and so's your chance to clear sourpuss's name. I'd take the hint if I were you. Besides, how long's he been alive? Hundreds of years? I'd bet he's done lots of bad stuff in his life way worse than what happened to Bernard. Maybe he deserves this."

I didn't say anything. Every word she spoke dropped on me like a tiny bomb. Not because I necessarily agreed with her, but because her point was painfully clear. Quitting would be what a lot of people do when they see their path is filled with rocks. That they're fighting a losing battle. That they just stepped in quicksand and they better pull their foot out while it's only an expensive shoe they're going to lose and not the entire leg.

Had Thierry done bad things in his existence? I mean, I didn't know half of it. A quarter of it. A hundredth of it, really. But I knew he had. The most recent skeleton I'd found in his closet was the group of hunters Bernard told me about who'd paid the ultimate price when Thierry had lost control of his bloodlust.

Was there an expiration date on evil acts? If you did something heinous a hundred years ago, did time and tide wash it all away? And if so, where was the line drawn? A century, a human lifetime, a decade?

How long did someone need to be actively redemptive before he was purged of all sins?

Yikes. My head throbbed just trying to wrap itself around questions like that. I wasn't the right person to make these sorts of determinations. I wasn't a lawyer or a judge or a jury. Had Thierry done enough in his six-hundred-plus years of life to land himself on death row? If so, did that mean he should be there now, even if it looked more like a luxury suite in a fabulous hotel?

And if I weren't in love with him, would I be so willing to forgive the things he'd done in the past?

So many questions, so few answers.

Such was my life.

All I knew was that he was a man with a great deal more history than I had. And, yes, those skeletons in his closet could fill an entire graveyard. A big one with tall iron gates.

But even though I knew this, it didn't change a single thing for me. Not a single damn thing.

I touched my left hand, feeling the loss of my engagement ring. *That's* when my bottom lip finally started wobbling.

"Puppy?" Victoria asked warily. I didn't bother to correct her on the nickname. I wasn't feeling quite as fierce as I had in the tunnels with the vampire girl. "Don't cry."

I couldn't break down, not in front of her. I didn't want her to see me totally lose it right now. "I'm not going to cry."

"He's not worth it."

That was debatable. "It's done. Until I figure out what to do next, I should get you back to Charles."

Her potentially psychopathic pseudo-daddy who'd be tracking us down any minute now.

She consulted her phone again. "I texted him. I left out the part about us almost getting killed. He'd probably blame you for putting me in danger."

I wasn't sure if I should thank her for this omission.

"Oh, he's just replied. He says for us to meet him at Blood Bath and Beyond in half an hour."

The blood addict wanted to meet us at a blood bank. That wasn't a terribly surprising location. "Fine. I could use a drink."

I could use a lot of things at the moment, but I'd start

with a little B-positive before I wandered the city homeless and directionless now that my main lead to help Thierry had a big piece of wood sticking out of his chest. It was an ironic end for a vampire hunter.

As we headed toward the blood bank, I started thinking about home and how I'd left mine to travel here with Thierry, assuming it would be the beginning of life on the road for us. They say that home is where the heart is.

It was only a little over a month ago that I'd finally moved in with him. He held tightly on to his privacy, but my previous housemate, George, had packed up and left the country to move to Hawaii and that left me homeless. I didn't have all that many things to gather, but gather them I did and I arrived at Thierry's doorstep like some sort of street urchin.

He opened the front door of his townhome and looked out at me. "You're here."

"With bells on."

"Come in."

My feet wouldn't move. They'd suddenly become a bit cold. "Thierry, I don't know. Maybe I should get my own place."

He just looked at me patiently. "Come in, Sarah."

I mean, we'd been engaged for a couple months by then. I wasn't shy. But the thought of sharing Thierry's house after it was like pulling teeth to get him to share *anything* about himself—well, this would take some time to adjust to. I'd been there many times before, but it always seemed so big and cold. I honestly couldn't imagine living there full-time. But there I was.

"How many square feet is this place, anyway?" I asked, glancing around at the large foyer.

"Sixty-eight hundred."

"Sixty-eight hundred square feet," I repeated. In that case, I hadn't seen more than half of it. "It's a cavern, not a townhome."

And it gave a new definition to the word sparse. All white walls with high ceilings, it held very few pieces of furniture except for the essentials. No clutter, no magazines, no friendly pets or plants. There were a couple cold marble statues that looked like they each cost a small fortune. If there was any dust, the dust was probably too intimidated to show itself.

"How often do you vacuum?" I asked.

His lips curved. "I have someone who comes in once a week to do that for me."

"Figured." I didn't know these things. Why didn't I know these things?

"I'm not looking for a maid, Sarah."

"I'm not offering." I looked around again. The chandelier above us was large enough to give even the Phantom of the Opera heart palpitations. "Never noticed how cozy this place was before."

"They say a home reflects its owner."

"You think so, huh? So you think you're cold, cavernous, and essentially empty?" I raised an eyebrow as I glanced at him.

That earned me a smile. "Depends on the day, really." He took my suitcase from me and leaned over to brush his lips against mine. "I'm glad you're here."

The cavern already felt about ten degrees warmer. "Really?"

"Really."

"Didn't think, despite the size of this place, that there'd be enough room for me here."

"Maybe not before. But there is now."

"What's changed?"

His smile widened at my trepidation about entering a house I'd been to many times before. "Would you prefer I charge you rent? Would that make you feel more comfortable calling this your home?"

"I don't think I could afford it."

He slid his gaze over the high ceilings, white walls, brass fixtures. "If you want to add anything you think would warm it up in here, feel free."

That sounded like an interesting challenge. "How long's it been like this?"

"Cold and empty?"

"Yeah."

He met my gaze. "A very, very long time."

"I guess it's definitely time for a change, isn't it?"

"Long overdue."

I grinned at him. "I'm up to the challenge."

I'd really only gotten started on that when we had to leave for his "offer he couldn't refuse." But I'd done what I could to warm the place up. I'd started with a welcome mat. It had a happy face on it and was bright and color-ful. It didn't say "Welcome." It said "!!!WELCOME!!!"

I knew he wouldn't like it. I considered it more of an amusing test to see how open he was to change. He'd let me move in with him, but how flexible was he really willing to be?

It disappeared the day after I placed it by the front door. It was just—*poof!*—gone. When I imagined the shocked look on his face when he would have first seen it, a spot of wacky and whimsical color in his other-wise monochromatic world, I started to laugh hysteri-cally.

Thierry entered the foyer to see me standing there with tears streaming down my cheeks. He immediately came toward me and took me by my arms. "What is it, Sarah?"

"My . . . welcome mat . . . it—it's gone. . . ." I couldn't catch my breath. My laughter came in hiccups now.

He didn't realize I was laughing; he only saw the tears. His expression was now etched with regret. "I'll bring it back."

I just stared up at him with surprise. "You will?"

He stroked the hair back from my face. "Of course. If you really want it here, I—I can find a way to accept the mat. If you like it, then I'll like it, too."

A smile spread over my face. "I don't care about the stupid mat."

He looked at me then like I was completely insane. Maybe I was.

At that moment, I finally felt like I was home—as long as I was with him.

Yeah, it was cheesy, but that's how I felt. So sue me.

"Sarah, good to see you again!" Josh, the owner/manager of Blood Bath & Beyond, greeted me in the coffin room.

"You too. I seriously need a drink," I told him. "It's been a rough day . . . and that's a huge understatement."

"I hear you." He put his hands on his hips and bent over toward Victoria. "And what's your name, young lady?"

"Back off," Victoria replied. "I don't do cute."

Josh shot a surprised look at me and I shrugged.

"Victoria does do cute, but she needs a larger audience for it first."

"I see. Well, allow me." He creaked open the door to the coffin and the three of us stepped into the Starbucks blood bank.

I scanned the place. "I guess Charles isn't here yet."

"Charles?" Josh asked.

"Victoria's . . . friend. He's the one who recommended this place to me." I flicked a look at the tiny vamp. "What's his last name, anyway?"

"Manson," she offered, then grimaced when I blanched. "No relation, I swear."

Oh boy.

Feeling even more uneasy than before, I ordered my shot of blood and a regular brewed coffee and paid for both mine and Victoria's out of the small amount of cash I had in my wallet. Sure, Charlotte took my ring but left my purse behind. That made sense. For a thief, she was a lousy one.

The B-positive didn't help today. I hadn't really expected that it would.

Charles Manson. Unbelievable.

"Hey, kid," Josh said with a grin. "Check this out."

He moved toward Victoria and touched her ear, pulling out a large gold coin. She stared at it for a moment before her eyes went wide and a big smile stretched across her face.

She clapped her hands excitedly. "Do it again!"

He did it with the other ear, this time pulling out a silver coin.

"Neat trick," I said. "Is that part of your act at . . . where did you say you have a show? Club Noir?"

"You got it. Vladimir Nosferatu the Great." He laughed. "Although I might be changing that to something a bit less corny soon. I use props from the store. Some magicians have their assistants escape from wooden boxes. I do coffins. Instead of live doves—bats. Fake ones at the moment, but they look pretty cool. I also have a segment with a kitten wearing a tiny Dracula cape."

I couldn't help but grin at the mental image. "That's ridiculously adorable."

He shrugged a shoulder. "I try."

"How's business for the shows?"

"Not bad. Could be better, but there's a lot of competition in town. I share the stage six nights a week with Kristopher the Magnificent."

"Another magician?"

"No, he's a psychic."

"I can sing and dance," Victoria offered. "And I'm looking for a new gig if you're looking to expand the evening of entertainment."

Josh eyed her. "You?"

"She's actually a hundred and two," I explained. "And currently unemployed."

"Ah. Well, I'll keep you in mind if a spot opens up, Victoria. Not sure it's quite the act I'm looking for, though. Kristopher keeps things pretty interesting for the audience as he reads minds and communes with spirits from the other side."

That made me sit up taller with a jerk. A bit of the hot coffee splashed onto my lap. "For real, or is it just an act?"

"Good question. I like him—I really do—but he's a bit strange. He's always at the theater, too—I think he practically lives there. I get this gut feeling that he's got some serious, legitimate skills, but something's preventing him from tapping into them as much as he could. I have no idea why he's stuck working at a dive like Club Noir."

His cell phone rang and he put it to his ear, talking quickly with someone on the other end of the line. When he ended the call, he looked at me, his expression apologetic.

"I have to deal with a problem."

"Something wrong?"

"Just a new employee of mine. He's . . . a bit of a hothead. Likes to scream at customers. Had no idea he was a vampire with human issues when I hired him a week ago. Afraid he's going to go postal if I fire him, but looks like it's going in that direction."

"Sorry."

"Yeah, me too." The strain on Josh's face was hard to ignore. "See you later, Sarah."

"Good luck."

He disappeared through the coffin door, leaving me there thinking hard.

A hothead employee—a vampire one—who'd been working here for a week. Everybody was looking like a suspect to me right now. I thought I'd said I didn't care about the serial killer? I only cared about Bernard's murder?

Right. The murder I hadn't been able to figure out yet and probably never would.

Ah, yes. Those were the chiming bells of doom echoing in my ears. I recognized that tune very well.

"Finished?" I asked Victoria.

She nodded, setting aside her tiny cup of O-positive

and bottle of chocolate milk. Her face was still lit up from before. "He did magic!"

"That's what magicians do." I'd take a stage magician any day over a real witch or wizard. Coin tricks were way more fun to deal with than curses, no question about it.

We slowly left the Starbucks and wandered through the massive vampire-themed store toward the front entrance. A stuffed bat swooped so low overhead that it nearly got caught in my tangled hair. As we passed the slot machines, I decided to try one more time. In went a quarter and out came . . .

Nothing.

Again, it was a straw and camel's back situation. Such a tiny failure made my eyes start to sting. I kept walking and ran my hand under my nose, trying to give myself a pep talk, only to find my inner cheerleader had gone on her dinner break and I had no idea when she'd be back.

"Oh, there you are." Charles was waiting outside, his arms crossed. Victoria ran directly to him and gave him a big hug. He shot me a look of impatience. I shot him back a look of suspicion.

It was on the tip of my tongue to ask him about the blood I'd seen smeared on his lips earlier. Was it from a blood bank or from the latest serial killer's victim who'd dropped dead right in front of me?

But I kept my mouth shut. About that, anyway.

"How long are you staying in Vegas?" I asked as calmly as I could.

"Our flight leaves tomorrow night."

"Flight to where?"

"Why, Sarah? Are you planning on staying in touch?"

I didn't really like his sardonic tone. I'd been friendly enough with this guy—to his face, anyway—given my doubts about his potentially murderous nature, plus I'd done some free babysitting today. Unexpected kidnapping notwithstanding. In my opinion, he should be friendlier. "Maybe I am. Maybe me and the kid bonded this afternoon."

"That's sweet. We live in Seattle. Having a connection to the Ring might be nice. Yes, please stay in touch."

"I'll send a postcard."

This guy gave me the creeps. Big-time. All I could see when I closed my eyes was him slicing that blade into Thierry's chest. The image morphed into him slicing his fangs into unsuspecting human necks.

I don't trust you, buddy.

"I'll see you again before we leave," Victoria said. "Won't I?"

"I don't know," I replied, wondering how I could gather more information about Charles Manson's shady background as a vampire hunter. "Do you want to?"

"Of course I do!" She left Charles's side before flinging her arms around my legs and giving me a tight hug. "I'm going to miss you so much!"

My heart melted. Then again, it *was* really hot out today.

I swallowed past the lump in my throat. "I'll miss you, too. Even though you call me puppy."

"I love puppies! Don't you?"

"Well . . . yeah. Who doesn't?" This kid was an enigma if ever I'd met one.

"What are you going to do now?"

My lump only got thicker. "I don't know."

"Forget him," she advised. "You should come back to Seattle with us. You could be my mommy. It would be so much fun!"

This kid was seriously bipolar and I couldn't believe she had worked her way under my skin given her roller-coaster personality. But she had. "Um, thanks for the offer, but I—I kind of have to deal with some stuff. Grown-up stuff."

Her smile fell and the harder-edged Victoria appeared again. "Don't patronize me, puppy."

"I'm not! I'm just saying . . ." I sighed. "I can't leave him. Not like this."

"It's too late to help him. The hunter's dead. He's next. Just cut your losses and let him go. That's what he wanted you to do, right?"

Knowing Thierry, that was exactly what he wanted. He'd ensured my safety with Markus last night, knowing full well that might mean we'd never see each other again. As long as I was safe, he'd be satisfied.

The thought only made me feel worse.

"Victoria?" Charles prompted. "Time to go, kiddo." She moved away from me to hold on to his hand.

"Bye," she said sadly.

I watched them walk away, looking very much like father and daughter. A family. A really screwed-up family, but still two people who clearly cared about each other. I didn't doubt her safety around him. I doubted just about everything else about him, but not that.

I stayed on the sidewalk in front of Blood Bath & Beyond watching tourists stroll past. Watching the whiz of cars move up and down the Strip. Feeling the hot air and scorching late-afternoon sun sink into my skin. I spotted Vampire Jesus handing out his apocalypse flyers across the street. The man was a firm believer in what he hoped was a better future. I, however, was losing hope by the minute.

Last night, after I'd left the airport, I'd been certain I'd be able to save Thierry. I failed. Duncan was dead and I'd nearly been staked trying to find out who hired him to kill Bernard.

I wanted to prove that Thierry had nothing to do with it, that he'd been set up, but I was no further ahead now than I was last night.

I can't do it.

The realization hit me with the force of a Wayne Newton tour bus. There was no way I'd be able to prove Thierry's innocence by the time Markus finished whatever murder investigation he was conducting. The death of someone from the Ring—which Bernard still was at the time of his death—likely wouldn't be swept under the carpet. Thierry wouldn't get off with a slap on his wrist. He was going to die.

I'd failed.

Was Victoria right? For whatever crimes Thierry might have committed in his long and difficult existence, did that justify his execution at the hands of the Ring's enforcer now, whether or not he was guilty of this particular murder?

Some people might say yes.

I, however, was not some people.

"Time for plan B," I murmured, and zipped open my purse to glance inside.

The dart gun I'd swiped from Shane, the unconscious

vampire hunter, lay at the bottom, next to a discarded bubble gum wrapper.

It was quite simple, really. If I couldn't free Thierry from that hotel suite by proving his innocence, then I was just going to have to break him out of it.

Chapter 14

Charlotte had been surprised I was fiercer than she'd expected—a fighter. Did I really look like that much of a pushover at first glance? There was a time when I was much more passive, lounging back in my boat without oars, content to let the current take me wherever it wanted while I simply enjoyed the view. I called those the first twenty-seven years of my life.

Since the view had recently changed to things that could kill me, I'd whittled an oar. Quickly. And I'd begun paddling as fast as I could to get away from the dangerous waterfall looming up ahead.

No waterfalls here. But there were fountains. The Bellagio fountains surged upward and waved happily to me as I passed them. They seemed to be in a much better mood than I was.

However, I was determined. I was focused. I was going to try first to talk my way past whoever was guarding Thierry's door, but if that didn't work, I was going to garlic dart him in the forehead.

All I could do right now was pray that I wasn't too late.

Markus had said something about a "day or two"

between Thierry being sequestered in the suite and the enforcer's determination of his guilt or innocence.

It had been a day. A little less than one, actually. It was closing in on six o'clock, but the sun wouldn't set for a couple more hours. This couldn't wait until dark.

Apprehension, not exertion, made my heart thud hard and loud as I took the stairs—the elevators seemed too risky and confined at the moment. I pushed open the door to the hallway. Our room was just around the corner up ahead. I moved steadily toward it and sneaked a peek.

A bad sign would have been to see nobody in the hall. That would mean there was no one there who needed to be guarded. It would mean I was too late. The moment between not knowing and knowing nearly killed me.

But there *was* someone in the hallway outside the door to our suite. A big someone I recognized immediately—the thug with the cheesy seventies mustache.

Relief nearly buckled my knees. Thierry was still alive.

Problem was, this guy was going to easily recognize me, since he'd helped take me to the airport. I hitched my purse up higher on my shoulder. I kept it unzipped, my hand partially inside brushing against the cool metal of the dart gun. I'd already checked to see there were still three darts available.

I took a second to summon my courage.

"I can do this," I whispered. "I'm a fighter. I'm a fierce warrior protecting the man I love. There is no other option here other than walking away, and I'm not doing that."

As they say, fake it till you make it. If I wanted to be a fighter, I had to force myself to fight. Not flee.

This dude was going *down*.

I stepped out from behind the corner and put one foot in front of the other as I approached Markus's thug, every step closer reminding me how big and muscular this vampire was, like some kind of Ultimate Fighter.

He frowned at me as I drew closer and he cocked his head to the side. "I know you."

"Hey there," I said with a big smile. "Yes, you sure do. Great to see you again."

"You shouldn't be here."

"I know."

"Go away." If anything, he looked annoyed that I would approach him boldly like this. I saw the tips of his sharp fangs just under his thick mustache.

"What's your name?" I asked.

It took him a second to answer, as if he was surprised that his fearsome glare wasn't enough to make me scamper away with my tail between my legs. "Jake."

"Jake, I don't think we were properly introduced before. I'm Sarah."

"Why are you here, Sarah? Markus is going to be pissed you didn't get on that plane. And he's going to be pissed at me that I didn't check to make sure you arrived back in Toronto."

"How much is it going to cost for you to open that door for me and look the other way right now?" I asked sweetly, even putting a little flirtation into it. Shave off the mustache and this guy really wasn't half-bad-looking in a large-thug-bodyguard kind of way. He was, however, in desperate need of a makeover.

"More than you got."

He wasn't reaching for a phone to call in backup, so I took that as an encouraging sign that he might be willing to negotiate. I pointed at the door. "I need in that suite."

He crossed his arms and his bemused expression grew colder. "Not going to happen."

"Pretty please?"

"Are you for real? No. Nobody gets in, nobody gets out. That's how Markus wants it and that's how it's going to stay. Leave now and I won't tell anybody you were here. No one has to get in trouble."

I hissed out a breath as my confident exterior started to slip. I couldn't stand here arguing all day. "I'm not leaving."

"What? You think you're going to fight your way past me?" he asked, now with a smart-ass grin. "I'd like to see you try."

I pulled out the dart gun from my purse and aimed it at him. "This gun is filled with garlic darts. I shoot you and I get at least a twenty-minute free pass. Maybe more."

He raised his eyebrow and looked down the barrel of the gun. "I actually didn't expect that."

Ha! Confidence surged through me. "Well, maybe I'm unpredictable."

"You are. But so's my friend David."

"David?"

The gun was snatched right out of my sweaty hand so fast I barely saw it move. One moment it was there; the next it was gone. My heart sinking, I turned slowly to look at Markus's other thug, who'd silently approached from behind me.

"Stealthy," I said.

"I am," he agreed.

Then he shot me in the chest.

I looked down at the dart with shock. Twice in one day. That had to be some kind of a record.

The next moment, darkness crashed down around me.

It might have been minutes—it might have been hours—before my eyelashes fluttered open again.

Which, if nothing else, was a good sign that I was still alive.

My plan had gone horribly wrong. I'd been disarmed and tranquilized in two seconds flat. Some fighter I was.

For a second there, I knew I'd had that first guy at a disadvantage because he'd underestimated me. I saw it in his eyes.

Too bad about the other one.

Dark room. Curtains closed. I lay on a bed—but it was one I thought I recognized. I was in the hotel suite. Then again, I guess most rooms in this hotel had the same bed.

I groaned as I tried to sit up. My head felt like a herd of elephants had been merrily tap-dancing on it. I scanned the dim room until I finally saw a familiar outline leaning against the wall to my left, arms crossed over his chest.

My heart skipped a beat. "Please tell me you're not just a dream this time."

"I'm not a dream."

As reserved as he usually was, sometimes it was extremely difficult to tell how Thierry felt. That wasn't a problem right now. Currently, his voice was low, controlled, but there was something in the tone of it—like something dangerous he'd locked in a cage. It was enough to let on that he wasn't a happy camper.

No, he was very angry. At me.

"I can explain," I began.

"You were supposed to be on that plane last night, Sarah." He continued to speak in that quiet way that made me very uneasy. "Do you think Markus does favors like that often? Don't you think it would have been much easier for him to also blame you for Bernard's murder, since you were with me? His job is to assess and to eliminate problems. The fact that he allowed you to leave was the only moment of relief I felt about any of this. At that moment, I knew you would be all right."

"Thierry—"

"But you're not all right. You never even left." He exhaled slowly, evenly. He didn't move from the shadows, but I could see the tension in his shoulders. "You have no idea how much trouble you're in right now, do you? It's one thing staying in Vegas, and another thing altogether to return to this hotel. It was irresponsible. Completely and utterly irresponsible. Those men could have killed you on sight. Frankly, I'm surprised they didn't."

I sat up in bed and watched Thierry with steadily narrowing eyes. I'd gone from relief that he was still alive to mad as hell that he was being this way with me. For some strange reason, I thought he might be happy to see me. Guess not.

"Does it help to scold me like a ten-year-old child who's been naughty?" I asked thinly.

"If that's what you insist on acting like, then, yes, it does."

"I'm very sorry I didn't want to just sit around passively and do nothing. Looks like you've got that covered."

"Is that what you think I've been doing?" His words were frosty at the edges.

I shrugged. "You're still here, aren't you? It's been a whole day and you haven't budged from this hotel room. Maybe things didn't turn out the way I expected, but at least I was out there trying to do something about it." I pushed up out of the bed. It took a second before the dizziness faded.

"Passive," he repeated the word with distaste. "Sometimes, Sarah, it's important not to jump into a swamp until you've properly assessed how many alligators there are."

"You can justify it all you like, Thierry. Point is, I took action to try to fix this mess and you didn't."

"And here you are. Recovering from being shot with a tranquilizer."

"And here *you* are, waiting for a miracle to save your ass."

"I don't believe in miracles."

"Maybe you should start."

"Unlikely. What have you been doing around town, exactly?"

I crossed *my* arms now. "Maybe that's none of your business."

I felt his glare through the darkness before he glanced toward the door leading to the rest of the suite. "They've called Markus. He'll be here in half an hour to deal with this situation."

"How do you know that?"

"They made the call when they brought you in here unconscious."

Something inside me went cold at the thought that the enforcer was on his way here, but I ignored it. "Good. We need to sit down and explain everything to him."

"Explain what, exactly?"

"That you're innocent. That someone else hired Duncan to kill Bernard and you had nothing to do with it."

"Is that what you've been looking into today?"

"Maybe."

"Find anything useful?"

"Afraid not."

He was silent for a moment. "So that's why you're here. You planned to help me escape from this hotel because you're certain of my innocence but can't prove it."

I hissed out a breath. "Maybe it's because I want to play blackjack tonight and I really needed a little cash."

Silence stretched between us for longer than was comfortable. "I despised Bernard and the feeling was mutual. To have him gone from the earth is not something I'm spending much time mourning. Maybe I did hire Duncan and have been lying to you."

I let out a frustrated, muffled scream. "Sometimes I really want to punch you in the stomach."

His brows shot up. "Is that so?"

"Are you thick or something? This is me, Thierry. I'm not your enemy. I stayed here in Vegas so I could prove your innocence. Sure, I failed, but at least I tried."

"I know that."

"Then what is your problem?" I crossed the room and was right in his face. Although, with our height difference and me currently without high heels, I was really more in his upper chest.

He grabbed my arms so tightly that I flinched.

This close, I noticed for the first time that his expression was not passive like I thought it was, not annoyed that I was causing yet another problem for him to have to deal with. No, it was tense and his gray eyes flashed with anger and something else . . . anguish.

"You were safe. I thought you were back in Toronto and away from all of this."

"Well, you were wrong." I glared up at his strained expression. "Get it through your thick head, will you? I love you, Thierry. I never left you. And I never will."

He let out a growl of frustration from deep in his throat. I thought he was going to turn away and leave the room, but instead he took my face between his hands and crushed his mouth to mine in a hot, deep kiss that scorched a line right through the center of my body. I hadn't realized how cold I was until his kiss warmed me up in seconds.

When the kiss ended, I looked up at him, stunned. The heavy weight on my heart finally lifted and I managed a smile. "See? That's much better."

"Damn it, Sarah, you shouldn't be here right now," he whispered against my lips.

"And yet, here I am. I'll stay by your side as we talk to Markus. I still have hope."

"That makes one of us."

"Better than none."

His jaw set. "Fine. This changes things, but there's no other choice now."

He kissed me again. And then took my hand in his and drew me out to the seating area with him.

Together we could figure this out. We could talk to Markus and explain our theories. He would listen because he didn't strike me as a man without empathy—despite what Thierry might think. Markus had let me leave at Thierry's request last night. He'd listen to what we had to say today.

Thierry moved toward the door and knocked softly on it.

"What?" Jake barked through the barrier.

"I need to talk to you about something important," Thierry said. "Please open this door."

Jake groaned. "Markus will be here soon. Can't you wait?"

"I think I've proven by now that I'm in no rush to escape, since I know your employer will only hunt me down."

There was a long pause. "Fine. Back away from the door first. And don't even think about trying anything. I have a stake and Markus has authorized me to kill you if you give me any problems."

"Understood."

Thierry returned to my side and I looked at him warily. "What do you want to talk to him about?"

"I need something from him and the other guard before Markus arrives."

Was he going to try to buy them off? It hadn't worked for me earlier, but maybe it was all in the delivery. The door opened slowly and Jake glared in at us. David stood next to him with his arms folded. I didn't think it was possible for anyone to have shoulders that wide. He was like a tattooed mountain. They both came inside and David shut the door behind him with the heel of his boot.

Jake's gaze flicked to me and he nodded. "Your girlfriend was determined to get in here and see you. You must be quite a stud."

"Is that what you think?" Thierry asked.

"Why else?" He shrugged. "But I'm surprised. You master vamps are usually all the same—all talk. I'm surprised you have any action to give. She's just a fledgling, right?"

"She is."

Jake's gaze leisurely moved over me. "Just like Bernard's wife. You know she was screwing around behind Bernard's back, right? Fledglings can't take it for long. They need more passion in their lives than what an ice-cold master vamp can offer."

"Is that so?"

Jake nodded. "I've only been a vamp for a little over twenty years. I'm still considered a fledgling, so I still like it hot." He grinned under the mustache. "Sarah, sweetheart, you can call me anytime if you get sick of this guy. Not that he'll be around much longer."

David shot him a look. "Stop trying to provoke him."

"Me, provoke? Nah. I wouldn't do something like that after he's been all nice and well behaved so far." He grinned white teeth in a feral manner. "He's way more pussycat than any lion I've ever seen."

Thierry looked utterly unenthused about joining this particular conversation. "Sarah? Are you interested in seeing other men?"

I looked at him with shock. "Are you serious?"

"Laura cheated on Bernard, starting shortly after

they were married. Trailing after him with his job as consultant bored her, so she found other ways to . . . amuse herself. This was not a secret, even though she thought it was."

"I hear he did the same thing. What's your point?"

"Bernard tolerated her infidelity because it kept her happy."

"Are you asking if I'm thinking of cheating on you in order to stay happy?" My mouth dropped open and my cheeks flared with heat. "This is ridiculous."

"You can't blame me for being curious."

My anger from before cranked back up again as I glared at him, speechless.

Thierry's gaze moved to my hand. "We've only been apart for a day and yet I noticed you've already stopped wearing your ring. What am I supposed to think?"

It reminded me again about the light-fingered underground vamp. "My ring was—"

He raised his hand to stop me before I could say anything else. "Hold that thought, please."

I just stared at him, stunned that he would ask me these things in front of an audience.

Jake watched us like a tennis match, his lips twitching with amusement. "Trouble in paradise, huh? Fledglings and masters are not a good combo. You're right to wonder about a sexy little thing like her, Thierry. Personally, I like to keep my women on short leashes."

David studied Thierry for a moment. "What did you want to talk to us about? Let's get to the point."

"Yes, you're right," Thierry said. "It's time we did."

I wasn't exactly sure what happened next. All I knew was that one moment they were standing there smug and amused and the next moment they were both flat on the ground. David was unconscious, but Thierry had his knee against Jake's chest to hold him down and the thug's own silver stake in his hand. Thierry pressed it to Jake's jugular hard enough that a trail of blood trickled down his throat.

What the hell? Had Thierry moved that fast or had I just blacked out for thirty seconds? I knew he could move quickly when necessary, but I'd never seen anything like this before.

Jake gurgled and attempted to fight Thierry off, but it looked like a losing battle. Thierry dug the stake in closer to the other man's throat.

"I'm not a pussycat," Thierry said evenly. "Master vampires are not always what you might think we are. Time has taught us the patience to wait for others to let their guards down so we can be lions when absolutely necessary. Do you really want to hear me roar?"

For such a large and dangerous man, Jake was now staring up at my fiancé with actual fear as if he saw something on Thierry's face that scared him to the very center of his being.

"Thierry," I said. Then when he didn't seem to hear me, I shouted it. "Thierry!"

He glanced over his shoulder and my breath caught in my chest. His eyes had turned black and soulless. Maybe it was the bit of blood on Jake's neck that set him off, but he was close to the edge of his control right now.

"Don't kill him." I forced myself to say it very calmly and put as much strength behind it as I could. "He's only doing his job."

Thierry narrowed his black eyes and returned his attention to the vampire he had pinned. "You're right."

He tossed the stake away and it clanged to the ground over by the flat-screen television. Then he grabbed Jake's head and slammed it down against the marble tiles. That would have been hard enough to crush a human's skull, no doubt, but despite the vampire going very still, his chest moved to show he was still breathing.

It reminded me to breathe, too. I'd forgotten to do that for a minute.

I watched Thierry carefully, waiting for a sign that he was okay. Black eyes worried me at the best of times. Especially when it was Thierry who was sporting them. He patted Jake down and retrieved his cell phone from the man's pocket before slipping it into his own inner jacket pocket.

Finally he pushed up to his feet and looked at me. His eyes were back to their normal shade of gray. The sight made me dizzy with relief.

"Ready to go?" he asked.

"Definitely." As we left the suite I turned to look at him. "You said you needed something from them before Markus got here. What was it?"

He met my questioning gaze. "Their lack of consciousness."

Chapter 15

My fantastic plan to rescue Thierry had come off without a hitch.

Well, maybe one or two. But the results spoke for themselves.

Again avoiding the unpredictability of taking an elevator, we made it to the stairwell and began heading downward.

I glanced back at him. "Do we have a plan?"

"I had one. It dissolved about half an hour ago."

"What was your plan?"

"Doesn't matter anymore. I'll revise."

My stomach sank. "You *did* have a plan. A good one, too, right? You weren't just sitting in there like a passive victim—you were biding your time. I screwed everything up when you were busy biding."

"You didn't screw it up. But you did scare the hell out of me." He pulled me to a stop as we reached the fifteenth floor. "When they brought you into the suite unconscious, I thought the worst. For a moment, I thought they'd killed you." His expression darkened. "Do you have any idea what that did to me?"

"You were happy you wouldn't have to deal with a troublemaker like me anymore," I guessed.

His gaze firmly held mine. "Try again."

"Your heart shattered at the thought of losing me and you wanted to kill everyone within a one-mile radius to help ease your grief and rage over my death."

A glimmer of a smile touched his lips. "More than a mile."

My heart beat faster and I almost returned the expression, but I still felt deeply uneasy about what had happened. "What was that in there? With Markus's men? I've never seen you move like that before. In fact, I didn't see you move at all, it was just . . . done. And the look on your face afterward when you had Jake on the ground and his stake at his throat . . ."

His expression was unreadable. "We needed out of there and they were both very strong. I had to use whatever I had at my disposal in order to get past them."

"And that's something you had at your disposal? What, is that a tool you've been keeping in a box that I never knew about?"

"I can do certain things, Sarah. Those who've been around for as long as I have—have access to these . . . *tools*, as you say. It doesn't mean I want to use them all the time—or even that I *can*. But sometimes it's possible."

I shivered despite myself. I was learning more about my fiancé every day. "Sounds dangerous."

"It certainly can be." He had my hand in his and he brushed his thumb over my ring finger. His eyes met mine again. "Your ring?"

"Stolen. When I was tied up in the tunnels under the city, a greedy vampire chick took it from me as payment to help me escape a couple hunters."

He just stared at me. That was a lot of information to pack into one sentence.

"Tied up by hunters?" he asked after a moment, his voice tight.

"It's been kind of a crazy day," I admitted.

"Tell me more."

I did. Quickly. I told him about my plan to talk to Duncan and how badly that went, starting with the hunters in the tunnels, the subterranean-living, black-eyed vampire, the hunter bar, and finally Duncan getting a pool cue through his chest before I could get him to confess who hired him to kill Bernard.

The taste of my failure was bitter. Kind of like the tea an aunt of mine always insisted I drink whenever I went to her house for a visit back when I was a kid. How hard was it to make tea that doesn't taste nasty? I mean, seriously. Ever since, I'd been a coffee person. But I digress.

"Duncan is dead," Thierry finally said after he'd processed everything.

I just nodded. "I'm sorry. I know that would have been the perfect way to find out who hired him. He was willing to talk to me for a price. And now . . . he's gone. This is all my fault."

"He would have been killed today with or without your presence. It wasn't you who killed him, it was someone else who wanted him dead."

I raked a hand through my still-tangled hair. "I thought Laura could be the one to blame. I talked to her, but it wasn't her. I'm positive about that. She actually gave me back Bernard's key to your mysterious safety-deposit box—or, at least, I'm pretty sure that's what it is." I touched my jeans pocket to make sure it was still in there. "She probably didn't know it led to a bunch of diamonds. She can't think straight—she's completely destroyed by his death."

"I never suspected Laura. She needed Bernard and his checkbook too much. Dead, he's no good to her."

I blanched. "It just makes me feel sick."

"Which part?"

"All of it. I believed they were madly in love, a fledgling and a master vamp. They reminded me so much of . . ." I bit my lip. "Well, you know. I wanted them to be a good example of that, to give me hope."

"We do share many significant similarities."

My chest tightened. "But she was cheating on him. And now you question whether I'm looking at cheating on you. I mean, what was that?"

He exhaled. "Sarah—"

I knew we had to get out of this hotel as soon as possible before Markus arrived, but I needed to get this out before it started to fester. "You didn't have to ask me to marry you, you know, but you did. And I said yes. That means something to me, Thierry. It means that, despite everything, you want to be with me now and in the future and vice versa. So am I thinking of acquiring some new man candy the moment that my eye starts to wander? Absolutely not. And, FYI, I'm mad as hell that you'd even think something like that."

He'd drawn back from me a little during my rant as my voice echoed in the stairwell.

I waited patiently for his rebuttal.

"Actually," he began, "I said those things merely as a way to distract Markus's men so I might get the upper hand when the time came. But I do appreciate you clarifying these points for me and am quite pleased with this confirmation of your fidelity."

I glared at him as his lips started to curve. "Don't laugh. This is not funny."

"I'm not laughing. I'm smiling."

"I'm so glad I amuse you."

"So am I. You truly have no idea." Smiling changed Thierry's entire face—from stern and coldly hand-some, to open and totally heart-stoppingly gorgeous.

But I still wanted to punch him in the stomach.

I blew out a breath and tried to fight against my own grin appearing. "So what's your new plan now that the original one imploded thanks to me?"

"First, I need to get you to safety."

"And then?"

"By escaping that hotel suite, I've signed my own death warrant. Markus will assume my guilt now instead of having any doubt about it and attempt to hunt me down." He must have seen me blanch at this. "It's not your fault. I'd planned to leave the suite tomorrow morn-ing if nothing had changed. I am patient when I need to be, but I have no interest in being executed for a crime I didn't commit. Knowing you were safe helped ease my mind. If I'd had any idea you were still in Vegas . . ." He sighed. "I need to get you to a safe place where no one knows you and Markus can't track you."

"And you?"

"I'll put distance between us. Perhaps, eventually, Markus will stop his search."

I blinked. "We won't be together?"

"You would be in danger. So no." His previous smile was only a memory now and his dark brows drew together. "It was a mistake bringing you here in the first place. You're too—"

"—much trouble?"

His gaze flicked to mine and again that smile tugged at his lips. He brought his hand up to cup my cheek. "Too important to me."

My heart twisted. I didn't like this plan at all. "I don't want to leave you."

"Trust me, Sarah, if there were any other choices, this would not be my first."

There had to be another way. Thierry's plan was to separate us, to put me somewhere nice and safe and hidden—which, quite honestly, sounded like hell. And for him to go on the run, trying to stay one step in front of Markus, who'd now kill him on sight.

My life had been complicated ever since I'd first been bitten, but this felt as bad as it got. There had to be another choice here. Because, even though Thierry had a plan that would do in a pinch, it was far from perfect.

I mentally retraced my steps today—all my leads that led to dead ends. I kept feeling hope that I was getting somewhere, only to have that hope land face-down in a muddy puddle.

"There was something," I said. "Josh—he's the vamp who runs the blood bank, Blood Bath and Beyond . . . Well, he's a magician, too, with a show here in town at a place called Club Noir. He's got an opening act, a guy who can contact the dead. Josh seemed to think he's legit."

"Are you really interested in taking in a show before we flee the city?" Thierry asked wryly.

I chewed my bottom lip as I considered everything. "What if we tried to contact Duncan's spirit? I wanted him to admit who hired him when he was alive, but if there's a chance to do it now that he's dead . . ."

"A real psychic who can contact the dead is a very rare find. Most are fake or they're fooling themselves that they have any supernatural ability at all."

"But there *are* real ones? You've come across them before, right?"

He was silent for a moment, as if mulling it over. "I have. Not often, but I have."

"Do you know any in the area we could go to instead?"

He shook his head. "What is this psychic's name?"

I wracked my brain to remember what Josh told me. "Kristopher . . . the Magnificent. Do you think it's worth checking out?"

"Do you?"

I nodded. "If there's any chance of finding out the truth, then we need to do it. If we can prove your innocence to Markus, then he won't keep hunting you."

Before he replied, I began to realize after what I'd seen upstairs in the suite with Jake and David, what might happen when and if Markus ever caught up to Thierry. Did the enforcer know what a master vampire could be capable of? Did he take special precautions when hunting one?

I'd bet money that he would. Which meant whatever special vampire-ninja skills Thierry had that I was previously unaware of, they'd be of little use against someone like Markus. Maybe he was a vampire ninja, too.

He nodded. "Then we'll go and see this Kristopher the Magnificent. However, try not to get your hopes up that it will make any difference."

"How about we try this—I'll be the optimist and you be the pessimist?"

That earned me another smile. "If you insist."

We headed down the rest of the stairs. "Saw one of the serial killer's victims up close and personal today on the street," I told him. "Just seconds before he died. Maybe if the psychic is legit, we can summon his spirit and find out who killed him. Although I've got this weird feeling I already know."

Thierry looked disturbed that I'd brushed up against more danger today like a friendly cat, but he chose not to press me about it. "Who?"

"Charles. Victoria's guardian . . . or whatever he is to her. He's so shady he's practically an umbrella. He's got a blood addiction—sort of like . . ." I cleared my throat. "Well, let's just say he's got a blood addiction. Can't seem to stop slurping the stuff up. Saw him with some blood on his lips earlier and that was about a minute and a half before the victim came staggering toward me. And, if that wasn't bad enough, his full name is Charles Manson. Talk about a big neon arrow pointing at him, if you ask me."

"Charles Manson didn't commit his own crimes. He had people kill on his behalf."

"Still. It's creepy. And what was even creepier was that when the man died right in front of me, I swear I could feel the moment his life left his body. I sensed it, Thierry. It freaked me out."

He pulled me to a stop again just as we'd reached the ground floor. "You felt it? How?"

"I don't know. Like, inside of me I could feel the difference between dead and alive. I figured that's just another vampire trait that everybody else has."

"Not everybody." He swept his gaze over me with interest. "Have you ever felt that before?"

"Well, I haven't been around that many humans who've been killed, but . . ." I thought hard about it. "No. This is a recent development."

"Hmm."

I eyed him warily. "Hmm, what?"

"I guess we might find out soon."

"Can you be more cryptic?"

"It's possible. If I tried really hard." He pushed open the door leading us out of the stairwell and we made our way across the lobby. Had it been only two days ago that we'd arrived? Seemed like two weeks. I didn't even glance up at the crystal flower ceiling this time; my gaze was too focused on our path ahead.

Suddenly Thierry's grip on my hand tightened and he pulled me back. It took me only a moment to see what caused this reaction. It was Markus.

I stopped breathing.

He'd arrived earlier than expected and was speaking to someone by the reception desks. I watched as he shook a man's hand, then began moving in the direction of the elevators. I was certain he was on his way to the thirty-second floor, where he'd been called in to deal with the most recent development to do with Thierry's imprisonment—namely yours truly.

Markus began to walk with purpose away from us. But then he stopped, cocked his head, and glanced over his shoulder. There were many other people in the area and we were blocked by a gathering tour group. But it was as if he sensed something wasn't quite right.

Then, after a solid ten seconds of Markus sniffing the air like some sort of blond hellhound, he turned back, his black coat swishing around his calves, and walked away. It wasn't until he disappeared completely from sight that I started to breathe normally again.

A lot of things in this world freaked me out. But I'd decided that enforcers—smart, savvy, immortal, and completely deadly—had graduated to the very top of my list.

Chapter 16

Club Noir wasn't on the Strip. It wasn't a casino or hotel. It was just a little run-down theater that had a dinner show of half-naked and slightly past-their-prime showgirls, followed by a break, followed by a little magic and psychic entertainment at ten o'clock, when the audience was mostly too drunk to care.

We arrived too early for any of the main entertainment, but the showgirls were milling around the dining area trailing cheap feather boas and sour expressions when they thought no one was looking.

Just like Josh had hinted to me earlier, Kristopher was already here. Thierry paid off a man in front to take us back to meet him. It hadn't cost very much. The man even confirmed that Kristopher rarely left the club. He didn't work two jobs like Josh did.

Thierry and I exchanged a glance when the club owner left us alone with the psychic in a back room that looked as if it doubled as a dressing room. It also contained storage—cardboard boxes piled high to the ceiling. Torn wallpaper. A cracked mirror surrounded by lights.

Kristopher was either meditating or napping sitting

up with his legs crossed on a worn vinyl couch. We stood at the open doorway and waited for two solid minutes, but Kristopher didn't open his eyes.

Finally, I cleared my throat.

One of Kristopher's eyes popped open and his brow went up.

He had longish black hair and pale skin. His eye was a muddy brown shade. He wore a ruffled white shirt and black leather pants. Black liner was smudged around his eyes, which made him look like a Goth pirate.

"Hello," I greeted him. "Sorry to disturb, but can we talk to you?"

The other eye popped open—and, surprisingly, it wasn't brown like the other. It was pale blue and the mismatched eyes gave him a spooky look. He swept his gaze over me before doing the same with Thierry. "You're vampires."

It was always on the tip of my tongue to deny a statement like that, but considering he worked regularly with Josh, I was going to assume he knew that we existed and that not all of us were serial killers. Still, I didn't immediately nod my head and let him know he was right. A little uncertainty never hurt anyone.

"You're Kristopher, right?" I asked. Best to make sure just in case we'd been led somewhere incorrectly.

"That's me. Kristopher DeMon."

I blinked. "How do you spell your last name?"

He looked at me with a glimmer of amusement in those mismatched eyes. "D-E-M-O-N."

I shifted my feet. "Yeah, that's how I thought it would be spelled."

Stage name, I told myself. *It's his stage name, just like Vladimir Nosferatu.*

Besides, if you were a demon in disguise, would you really announce it to the world? I mean, was Criss Angel really an angel?

I had heard rumors to that effect, but that didn't mean it was true.

"Um, I'm Sarah Dearly. This is Thierry de Bennicoeur."

"Charmed, I'm sure," he said.

"Meditating, huh?" I scanned the room looking for something that might help me decide if this guy was a big faker or not. "That's relaxing. Clears the mind, helps concentration. I keep meaning to take it up."

"To meditate, you need to be capable of stilling your mind and thinking of nothing at all. Those unable to control their worries and stresses and those who are impatient find it nearly impossible—but they're the ones who need it the most. It's a quandary."

"Yes, that is . . . a quandary," I agreed.

"What do you want? I'm preparing for my show tonight."

"Josh gave me your name," I said. Thierry remained silent beside me. He watched me curiously, as if amused that I had taken over. I wasn't sure why I had, exactly, but it was my decision to come here in the first place, so I might as well put my money where my mouth was. "He said that you're a psychic who can speak with the dead."

"And you want me to help you speak to someone you've lost."

"Yes. You could say that."

"Some dearly departed relative whom you miss with all your heart."

I glanced at Thierry.

His expression was grim. "Very intuitive, don't you think? He can read you like a book."

Smart-ass. I wasn't giving up so easily.

"Can you do it?" I asked. "For real?"

Kristopher's gaze shot to me. "You doubt my powers?"

"Well, I mean, I'm not sure. That's why I'm wondering. What can I say? I'm a skeptic."

"I am as real as they come." He narrowed his eyes at me as if concentrating. "I can glean your name from the fabric of the universe. It's . . . it starts with a . . . a . . ." He nodded his head toward me, staring right into my eyes. "A *C*. Yes, a *C*. I can see it. Your name is . . . Catherine. *Cathy*."

I grimaced. "Close. It's Sarah. I just told you that a minute ago, actually. Remember?"

"Right, yes. Sarah. But you know a Catherine. She means a great deal to you. She is the one who has passed on. She was a . . ." He leaned forward again, rocking on his black steel-tipped boots. "A . . . an aunt. Yes, an aunt. Your aunt Catherine is with us, Sarah. She wants me to tell you that she loves you very much."

I couldn't believe this. I'd thought this might be something helpful, but instead I got this jackass. I'd put my entire future happiness in the hands of a jackass in a frilly shirt. Instead of making me sad or upset, it just made me angry.

I poked him in the chest. "You suck, you know that?"

"Excuse me?" When he rubbed his chest, I noticed

he wore a strange ring. It covered three fingers and had two short half-inch spikes.

"You're a terrible psychic. How do you even get a job with skills that bad? It's painful, really. People pay you for this? You don't get thrown out on your butt? Is that why you have that pointy ring on your hand, so people don't get too close?"

He frowned a little. "I'm offended."

"That makes two of us."

"There is a Catherine. She's here with us right now, telling me that you used to go for long walks on the beach—Malibu, right? You're a California girl."

My mouth was wide open. "Wow, you're not even close. Born and bred in Ontario. Swap the beach with snow and you're in the right territory."

"Sarah . . . ," Thierry said.

I put my hand up. My disappointment and frustration with everything was manifesting as anger directed at a fake, spooky-eyed psychic. "Just give me a minute here to tell this chump off, Thierry. We came all this way, hoped that he might be more than just another . . . I'm going to use the word 'chump' here again, because I can't think of anything better right now. This is pathetic. Completely pathetic."

Kristopher spread his hands. "I'm sorry if my gifts are not to your satisfaction. I channel the secrets of the universe and use them to help those in need."

"Just great. Now we're stuck exactly where we were to begin with." I turned to Thierry. "We can figure something else out. Just because he's a fake—"

"He's not a fake." Thierry's attention wasn't on me; it was on Kristopher.

"What?"

"He's real."

"Of course I'm real," Kristopher said thinly. "I think I just proved that to you with an absolutely free reading."

Thierry had his arms crossed over his chest and he studied the psychic carefully. "I'm not really sure what game you're playing to go to such extremes to appear incompetent."

"I don't know what you're talking about."

Thierry's gaze moved to his unusual jewelry. "And you're more powerful than my first guess. I see you have the tools to work blood magic. I haven't seen a sickle ring like that in over a hundred years."

"It's time for you to leave." Kristopher's voice grew darker.

"Where do you get blood in the quantities required? And are all your donors willing?"

"Maybe I just think it's a nice piece of jewelry that makes me look badass."

Thierry glanced at me. "A sickle ring has many uses, primarily being a dark wizard's tool for delving deeper with his magic. Blood magic—it's a powerful thing. But very dangerous to the wizard himself, since it often backfires."

Uneasily, I took another glance at the ring. It looked like something you might find at Blood Bath & Beyond, a random Goth trinket to make someone look dangerous and edgy. The ring itself was deeply etched with small symbols on the burnished silver. And the spikes themselves . . . now that I was paying attention, they looked a whole lot like sharp vampire fangs. Stab this in a victim's jugular and the resulting wound would look exactly like a vampire bite.

My mind immediately went to the serial killer—the last victim grabbing hold of me and trying to tell me who'd killed him: *Vampire*.

Kristopher, at first glance, looked exactly like a vampire should if you didn't know any different.

And . . . did Thierry just say *dark wizard*?

"You're right," Kristopher finally said. "It is dangerous. Which is why I use it only rarely and when absolutely necessary."

"Then why wear the ring now?"

"Because it looks badass." Kristopher smiled, but it didn't look friendly. His spooky eyes took in both me and Thierry as if seeing us for the first time. "What do you want from me?"

"We want you to summon one who has recently died so we can question him." Thierry didn't ask if Kristopher could do it. The confident look on his face was enough to show that he was totally convinced that this guy was legit.

"Difficult," Kristopher said.

"For someone with as much power as I can sense from you, I find that hard to believe."

Kristopher's unpleasant smile held. "Sometimes those with power are unable to fully tap into it."

"Oh? How so?"

"Let's just say I have limited access to the full extent of what I can do."

"Is that your own doing or did someone else put these restrictions on you?"

Kristopher looked at Thierry with a distinctly unfriendly expression. "You are a bit too insightful for your own good . . . Thierry, was it?"

"I'm just a good judge of character."

"And what do you see in my character?"

Thierry's eyes narrowed slightly. "A man who is hiding from what he really is and his full potential. Why would one who has touched dark magic be working in a low-end dinner theater telling fortunes for pennies?" Thierry studied him for a moment. And I studied Thierry, surprised by just about everything that was happening here. "It's a punishment. You're condemned to be this way for some crime in your past. Being here, putting up with regular humans who look at you as no more than momentary entertainment, it must be torture for someone like you."

Kristopher's expression tightened. "You have no idea."

"You might be surprised." Thierry was silent for a moment, as if mulling over what he'd gleaned. "What happens when you access your true power and don't just put on a flashy show to distract from the truth? What do you lose that you value more than anything? What is the punishment?"

"Stop," Kristopher warned.

"Is it pain? No. Beneath the frills and makeup you think masks the real you, you strike me as someone who can take a great deal of it. Is it someone you love you're concerned with hurting?" He cocked his head. "A woman who meant everything to you? No, I don't think so. My guess is if there was anyone like that, she's gone—a long, long time ago."

A split second later, Thierry flew backward and smashed against the wall next to the door. His eyes flashed and moved to me, but the rest of him seemed pinned. For the first time since we'd arrived here, an edge of worry went through his previously confident and assessing gaze.

Kristopher's arms were tense, his fists clenched, and he stormed toward Thierry. I cut him off, putting myself between the two men.

"Take it easy," I said, panicky. "Seriously, just relax. I'm sorry for what Thierry said. . . . Sometimes he can be a little too blunt for his own good. Just don't—don't hurt him. Please."

Kristopher's gaze snapped to me and beyond the fury in his strange eyes, I saw something else now—madness. It hadn't been there before. Only since he used whatever magic he normally kept under lock and key.

He shook a little, but I wasn't sure if it was from anger or frustration. "Why did you have to come here?" he demanded.

"I've heard they make a fantastic Tequila Sunrise." I tried to breathe and do whatever I could to defuse this particular bomb. "And also, because we desperately need your help."

"Get out of my way."

"Not a chance."

He shook his head, his face etched in misery and that touch of crazy. I suddenly realized that was what Thierry had guessed at, although he'd been wrong and only provoked the man further. There was a price to pay for Kristopher tapping into his magic. It was his sanity.

"You think you can protect him from me?" A dark smile flashed on his face. "You're barely powerful enough to continue breathing."

I didn't budge. "You have no idea what I'm capable of."

He stared fiercely at me for a long time—maybe a full minute. I forced myself to hold his gaze and not flinch or look away. Thierry didn't move, didn't make a sound. Whatever Kristopher had done to him had stopped him cold and kept him immobilized. I could only assume he'd be able to kill Thierry just as easily if he wanted to. It was a chilling thought.

Finally, Kristopher glanced past me at Thierry. "You're a lucky man. Many women would flee the moment they felt threatened, not stay and defend someone else when they're obviously outmatched." Sanity had slowly returned to his gaze.

"Release him from whatever this is," I said firmly.

"I don't like him."

"You don't like him only because he hit too close to home. There was someone who meant everything to you and you lost her, right? And now you want to take it out on someone else."

His eyes slid to mine. "Believe me, I've taken it out on many over the years. But here we are. If I kill this vampire with my magic, I will go completely insane. Would it be worth it?"

A violent shiver went through me. "I'm going to vote no."

"I don't know. It might be."

Did anyone else have any idea who Kristopher DeMon the Magnificent really was? Or was his Goth pirate persona enough to fool everybody except Thierry?

Sometimes that man *was* too insightful for his own good.

"I'm sorry for whatever you've been through." I sounded totally sincere because I was. I hated seeing anyone in pain and it didn't really matter who they were. I didn't know what Kristopher had done in his life, but the fact that he'd all but admitted he'd lost someone he loved was enough to coax out a tune on my heartstrings. "But we still need your help. If we don't find answers, then we're going to be torn apart, too—and I bet it's going to end just as badly as whatever happened to you. So please, help us contact somebody."

"I don't usually help vampires. I don't count them among my friends."

"What about Josh?"

He laughed softly, humorlessly. "Yeah, that fool. I'll admit it. Over his head and overworked. When he's not working, he's got a grand thirst for the roulette tables. Keeps channeling what money he has left into losing ventures like that money-suck of a store of his. And that new vamp show that's opening next week is sure to be another failure."

"You mean *Fang*?" I said, surprised. "Josh is an investor?"

"He is. I want to help him out, but he wants to do it all on his own. So be it."

I smiled. "You want to help him—a vampire. You see a friend in need and you want to lend a hand. I knew you weren't unredemptively evil."

He glared at me. "Don't try to see light where there's only darkness, vampire."

"You might be a dark room, but there's a night-light glowing in the corner, even if you don't believe it. So are you going to help us or what?"

His glare wavered just a little. "You don't exactly make a great bargain for yourself. What does it get me?"

"The satisfaction of helping two people in need, and knowing you did it to help that glimmer in the corner get a little bit brighter."

He stared at me so long I was afraid he was going to hypnotize me with those mismatched eyes and make me start clucking like a chicken. Or worse.

"Say please," he said.

"Please."

Thierry gasped from behind me and was finally able to move. I hadn't realized it before, but he hadn't been breathing until now. He'd been suffocating. Vampires didn't need to breathe as much as humans, but they did need to breathe. I wasn't totally sure if suffocation could eventually kill us, but it would be extremely unpleasant. He recovered quickly and came to my side, sliding an arm around my waist. I looked at him with concern, expecting him to do something in retaliation, but other than that firm grip on me, the tension in his body was kept under control . . . although I felt the potential violence humming all around him.

"Let's get this over with." Kristopher held out a hand to me. "Give me something that belonged to whomever you wish to contact."

I stared at his hand. "You need something, like, specific?"

"Yes."

"You can't just pull a spirit out of the air if we give you a name and description?"

"No. Spirit magic is different. I need something to

ground me, to help me pick through the world of the dead and summon their ghost here."

"I can go find a Ouija board for you if it'll help."

"That won't do it." His hand was still extended. "If you don't have anything, you yourself can work as an anchor if he touched you. It's more difficult, but there's still a chance."

My stomach sank. I'd been consciously avoiding any physical contact at all with Duncan and I knew I'd never touched him once. "There has to be another way."

"There isn't."

I looked at Thierry. "Did you know this?"

"That to summon the ghost of one who has died you must be in possession of something he or she owned? Yes, I knew that."

I stared at him blankly. This was bad. Another dead end, after everything we'd just gone through to convince Kristopher to help us. He was willing, ready, and able to do just that—but now we were stuck again.

"If you knew that, why did you even agree to come here? I have nothing of Duncan's . . . unless you do? I mean, he was an informant for you, right?"

"Correct. But I have nothing of his. Any money that passed between us went in one direction only, from me to him."

Hope was slipping away from me with every second that passed. "So how are we supposed to summon Duncan's ghost?"

"We're not," Thierry said simply. He was so calm about this that it was driving me in the opposite direction as my anxiety and confusion grew bigger and bigger.

"Okay, then why did we come here at all?"

"To summon a ghost. But not Duncan's." He raised an eyebrow at my bewilderment.

"Then, whose?"

He pulled me closer to him, my back to his front, and slid his hand into the front pocket of my jeans. My eyes widened. This felt a bit too intimate to be done in front of someone else.

"Thierry . . ."

He pulled the safety-deposit key that Laura gave to me out of my pocket and looked at it for a moment. Then he handed it to Kristopher. "Use this."

Kristopher took the key from him and formed a fist around the small piece of metal. "Do I have a name to work with?"

"Bernard DuShaw."

"You think Bernard knows who hired Duncan to kill him?" I asked breathlessly as I felt magic begin to charge the small dressing room. The fine hair on my arms stood up.

Thierry's expression was unreadable, as usual, but he flicked a glance at me. "I do. And we're about to see if my guess is right."

Chapter 17

Before I had a chance to ask any questions, it felt as if a tornado had just entered the room and my hair blew straight back from my face. The temperature in the room plunged twenty degrees in five seconds and continued dropping. Kristopher held the key clenched tightly in his fist and was chanting something. His hand started to glow. His lips moved, but I couldn't make out the words. His eyes—they freaked me out. I thought that black eyes on a vampire were scary enough, even when they were mine, but on a witch or wizard—try dark red on for size. Kristopher suddenly looked in major need of about a quart of Visine.

Finally, as I held tight to Thierry's arm so I wouldn't get knocked off my feet, the violent wind ceased and the room was still again. The crack in the mirror had only grown larger.

"He's here," Kristopher announced, his eyes still that scary shade of red. The room remained cold enough that a shiver went through me.

"Yeah," I said. "I can see that."

And I could. Bernard DuShaw now stood to Kristopher's right, looking at me and Thierry with complete and utter shock.

Kristopher frowned. His face was strained and his fist glowed with bright red light from where he held on to the key. "You can see him? Even I can't see him. I'm supposed to be the medium and tell you what he says."

I looked again, now not positive that I was seeing what I was seeing. But it was true. Bernard stood in the room with us as if he was really here and totally alive.

"*Quoi?*" Bernard said, glancing around.

"You can really see him?" Thierry asked, touching my shoulder.

I looked up at him, stunned. "Yeah."

A glimmer of a smile played at his lips. "I had a feeling you might be able to. After what you said about sensing death earlier."

"So, what? Now I can see ghosts?"

He nodded. "It's a rare ability for some vampires."

"Can you do it, too?"

"Yes." His smile widened. "And here you thought we had nothing in common."

"Great," I murmured, my heart pounding. "We can start a ghostbusting business together."

"What the hell is going on?" Bernard boomed. "Where am I? What happened?"

"Those are all very good questions." Thierry swept his gaze over the length of the other man. Bernard looked exactly as he had last night at the after-pageant reception out on the terrace balcony. He wore a tailored designer suit with Italian leather loafers, and had that pinched look on his face he got whenever Thierry was around.

"Well? Answer me, de Bennicoeur."

"For starters, you're dead."

"What?" Bernard's eyes bugged. "How?"

"Don't you remember? A hunter staked you in public right in front of a crowd of humans and an enforcer. It was chaos."

Bernard frowned deeply. "But—this is impossible. How can I be dead? I feel alive. I feel fine."

Thierry moved closer to him before thrusting his fist into Bernard's chest. It passed right through and the part of Bernard that was breached swirled like smoke, leaving a hole behind. When Thierry removed his hand, Bernard's chest re-formed itself into something that only looked solid.

He glanced down at himself with shock. *"Merde."*

"We summoned your ghost for a short time to find out the truth," Thierry said very calmly. How could he be calm about any of this? Was he really this calm or was it just an act?

Bernard's expression was bleak. "And here I am."

"Tell me the truth of what happened, Bernard," Thierry said. "You have nothing to lose anymore. It's over. You're dead and gone. The world is moving on without you as we speak."

"Laura," Bernard said. "What about Laura? Where is she? Is she all right?"

His question surprised me. That she would be the first thing he thought of after he'd gotten over the shock of what happened wasn't something I expected. I'd come to understand that he was well aware of her infidelity, but he tolerated it to keep her happy. He knew she was only married to him for his money and power.

One part of that stood out beyond all else: He tolerated it to keep her happy.

He wanted Laura to be happy.

"Did you love her?" I couldn't help but ask it. "You

and Laura—I'd begun to think it was only a marriage of convenience. She got money and protection and you got something young and sparkly for your arm. But was it more than that? Was it *ever* more than that?"

Bernard's gaze flicked to me and narrowed maliciously. "Why, Sarah? Are you worried for my happiness in the past or for your own in the future? Do you want confirmation that someone as old as I could truly love someone as young as you? I was very fond of Laura, but I've been fond of many women over the years. Did I think our marriage would last forever? No. But it was amusing to me while it did and I thought of Laura much as one would a beloved pet. I'm sure Thierry feels much the same toward you."

I glared at him. "Even dead, you're kind of a dick, aren't you?" A low groan from Kristopher caught my attention. His hands were trembling and there was a sheen of perspiration on his forehead. There was that look on his face again, that madness from before. It was growing the longer he held this connection between the living and the dead open for us. "Thierry, I think we need to speed this up."

Kristopher gasped, blinking quickly. "All gone, spinning and spinning away from me. Bring her back! Please . . . I'd do anything, give anything. I'll kill them. I'll kill all of them!"

The pain in his voice equaled the craziness and it made my heart hurt. How much longer could he hold on before he totally lost it? Was this what he had to face whenever he used his magic? But his words also chilled me. Who was he willing to kill?

And, considering that sharp fangish-looking ring of his—had he already started?

"I need to know the truth, Bernard," Thierry said. "And you're going to tell me."

"This is all your fault. I gave you a chance. I was willing to make you a deal. I know how much your precious treasure means to you." This was said with a sneer. "You made that crystal clear when you threatened my life at my very mention of it. But it didn't have to end like this."

"I think it did, but I wasn't the one who had you killed."

"There's no hiding anymore. It will be used against you, whether by me or someone else. You know that, don't you?"

"Let me worry about that." Thierry's face was stone. "Last night, you saw Duncan talking to me in the casino, didn't you? You knew anything he did would trace back to me, especially after I publicly lost my temper with you the night before. You hired him, since you knew his loyalty could easily be bought."

"You—you think that Bernard hired his own murderer?" I managed.

Thierry's expression didn't change and he kept his attention fully on the ghost of the dead vampire.

Bernard laughed. "Even your fiancée thinks it's a ridiculous suggestion. You're grasping at straws, Thierry. What kind of a fool do you take me for?"

Thierry crossed his arms. "I don't take you for a fool, Bernard. I know how smart you are, how cunning when there's something you want on the line. I know to what extent you will go to achieve your goals. I never doubted it for a moment."

Bernard nodded. "You know because we're so much alike."

"Maybe once."

"Fool yourself if you like, Thierry. But we're still the same. We'll do whatever it takes to get what we want. To survive."

"This was extreme, even for you, Bernard."

"I saw Markus Reed at the party. Has he been after you?" Bernard raised an eyebrow. "The most deadly of all the Ring's enforcers must be making your life difficult now, isn't he?"

He said it with so much glee that the pieces began clicking together for me and I actually gasped out loud.

"Wait. It *was* your goal for Markus to be there and to witness what happened. For him to assume that Thierry wanted you dead."

Bernard snorted. "Foolish girl. Why would I ever sacrifice my life in order to destroy his? I valued my life. It makes no sense."

I hated to admit it, but I had to agree with him there. Bernard might have disliked Thierry, might have wanted to get his hands on those cursed diamonds they had hidden away, but was it worth dying just to get Thierry in trouble? Seemed kind of insanely extreme to me.

I kept working it over in my head, trying to figure it out, but the last piece wasn't clicking in yet.

"You're right," Thierry said. "It makes no sense."

"Then it's settled. Now let me go to wherever it is I'm headed. And you can face the punishment that's been coming your way for too many years to count."

The piece finally clicked and another gasp escaped my lips. "Wait a minute. Duncan screwed up, didn't he?"

Thierry finally glanced at me and he looked pleased. "You think?"

My mouth felt dry. "Wow, this is incredible, but it finally makes sense to me." I turned to face the ghost. "You did hire Duncan to kill you . . . but you wanted him to fail."

Bernard's smug expression soured with every word and I saw the confirmation of what I was saying reflected on his pale face.

Thierry nodded. "An attempt on your life would have been more than enough to frame me for attempted murder. But Duncan didn't play by the rules, did he? It's a harsh lesson to you that comes too late—never pay them up front. He got his money and he had a master vampire who had asked for a stake through his chest. It was just your bad luck he decided to go for the heart."

Of course! Bernard had hired Duncan—not to kill him, but to make it *look* like he wanted to. All signs would point to Thierry as the suspect, just as they did now. Only Bernard would still be alive and be in a position to "help" Thierry. If Thierry had wanted to get out of this mess, he would have had to do Bernard a favor: hand over his key to the safety-deposit box.

All of this for a handful of cursed diamonds. Unbelievable.

Here I thought I was the magnet for trouble, but with luck like Bernard's, I think I was doing okay.

Bernard stared at us, haunted. Regret was etched into his every feature.

"I did what I thought I had to do," he finally said.

"That's not much of a confession." My voice shook.

"No, it's not. What, do you think you can use

evidence from a dead man as a way to prove Thierry's
innocence? I knew every single shred of it would point
toward him, not away from him. I waited until the
enforcer was at the hotel—I didn't know he was at
the party. That made it only more spectacular." He
frowned. "I wish I could have seen it."

Kristopher dropped to his knees. Sweat poured
down his face now and I ran to his side to support him
before he fell all the way to the floor.

"Thierry," I said sharply. "We need to stop this now.
You have your answer and it's not going to do us any
good anyway."

Thierry stared at Bernard glared at each other.

"I'm sorry," Thierry finally said.

Bernard's brows went up with surprise. "You are?"

"I'm sorry it had to come to this, Bernard. There was
a time we were true friends. Do you agree?"

Bernard didn't say anything to that, but after a
moment he inclined his chin in a shallow nod.

Thierry exhaled slowly. "You needn't worry. I'll
make sure Laura is looked after."

I'd started to pry Kristopher's hand open. The key
was glowing, actually glowing, and it seemed to be
causing him deep distress.

"It's okay," I told him. "You can stop now. Let go of
the key."

"My mind . . . I feel it pulling away from me. I'm
bombarded with images from my past. . . . Too many
of them . . . I can't escape."

My focus had shifted from the discussion between
Thierry and Bernard to the dark wizard going insane
on the floor of a run-down dressing room.

"No, be strong." I shot a look toward the other two men. "Thierry!"

Thierry swore under his breath. *"Au revoir,* Bernard."

Bernard frowned at him. "You don't hate me for what I did?"

"Hate is a poison that destroys the one who hates, not the one who is hated."

"You can pretend you've changed, but I know differently." Bernard glared at him. "She doesn't know everything about you, does she? This pretty little fledgling you've taken as your new pet. She doesn't know anything about—"

I finally pried the key out of Kristopher's hand. It dropped to the ground and the glow extinguished. As it did, Bernard's ghost disappeared. One moment he was there; the next he was gone, as if I'd flipped a switch.

However, I had heard what he was trying to say. Some piece of Thierry's past—some rotten part he thought might bother me. Thierry had tried to make amends at the end, but Bernard continued to be a dick.

"Bon voyage, Bernard," I said under my breath. "Don't bother sending us a postcard from wherever you end up."

Kristopher collapsed against me, unconscious. I sat on the dirty floor supporting his weight and looked up at Thierry.

"So," I said, "if that was the preshow, I think I'll skip the main act."

He looked tired, which was a rare look for Thierry. "It was just as I thought. Bernard hired Duncan. Now both of them are dead."

"What if you explain that to Markus?"

"Would you believe such a far-fetched story coming from the main suspect's mouth?"

I sighed. "Probably not."

"And what he was attempting to say at the end . . ." He looked at me cautiously.

"Some last nasty detail to try to turn me against you?"

"Yes."

I shrugged. "Grain of salt, Thierry. I don't care what he had to say."

"But you think the two of us are so much alike."

"No," I said firmly. "If I ever thought that, I was totally wrong. Except for your stellar taste in fashion and your preference for adorable younger brunettes, you're nothing like Bernard DuShaw."

He didn't agree or disagree with me verbally, but his tight expression relaxed just a fraction.

Kristopher slowly regained consciousness. He looked up at me with deep confusion; then his brows drew together. "What happened?"

"You summoned Bernard's ghost and then you lost your marbles. How are you feeling?"

"Better." He pushed himself up to his feet and scrubbed a hand through his black hair. "I've never summoned the spirit of a vampire before. It was . . . different."

"Different good or different bad?"

"Different bad." He looked at Thierry. "Did you get the answers you were looking for?"

"I did."

Kristopher nodded. "Good. Now please leave." He moved toward the cracked mirror to inspect himself.

After a moment, he glanced over his shoulder at us. "Why are you still here?"

"If there's anything we can do for you," I began. "I know you think you're skinny-dipping in a big pool of darkness, but you helped us even knowing it might scramble your eggs a bit. We owe you. Whatever you're trying to deal with on your own, we might be able to help you."

Kristopher looked at Thierry. "Is she for real?"

Even though he looked weary from dealing with Bernard's ghost, he smiled. "Trust me—Sarah is entirely real in every way."

Kristopher crossed his arms over his chest and approached me, peering into my eyes. "Sarah Dearly, a vampire with a heart of gold. I'm going to assume that gets you into trouble, looking for the good in people even if they don't deserve it."

I didn't like the way he looked at me. Cold and predatory. Whether it was the real Kristopher or just part of his act, I wasn't sure.

"Sometimes it does," I admitted.

"Take a hint, Sarah. I did you a single favor. It's over. And now I want you to leave and never come back. You have no idea what I've been through in my life or what I've lost along the way. Cherish your innocence while you still have it, because, trust me, it will soon fade and leave only a ghost of who you once were behind."

I gaped at him, my hands on my hips. "Is everybody a member of the total dick club today, or what? You need to get over yourself, Kristopher DeMon, and accept help from people who give a damn. But don't worry—if I hold my hand out to a wounded dog and he tries to bite it off, I'm not likely to try it again."

"This wounded dog appreciates it." He gave me a very unpleasant smile.

I bent over and snatched the key off the floor and slid it back into my pocket. "I don't know your story. I'm not sure I want to know it. But there is good in you—I'm sure of it. And if you ever find it, feel free to look us up if you need some help. Like I said, we owe you one. Jerk."

Chapter 18

I didn't stick around so he could argue with me anymore. I turned and left the Goth pirate wizard who had imprisoned himself in this lousy little theater as surely as Thierry had been imprisoned in the hotel suite.

Then again, I now knew Thierry could have left any time he wanted to. I wasn't so sure it was the same with Kristopher.

"Seriously," I groused as Thierry and I left Club Noir. The area was surrounded with concrete and other seedy theaters and businesses, but not a lot else. The sun was starting to sink beneath the horizon and the heat of the day was finally easing off a little. "What was his problem?"

"Did you honestly think we could help him?"

"I don't know." I frowned and looked up at him. "Is it stupid of me that I try to see the good parts in people before I'm forced to see the bad?"

"Stupid, no." He caught my hand in his and pulled me to a stop. As I turned to him, I realized he was smiling at me, his weariness from dealing with Bernard now gone from his expression. "Naive, yes. Your heart"—he placed his hand flat against my chest—"is very pure, despite all you've faced these last months. Don't belittle how you feel. It makes you who you are."

"If it constantly gets me in trouble, maybe I should learn and change. Maybe I should look at everyone as a potential threat."

"You have learned and changed in the time since I first met you. You've grown in so many ways."

"You really think so?"

"I know so." His gaze slid down the front of me all the way to the ground. "For one thing, the Sarah I originally met would never wear flat shoes like those."

I looked down at my Keds. "They're incredibly comfortable. So what if I'm way shorter now?"

He bent over and brushed his lips against mine. "Thank you for standing by me through all of this, for believing in me. You don't know how much it means to me."

My previous doubts flew away as quickly as they'd arrived. "I can't think of anywhere else I'd rather stand."

"Come, I know someone in the city who can get us an untraceable car and some new identification. We'll leave tonight—it can't wait any longer."

"You really don't think there's any other way? We know the truth now."

"This, unfortunately, is not a truth that will set me free. I'll get you to safety and then I'll deal with Markus."

"Oh, now you're going to deal with Markus—you're not just going to avoid him?"

He cast a look at me and I didn't like the uncertainty in his gaze. I was used to him knowing exactly what to do at all times, even if he didn't share all the details with me. The doubt in his gray eyes made the ground feel like it was shifting beneath my feet.

He didn't reply. He didn't really have to.

There was only one solution here and that was for us to split up. My time with Thierry was coming to an end whether I liked it or not and I had no idea what our future held or if I'd ever see him again.

He was standing right next to me holding my hand and I already missed him.

"Do you think there's any possibility that Kristopher is the serial killer?" I asked, giving my suspicions a voice. Even though it was dusk, the streets were busier than ever. We'd quickly made it back to the Strip and were headed, apparently, toward a hotel where Thierry had some sort of contact who could help us for a price. Everybody, I'd learned, had a price.

"What makes you think that?"

"I don't know—emotional distress, lost love, a mysterious curse or magical punishment, bad fashion choices, and that pointy sickle ring of his. To me that adds up to a whole lot of potential for kookiness and instability."

"It's possible. But the serial killer is Markus's problem now. I believe my accusation of murder has removed me as Bernard's replacement as consultant."

He was right about that. "So can you tell me now what the offer you couldn't refuse was?"

"Does it matter?"

"I'm curious."

"It's past. I was willing to take the position for several reasons."

"But not entirely of your own free will?"

His expression darkened. "If I ask you not to press me on this matter, will you do that for me?"

I was frustrated that he wouldn't talk about it, but this wasn't the most important thing to deal with right now. "Okay, fine. No pressing. But it's just another secret you won't share, isn't it? You can't blame me for being curious."

"There is much of my past I'd like to leave exactly where it is. There's no logical reason to turn over every one of my rocks to reveal what's underneath. It's only a matter of time before you find something you might not be able to deal with."

"Maybe you underestimate me."

He gave me an amused sidelong look. "Frequently."

"I have secrets, too, you know," I said pointedly, although I was completely lying. I couldn't think of a single one I had locked away in a dark closet so no one would see the truth. "Big secrets. And you know what? You're never going to know what they are."

He still looked amused. "Noted."

The next moment I felt as if my arm had been yanked right out of its socket as he pulled me off the sidewalk and in through the doors of the Paris casino.

"What is it?" I asked as he walked briskly, almost more briskly than I could keep up with. I was fast now, but this was Speedy Gonzales–level fast.

"Markus," he said. Only one word, but it was enough to tell me everything I needed to know. He'd spotted Markus, and if the enforcer spotted us in return, we were in deep, deep trouble.

He swore under his breath again, which worried me. The more he did that, the more it meant that he didn't have everything under control.

"What do we do?" I asked, my throat tight.

"He'll be looking for us to be together." We hadn't stopped walking. We breezed past the slot machines and down a long carpeted hallway. "I don't want this, but we'll have to split up for a while. Go somewhere safe. I have my cell phone back from Markus's men. I'll call you the moment I have a car and we can leave the city together."

"How long will that take?"

"An hour. No more than that."

"I hate to ask, but can't we just steal a car?"

"We could, but I need my contact for more than just transportation. He will help us in other invaluable ways, too, and he has no affiliation with the Ring, so there's no risk of him selling us out. This must be done now. Call me if there is any problem at all, do you hear me?"

I nodded, my heart racing. "Okay, fine. I'll go somewhere dark and private where I can hide out for an hour."

He stopped walking and pulled me against him. "I'm so sorry for dragging you into all of this, Sarah. I never should have brought you here with me in the first place. I see now it was a terrible mistake." He kissed me hard before he pulled back and gazed into my eyes for a moment with regret and worry. "Be safe."

Then he turned and walked away from me. Before long, I lost him in the crowd of tourists and gamblers.

In hindsight, coming to Vegas and playing at being his fiancée slash personal assistant had been a bit of a long shot, I'd admit it. But his admission that it was a *mistake* left me with a sick feeling in the pit of my stomach. All of this still would have happened whether or not I'd been here, so I didn't think he was blaming me. However, escaping from Markus, and then dealing with the consequences, with a naive fledgling slowing him down every step of the way . . .

I could see his point.

I was a liability on many levels. I was a problem that had to be dealt with.

No news there.

Still, that "fighter" part of me didn't want to accept this as the truth. It wanted to yell at him and say that it wasn't a mistake. That I was meant to be by his side, in good times *and* in bad. And that he was lucky to have me when practically any other woman would have dutifully gotten on that plane last night and gone back to her safe and secure home, tail tucked between her legs, before getting on with her regularly scheduled life.

I wasn't that woman. And I might be naive, but I knew what I wanted. I wanted Thierry, secrets and all. I even wanted to help him with his job. Working with Victoria had shown me that being a consultant with the shadowy organization was a valuable position and it served an important purpose: lending a hand to vampires in trouble. Since I'd been one of those vampires for a while now, I saw the value in getting a little outside help now and then. Thierry and me as a team would have done a way better job than Bernard ever had. After all, we would actually care about the people we were sent to assist, not get distracted by pet wives, stolen diamonds, and misplaced revenge.

But that was over now. I'd be placed somewhere safe and given new identification like someone in the witness relocation program.

This was all so messed up. There had to be another answer, I just couldn't think of it yet.

Keeping an eye on my surroundings, I tried to blend in with the crowd. I planned to go back to my motel room and wait there until I got Thierry's call.

But then I saw him.

Not Markus, somebody else. Somebody that I didn't trust for one minute.

Charles moved down the sidewalk just as I stepped outside the casino. His hands were shoved deeply in his pockets and he looked nervously to the right and left as if checking to see if anyone had spotted him.

Victoria was nowhere to be seen. As far as I knew, the little vamp was safely tucked in bed for the night with her teddy bear.

And Charles had ventured out at sunset all by his lonesome.

Staying vigilant to Markus's potential presence, I trailed after Charles down the sidewalk.

"Are you prepared, my child?" a voice asked.

I looked to my left to see Vampire Jesus standing there in his familiar white robes, a cheery smile on his face that showed off his fake fangs. He thrust a lime green flyer out to me.

"No, I'm definitely not prepared," I replied.

"It will be soon. All of this will end. Everything you've ever known. The day is nigh when the vampires will rule the world and all humans will become their willing slaves."

I grabbed the flyer out of his hand, stared at it a moment, then crumpled it into a ball and tossed it at his face. It bounced off and hit the ground.

"Get a life," I told him.

A frown creased his brow. "But, my child—"

"Besides, any smart vampire wouldn't want a human slave. Way too high maintenance. Now go get a real job, you weirdo."

I turned my back on him and kept after Charles. He finally slipped into the M&M's store. I kept following him. I really wanted to know where he went when he left Victoria for long stretches of time.

Thierry said that the serial killer was Markus's responsibility now, and I totally agreed with that. I'd never wanted anything to do with it; all I wanted was to find out who had Bernard killed. Well, now I knew the answer to that—as bizarre as the answer turned out to be. My plate was clear.

However, if it *was* Charles, I couldn't just sit back and let him keep killing people, could I? The answer to that rhetorical question was a big fat no. I wasn't going to take him down and perform a citizen's arrest or anything if I found out I was right, but I could pass along word to people who could do something about it— even if it was an anonymous tip to Markus himself. While I didn't like Markus and he scared me deeply, I knew he was a damn good enforcer and would take care of the serial killer problem swiftly and permanently.

There was a door at the back of the chocolate-themed store that Charles opened up and walked through. When I reached the door, I pushed it open a few inches, trying to hear something—talking, screaming, I wasn't sure.

I couldn't hear much beyond the buzz of customers behind me in the store—and yet, farther down the hall there was a murmuring. Voices. Several of them.

A hand clamped down on my shoulder and I barely stopped myself from doing my best banshee impression.

A large bald man smiled at me. His hand was about the size of an oven mitt. "You don't need to be afraid."

My heart thudded against my rib cage. "I don't?"

"No, it's fine. We're all in this together." He had fangs. He was a vampire, too.

"We are?"

"Yes. Come along, then, I'll help you. The others will be glad you've decided to join us."

I gulped. "They will?"

"I understand the urges. We all do. Now, don't make a fuss. It'll all be better soon."

Oh my God. What had I just walked into? A serial killer party in the back of a chocolate store? I was supposed to be somewhere safe waiting for Thierry's call and now I was being led along a dark hallway to face my doom. I never planned to venture out of the main store where it was safe, but now it seemed too late. I really would have much preferred to learn the truth about Charles from a happy and healthy distance.

"Oh, I don't know." I tried to sound calm. "This doesn't feel right. I think I want to leave."

"We all said that in the beginning. It's only together that we can make sense out of everything. Trust me."

Trust him? I'm thinking . . . *no*.

He pushed open a door at the end of the hallway and six pairs of eyes turned and stared at me, including Charles's. His gaze widened.

"Sarah," he said with surprise. "What are you doing here? How did you even find out this place exists?"

The big bald man patted my arm in a friendly

manner as he let go of me. I wasn't immediately attacked and torn into small bloody pieces, which was a relief, so I decided my only chance to get out of here was to play along.

"You know, word gets around," I said as calmly as I could. "And here I am."

Charles shook his head. "I had no idea."

"Right." I glanced around at the others. Including Baldy and Charles, there were four men and three women. "No idea about what?"

"That you were one of us."

That was highly debatable.

Seven members of this group. And there had been seven murders to date that I was aware of.

Oh boy.

A woman approached me. She had a neat blond bob and looked like a professional—a lawyer, maybe. She wore a pantsuit that gave her a very Hillary Clinton look. "New members are always welcome. Please, everyone, have a seat and let's get started. Don't forget, there's coffee available to you all at the back."

I uneasily took a seat in a metal chair. Charles sat down next to me. He had a Styrofoam cup full of coffee. He gave me a small grin. "Sorry I've been kind of rude to you. I appreciate you looking after Victoria while I've been dealing with stuff."

"Dealing with what kind of stuff?" I asked cautiously.

"*This* kind of stuff." He glanced around the room. "It's been a tough month for me, so I'm here a lot, like three times a day, which is way more than the others. But they've been helping me deal with my issues. I know Victoria told you I used to be a hunter."

"She did . . . ," I said slowly. What else had Victoria shared with him? My guess that he was still hunting . . . only it was humans now?

"It's rough. But we need to deal. We need to accept what we are and make peace with it any way we can, even when it's difficult. *Especially* when it's difficult."

"I couldn't agree more."

This felt off somehow. When I'd entered this room, I'd been utterly convinced it was full of vampires who were indiscriminately killing humans and leaving their bodies in the open all over town. But I wasn't starring in a Stephen King movie and a serial killer meeting seemed extremely unlikely. So what the hell was this?

"Welcome everyone," the blonde said. She stood at the front and everyone's attention went to her. "Thank you all for coming out to our Thursday evening meeting. My name is Dolores and I am addicted to blood."

"Hi, Dolores," the group chimed all together.

Charles leaned toward me. "It's easier to deal with our addictions when we have people who understand what we're going through. Don't you think?"

I just nodded as the truth of where I'd found myself became abundantly clear.

This wasn't a serial killer strategy meeting.

This was a meeting of Bloodaholics Anonymous.

Chapter 19

The members of the group each got up in turn, introduced themselves, and related their story about how they'd faced difficulties. I could only equate it to Overeaters Anonymous more than Alcoholics Anonymous. You could abstain from booze completely, but someone addicted to food still had to eat to survive. Ditto vampires and blood.

Charles admitted to having impulse problems. He was spending heaps of money at blood banks, including Blood Bath & Beyond, to literally feed his cravings, and he longed for a day when he could drink like a normal vampire.

Finally, it was my turn. I stood on shaky legs, incredibly relieved by what I'd learned so far. But I still needed to play along. I didn't think anyone would be too thrilled to find out that I'd been faking.

"Hi, I'm Sarah, and I'm . . . addicted to blood."

"Hi, Sarah!"

I took a deep breath. "Just like the rest of you, I have problems with my thirst." I thought of Thierry and his issues. Had he ever been to a meeting like this before? I honestly couldn't picture it. "When I get even the smallest taste, I lose it. I want more and more. I'm afraid of hurting someone really badly—like, say, my fiancé. I've bitten him before and one time I nearly drained him. I was lost, crazed; it was scary. I try to keep a hold on it, but it's always at the back of my mind . . . blood. More. Always more. All I can do is try to stay away from the temptation completely and not drink blood at all."

There were gasps at this. I swept my gaze over the group and they all looked at me with shock. I'd been role-playing Thierry's situation, his difficulties with blood, but somehow with this reaction I wasn't sure if I'd said something wrong.

"What?"

"You sound like you have a serious problem," Charles said.

I frowned. I thought maybe I could get some insight on Thierry's issues by speaking them out loud. "Isn't that why you're all here? Because you're addicted to blood?"

"I'd never actually *hurt* someone. I just spend too much money trying to satisfy my never-ending craving, that's all. I've never lost control of myself like you're describing. As soon as I get a taste, I feel better, not worse."

I could see at a glance that this was a common feeling.

"It gets worse when you get older," I said.

"Aren't you a fledgling?"

"Um, yeah." I crossed my arms. "But, uh . . . maybe I have an old soul?"

Dolores, the group leader, looked at me with concern . . . and some wariness. "It sounds as if you're describing something that goes far beyond a simple addiction like we all share. Quite honestly, it sounds dangerous."

That was worrying. "I know someone else like this, too. He's—older than me. A lot older. He doesn't need to drink blood at all and when he does, it gets a little . . . unpredictable."

She nodded slowly. "I suppose it's possible. I know those older than five hundred years can survive for a very long time without any blood. But they should still be in control of themselves when and if they do drink. Masters are the most controlled of any of us. Practice makes perfect, and all that." She drew closer and pulled a card out of her pocket. She hesitated only briefly before holding it out to me. "If you find that either you or your friend is getting to a point where you can't control this dark thirst anymore and you feel that you might be putting others at risk by being around you, I strongly suggest you call this number to get help."

I took the card from her and looked down with dismay at the phone number and name.

Markus Reed.

Small world. I had a funny feeling I knew exactly how Markus would deal with a vampire with a severe and potentially deadly blood addiction. He'd prescribe one wooden stake to be administered straight through the heart. Problem solved.

The meeting ended a few minutes later with hugs and words of support. I tossed back a quick cup of black coffee with three sugars as I thought about what I'd learned. Basically that whatever it was that Thierry dealt with in regard to his particular kind of bloodlust, it wasn't something that could be helped at a typical

Bloodaholics Anonymous meeting. Just one more thing for me to worry about.

Charles approached me as the others filed out of the room. I was looking at the screen of my cell phone to see that I'd received a breezy text from Amy asking me how I was doing. I decided to reply to it later when I actually knew the answer to that.

"If there's anything I can do . . . ," Charles began.

I looked at him now feeling completely horrible for suspecting him of anything more than being an over-protective guardian of Victoria. "I'll be okay."

He didn't speak for a moment. "It isn't you at all, is it? It's just Thierry. Am I right?"

I cringed. "I'd rather not say."

"It sounds like he has a really hard time with it, but he's survived this long. Don't worry about him." He actually looked concerned for me, which was weird given our strained relationship before this. "I've got to get back to the hotel and make sure Victoria's okay, but I'm here for you if you need me. For both of you."

"Thanks. You go. I'll . . . well, tell her I'll be in touch when I can."

He promised he would and then left—after giving me a rather awkward hug of support.

I took my time leaving the M&M's store, thinking about what I'd learned and whom I'd met and what it all meant. I didn't even know why I was giving it this much thought. Thierry had his issues under control and he was way better than when we'd first met. I didn't constantly worry for the safety of my neck around him.

I stared at my cell phone again. It had been a little over an hour since I'd split from him. He should be calling me any minute and I could stop obsessing about stuff that didn't even matter in the grand scheme of things.

In the meantime, I didn't exactly feel secure standing in the middle of the sidewalk all by myself. I was right near Blood Bath & Beyond, so I headed toward the novelty store, feeling more paranoid with every step I took.

Had to say, though, I felt incredibly relieved about Charles. I'd been convinced that he was the killer—based mostly on gut instinct. It was nice to know my gut had failed me for once. He was just a person with problems he needed to deal with on a daily basis. I knew a lot of those. I was one of them.

I was glad he was legitimately interested in being Victoria's pseudo-daddy. I couldn't believe how quickly I'd grown to care about that kid and her wildly split personality. I wasn't sure which side of her I liked more—the fun-loving child who loved wearing pretty dresses and singing, or the no-nonsense business-woman who drank and smoked and had no filter in saying what was on her mind.

I still wasn't too thrilled with "puppy" as a nickname, but I supposed there were worse things to be called.

If given a choice, I would stay in touch with her and make sure she found a new way to pay her bills without doing any more pageants and placing herself in potential danger—some way that also didn't involve becoming a tiny jewel thief.

Just as I reached the front door of the store, the Elvira-costumed cashier was turning the sign to CLOSED. I pushed the door open and slipped inside before she was able to lock it.

"Sorry," she said. "We're closing early tonight."

"Why? Is Josh here?" This would be the perfect place for me to wait for Thierry and get lost among the aisles and merchandise. I hated to think that wouldn't be an option.

"We lost a ton of staff today and Josh has his magic show to get to. There are just not enough people around to keep it open till midnight like usual—and I'm sure as hell not sticking around. Not when I haven't had a paycheck that hasn't bounced in nearly a month." She glared at me as if daring me to question her about why she was being so open with this particular gossip.

I cringed. Kristopher had hinted that Josh's finances weren't doing so well. I guess this was only more proof. I couldn't imagine how much a place like this would cost to keep running on a month-to-month basis. It was huge and it had a ton of stock. When I'd been here before, it was busy with tourists, though. It wasn't like it was completely empty. Still, I guess it wasn't enough.

"Is he still here?" I asked.

"Yeah, he's giving Carlos his walking papers right now. Been putting it off far too long. That guy is a disaster waiting to happen, if you ask me."

I wondered if that was the vampire Josh mentioned earlier—the vamp who'd been here a week who had "human issues."

"Can I hang out here for a bit?" I asked. "I know Josh, so I don't think he'll have a problem with it."

She shrugged and pulled off her long black wig, revealing a platinum blond pixie cut underneath. "Whatever. Just promise not to steal anything."

"Cross my heart."

Without another word, she slipped past me and

went out the door before locking it behind her with a key she had on a key ring.

I checked my phone again. I didn't want to text or call Thierry yet and interrupt whatever he was doing. So instead, I browsed the store. Half the lights were off, but I could see just fine. This place was a lot of fun; I hated to think it wasn't doing well. Even before I was a vampire, I liked vampire paraphernalia. I'd been a big Anne Rice fan and loved all the vampire-slaying TV shows with sassy girls who liked kicking butt and quipping sarcastically as they sank stakes into chests. I wasn't quite as fond of Buffy as I once was, given that she was essentially a hunter in a short skirt and lip gloss, but it had its moments.

"You can't do this!" The voice was deep but whiny and came from the other side of the store. Since there was no one else in here and the organ music from the speakers had gone silent, it sounded louder than it normally might have.

Josh spoke next. "I'm sorry it came to this. I tried to give you a chance, but it hasn't worked out. You worry me too much."

"I worry you?"

"You punched a human customer. When his nose started to bleed, I thought we were going to have an incident."

The other guy—Carlos, I presumed—snorted at that. "What did you think would happen? I see blood and I automatically attach myself to the customer like some sort of sucker fish? I'm not a complete heathen."

"I don't know you and I have no idea what you're capable of. I'm just trying to protect my business."

I turned the corner in time to see Carlos—who was

as big as a football quarterback—grab hold of Josh's novelty T-shirt and push him back up against the wall hard. "You're right. You have no idea what I'm capable of."

His furious gaze flicked toward me and I fought the urge to take a step back.

"Sorry for interrupting," I said. "Or maybe I'm not so sorry. You okay, Josh?"

Josh pushed back against the huge vampire. "Yeah, I'm fine. Carlos was just leaving."

"I need to be paid," Carlos growled.

"I'll write you a check."

"Your checks aren't any good. I want cash or I'm not going anywhere."

Josh cast a look in my direction, one that was weary and defeated. "Fine. Follow me."

Carlos followed closely, glaring as me as they walked toward the cash register. Josh pushed a few buttons and it popped open. He counted out twenties and tens into Carlos's hand.

Carlos counted the money a second time before shoving the wad in his pocket. "You're pathetic, you know that? I almost feel sorry for you."

Josh's shoulders sank, but he didn't say anything.

"He paid you like you asked him to," I said sharply, pissed off on Josh's behalf at this jerk's rude behavior. I couldn't help but stick my nose into this even though I knew it was absolutely none of my business. "So why don't you get out of here and leave him alone?"

He glared at me. "Who the hell are you?"

"A friend."

"Josh doesn't have friends. Not anymore. He's too pathetic to keep any of them. Nobody wants his bad luck to rub off on the rest of us." He gave me a cold, fang-filled smile; then he moved away from the cash area and started toward the door. I was standing in his path, fuming at what a jerk he was being.

"Move," he snarled at me.

I put my hands on my hips. "Or what?"

"Or I'll make you move."

"Big tough guy, are you? You know what? In my experience, it's the toughest ones whose knees are the most full of jelly. I bet *you're* the one who doesn't have any friends. You were lucky to get a job here. Do you know how freaking cool this place is? But, no. Instead, people like you take everything and everyone for granted and don't even say a thank-you. Josh is way better off without you here." I was livid by now. "Oh, and by the way? You're ugly, too."

Carlos stared at me for a few moments before his bottom lip began to wobble. "Why do you have to be so mean?"

I immediately deflated, regretting that I'd let my rant get away from me. "Excuse me?"

"It's been a hard week, okay?" he managed, his voice breaking. "My girlfriend dumped me; I can't pay my rent; I'm a total and complete loser. I already know that! And now—now I'm ugly, too?"

I felt terrible. So much for my bluster and bravado in trying to take this guy down a notch. "You're . . . not ugly. You're really quite, uh . . . attractive, now that I get a really good look at you. I've always loved unibrows—very retro. Don't feel bad. It's been a hard week for me, too, so I understand what you're going through. Things will get better. Just . . . stay positive. Keep that chin up.

And stop hitting humans. You'd probably still have a job if you didn't do that."

"But my girlfriend left me for a human guy. Then he came in here to rub my nose in it by telling me how much happier she is with him than with me." His eyes glistened.

This was just getting worse and worse. "She obviously didn't deserve you."

"Whatever. I can take a hint. Women . . . you're all the same. You all just want to break my heart." He ran a big mitt of a hand under his nose and headed for the door. Josh caught up to him there to let him out and locked the door again behind him.

I grimaced as Josh turned around to face me. He was actually laughing now, his hands on his thighs, his face red. "Oh my God, I can't believe you called him ugly."

"Who knew he had self-esteem issues? I mean, he's a tank with fangs and a single eyebrow."

He finally got himself under control and raked a hand through his red hair, shaking his head as he looked at me. "That was awesome. Nearly worth the three hundred bucks I just shelled out to him."

"Glad to oblige. Are you okay?"

That sobered him up quickly. "I've had better days."

"Sorry to hear you're having problems."

"Me too." He shoved his key chain into the front pocket of his jeans. "Sorry, but I'm closing up shop early tonight. That goes for the blood bank, too."

"I'm not here for that. Will you be much longer? Can I hang out for a bit?"

"I have a few things I need to clear up—plus I have

to quickly do a count of the day's receipts. I'll be here another fifteen minutes." He looked at his watch and grimaced. "Damn, I'm running late. I need to be at the theater in half an hour or I'm in serious trouble."

"That place isn't what I expected."

He raised an eyebrow. "You've been to Club Noir?"

I nodded and shifted my purse higher on my shoulder. "I went to see Kristopher earlier."

"Really. Why?" He moved behind the cash register again and began to gather the money together.

"I needed his help. Thought he could use his psychic ability to contact someone for me."

He grinned. "I'm sure he loved that."

"If by 'loved' you mean he tried to pretend he had no real power at all, just before nearly suffocating my fiancé when the truth came out, then you'd be right. He's got a whole bunch of issues himself, doesn't he?"

"Oh yes. Kris is an interesting guy."

I ran my hand along the side of the counter and picked up a Beanie Baby bat that was seated next to a small display of black jelly beans. "Do you think he's dangerous?"

He flicked a look at me. "I wouldn't doubt it for a minute."

"Really? I mean, like, *really* dangerous? Like . . . kill somebody dangerous?" Ever since we'd left the theater, I hadn't been able to get that sickle ring out of my mind and picture the vampirelike wound it would make on a human's neck.

"I don't know," Josh said. "Kristopher's got a lot of secrets that he hasn't even confided in me and we've worked together for nearly a year now. Maybe if you had some real dirt on him, he might get a little hard to handle."

I didn't like the sound of that. I might be having nightmares of wizard pirates for many nights to come.

Josh scurried around the store doing cleanup and I leisurely followed him since he didn't seem to mind too much. I randomly put another quarter in the slot machine and received the same results as the other two times—nothing. I was beginning to think either I was deeply unlucky or the thing was fixed. Probably both.

"What's your plan with this place?" I asked. "Sorry for prying, but I'd hate to think you might close it down."

"I don't know yet. My money flow is . . . well, I won't bore you with my financial problems. Let's just say, I keep waiting for interest in the subject matter to grow. Who knew vampires would get to be so commonplace that nobody really cares about them anymore?"

Maybe I wasn't the only one with bad luck. I used to think we hid our existence from the world at large to protect ourselves from hunters or to make sure humans weren't scared, but lately the reaction to vampires being real might end up being one big "whatever."

"Is your blood bank the only one on the Strip?" I asked. "I haven't heard of any others. But I'd think the area would be big enough for more than one."

He flicked off some more lights, but even in the growing darkness I could see his immediate frown "No, a couple others just opened up."

"You don't look so happy about that."

"For a month, I was the only ticket in town, which was great for business and my profits helped me pay off a bit of my debt. My café had never been busier than after the two main Vegas blood banks closed down earlier this year."

Both had closed down? "Were they cafés like yours? Or bars? I've only been to the bar kind before."

"One was in a strip club. Kind of sleazy but the clients loved it. Their wives, not so much. Another was five-star all the way. A rooftop patio with a pool. Absolutely gorgeous. That's where the millionaires and the movie stars went while in Vegas."

I blinked. "Vampire movie stars?"

He gave me a grin. "There are a few."

I *knew* Botox couldn't be responsible for all that eternal Hollywood youth. Fifty was the new thirty— literally.

"You said they closed down? What happened to them?"

"The strip club burned to the ground. The rooftop bar also ran into a streak of bad luck—the owners kept falling off the top of it."

My eyes widened. "Falling? But that wouldn't kill them if they were vampires, right?"

"The wooden stake found among their remains would have taken care of that. Staked and pushed. Not a good combo for survival. Got to be careful here—for all its shiny surface, Vegas has a nasty mob underbelly."

I shuddered. "Yikes. But it sounds like more have opened up, so I guess the vamps who run blood banks are a stubborn lot."

"Yeah, two more," Josh said flatly. "And it's been hell on my café."

I felt bad for the guy. Owning a business with so

many bills to pay, and having to deal with competition from others who might offer more, or a better or more convenient product—it had to be rough. Josh had so many balls in the air with his store, his café, and his magic show . . . I had no idea how he managed it all.

"So what are you doing here, Sarah? If you're not looking for a quick drink in the back or possibly adding a lovely, hand-carved wooden casket to your home decor, I can think of a thousand places more interesting than here for someone like you. This is Vegas—there are shows, nightlife, you name it. Where's your fiancé?"

"He's . . . around. That's who I'm waiting for." I looked at my phone again. "I hope nothing's wrong. But, I mean, kick me out when you're ready to go. I can find somewhere else to hang out."

Or *hide* out. Same difference.

"I'm not quite there yet."

I shook my head, needing to put my thoughts into words. "I honestly don't know how you do it, Josh. Managing this place, having your magic show, and also I heard you're an investor in *Fang*."

"You heard that, huh?"

"Kristopher was chatty in between his bouts of crazy. But he's also concerned about you. For such a creepy and disturbed guy who enjoys frilly shirts a bit too much, I think he really likes you."

And now that I thought about it, the psychic had also mentioned something about a gambling problem.

This poor guy was bleeding out money from every vein.

"The feeling's mutual." Josh leaned against the counter, his expression troubled. "I can't say it's easy,

Sarah. I keep trying to make a go of it, but things keep crumbling all around me. No customers, no profit."

"And you think it's all because vampires aren't as edgy as they used to be?"

"Twenty years ago this wouldn't have been a problem—my store would be swarming with customers. Vampires were dangerous back then, scary, sexy. We've totally been defanged by the media, by entertainment, by the publishing industry. Once upon a time, we were horror novels—now we're heartwarming paranormal romances. There's no thrill there anymore to get a human's juices flowing when it comes to us." He cast a dark look toward a couple life-sized wax statues. "I mean, just look at these pathetic examples of vampires. This one doesn't even have fangs. I mean, how sad is that?" He walked toward one and poked the teen vamp in his gray peacoat.

"Fangless, yes, but still kind of hot," I admitted.

"Kind of hot doesn't cut it. I need humans to feel that fear again. It's like a roller coaster. People don't line up for two hours to go on a leisurely tour in a tiny, sparkly car that smells like roses and cinnamon. No, they want the excitement, the thrill, the illusion of life and death. Without that, it's just not the same." His expression grew bleak. "And the stage show is violence, glamour, death, and blood—with boobs and feathers, of course. I mean, this *is* Vegas. I won't even tell you how much debt I've gotten myself into because of it, and our presales are pathetic. Absolutely pathetic."

I shook my head. "I'm really sorry."

"Me too." He moved toward the door and looked out at the street. "You'd think there would be some sort of buzz going. With the murders right out in the open, that should start rumors. But they're not even in the newspaper. It should be front-page by now. National news. CNN should be here with vans and cameras. Word is not spreading that there's a dangerous vampire who is prowling the Vegas streets. If it was, I'd be rolling in money by now. How many more murders will it take?"

I had no idea Josh had even heard about the serial killer, but I figured word was spreading fast even with the Ring's intervention.

Talking about the murders made me feel ill, especially thinking about how wrong I'd been in my guesses so far about who was behind them. The more I considered Kristopher, the more I decided it couldn't be him. The guy had issues and I knew he was dangerous, but . . . I wasn't sure.

Josh honestly thought that having the rumor circulate that there was a dangerous vampire in Vegas murdering humans would be enough to spark interest in his store and show, and help him get out of his deepening debt. I could see his point of view there. And, quite honestly, he was probably right. As they say, there's no such thing as bad publicity.

A vampire serial killer wouldn't drive humans away from Vegas. They'd probably come here in droves, wallets in hand, wanting to be a part of something bigger and more exciting than their normal boring lives. The chance to rub elbows with something that could potentially tear their throats out could be a major thrill for some.

Yes, if word got out about the murders, Josh probably wouldn't have to worry very much about losing Blood Bath & Beyond. He'd be raking in the money and so would his stage show. Vampires would be cool again.

But nobody knew.

And Josh seemed really angry about that.

Almost disappointed, if you ask me.

And also . . . defeated.

Those weren't exactly normal reactions to a situation like this. He glared out of the door of his failing vampire business as he dealt with the frustration that the recent rash of brutal and horrific deaths wasn't working in his favor.

It was as if he'd expected it to be different.

Oh crap.

Suddenly, I had a brand-new suspect in the serial killings. And this time, my gut instinct wasn't just nudging me to believe he was the right one.

It was screaming at me.

Chapter 20

We were silent for a full minute and Josh's previous good-natured humor seemed to leave the store like a wisp of smoke. The expression on his face was haunted, strained, and deeply pissed off at the world.

"You ever ask yourself what it's all about?" he said quietly as he continued to stare out of the locked door.

"You mean, the meaning of life?" I was frozen in place. I needed to stay calm and get out of here, put distance between me and this vampire, and then have a chance to think everything through.

Maybe I was wrong about him.

No. Damn it, I wasn't wrong. Not this time.

"I thought being a vampire was going to be wonderful. I offered up my neck at the first opportunity I got. Nearly forty years ago, can you believe it? Feels like twice as long, actually. Every day's been a struggle. My sire never wanted me around. Never taught me the ropes. I had to learn everything the hard way. Being a vampire is work. Hard work. And I'm so, so sick of it all."

I cleared my throat. "Maybe you should try being a werewolf instead."

He let out a sharp laugh, but it lacked humor. "Too late to change. I have to make do with what I have."

My mouth had gone very dry. "You have lots, Josh. I mean, this place is fantastic."

"I hate this place. It's a weight around my ankle, pulling me down to the bottom of the deepest ocean of misery. The café, too." His gaze moved to me and the darkness there chilled me. Between Josh and Kristopher, I was surprised their audiences didn't go running for the hills. "If you had any idea what I'd done to hold on to this, you'd be shocked as hell."

Oh, I think I had a vague idea.

"So sell it," I suggested, eyeing the door eagerly.

"Tried. Failed. It's the cycle of my life. Try and fail."

"Me too."

He swept his eyes over me, unimpressed. "I find that hard to believe."

"Trust me—I'm as unlucky as they come." I twisted a nervous finger through my hair. "I met a woman recently who reminded me just how much I need someone to look after me and keep me out of trouble practically every waking hour of the day. She looks like me, too. And we're really similar in so many ways. Without her husband, she was completely lost in the world."

"You think you're like that. Lost without your fiancé?"

"I—I don't really know."

"Just a weak little lamb lost in the woods."

"That's me. I'll save my lamb impression for another time. It's not that good."

His gaze turned predatory. "Little lambs need to be aware of the monsters lurking in the shadows. The ones with the biggest appetites."

I forced myself to laugh lightly. "Very dramatic. Yes, you're quite the showman, aren't you? I definitely want to catch your show before I leave Vegas. You're on tonight, right? Aren't you running a bit late now?"

"Kristopher goes on before me. Looks like I have time to take care of some last-minute problems."

I really didn't like the way he said that. I rubbed my lips together and looked at my phone. "Gee, I wonder where Thierry is. You know, he's a master vampire. Very old, very powerful. Knows everybody. If you had any idea how much ass I've seen him kick over the months, you'd be amazed. Everybody's terrified of him."

"I'm sure. He sounds swell. So he takes care of you, Sarah? Like your little friend's husband did for her?"

"He tries his best."

"I guess he can't always watch over you if you're not with him. Who knows what danger you're going to find yourself in at any given moment of the day, huh? It's a dangerous world for a fledgling who doesn't know any better than to go places she shouldn't be."

"Totally." I kept my smile going as I jabbed my finger on my address book to call Thierry's phone. I pressed it to my ear.

Answer. Please, please answer.

Thierry picked up on the second ring. "Sarah."

"Hey, killer," I said as breezily as possible, winking at Josh to let him know that was my special pet name for my very dangerous fiancé. "What's taking you so long?"

"I'm almost finished." He sounded a bit uncertain. I couldn't blame him. Our nicknames for each other so far had usually been no more imaginative than "Sarah" and "Thierry." If nothing else, they were easy to remember. "Are you . . . well?"

"Yeah, me? I'm fine. Just fine. Just hanging out with Josh, a good pal of mine. Just chatting away. No problem. How long are you going to be?"

There was a short hesitation. "Where are you? Is everything all right? You sound very unlike yourself."

"Do I? No, I'm fine. Everything's fine and dandy. Anyway, when you're ready, you can find me at Blo—"

The phone was suddenly gone from my hand. Josh had moved toward me quickly and plucked it right out of my grip. He stared at the screen for a moment before he ended the call.

Terror gripped my chest. "I wasn't finished."

"Yeah, you were."

"Can I have my phone back, please?" I held my now-shaking hand out and tried to look stern.

"This?" He held the device between his fingers.

"Yes, that."

He bent over and placed it on the ground. Then he smashed it with the sole of his shoe. "Oops, sorry about that."

I raced for the door, grabbed hold of the handle, and pulled hard. It was locked. I grappled to find the lock, but there wasn't one. This was a door that needed a key on both sides. Before I could try to break the glass and get someone's attention on the sidewalk, Josh grabbed hold of the back of my tank top and hauled me backward. I staggered six feet away before going over on my ankle and hitting the ground hard. Panic raced through me as I stared up at him.

"So here we are," Josh said, spreading his hands.

"I want to leave."

"Too late for that."

"I don't understand why you're doing this."

"Wrong, Sarah. You know, I've met many people over the years. Part of being a magician unable to do any real magic is acquiring the skill of reading faces. The eyes are the windows to the soul. I can see it—and I can get a sense of who somebody is when I meet them for the first time. It's all in their eyes."

"My eyes?"

"A lovely shade of hazel. Brown with flecks of green and amber. I studied them before—when you were in my blood bank. You're sincere. I saw that easily. No guile. I hate guile."

"Guile sucks," I agreed as I began to slowly back up, crablike, away from him until my back hit a low shelf.

"You weren't trying to trick me then, find out more about me, other than genuine curiosity. I liked you, Sarah."

"Liked," I repeated. "That's past tense."

"Yes, it is."

"I don't understand why you're doing this, Josh. I thought we were friends."

"No, we weren't. But we were well on our way. See—like I said, I can read people. Before you had no agenda with me. But that changed tonight in an instant. I could see it in your face. In your eyes. Trust and friendliness shifted to doubt and suspicion." His lips thinned. "You know, don't you?"

"I don't know anything." I put as much conviction as I could into my guileless hazel eyes.

"Yes, you do. I think you know more than people realize. They look at you and see a pretty but meaningless fledgling who might be connected to a powerful master."

"That's all I am," I admitted. "And thank you for

calling me pretty. I've been having a really lousy hair day today, you have no idea."

"This friend of yours, the woman who reminded you of yourself. Where is she now?"

"Lost," I said. "Looking for a new path."

"And you think you're like her?"

"I don't know what I'm like."

He folded his arms over his otherwise friendly "Vampilicious" T-shirt. "There are two kinds of people, Sarah. There's only one way to tell the difference—and that's what they're willing to do when their survival is at stake. Half will give up and accept their fate. The other half, however, will fight to keep breathing, fight to survive and protect those they care about, no matter how much the odds seem stacked against them. It sounds like your friend falls into the first category. Do you as well?"

Suddenly, I wasn't feeling all that share-y. "I don't know. What category do you put yourself in?"

"Forty years, bad luck all along. I've been in the first category for too long to count. One day I got sick of being pathetic and weak, so I decided to change. I decided to do whatever it took to survive and not sit back and let fate keep kicking me in the face."

"You killed them," I said quietly. "One a day for the last week. You left them out in the open, hoping that the news of the vampire attacks would cause some major publicity. So your business, your show, would be successful. So you could pay off your debt from your lousy business decisions and gambling. And you even set it up so if suspicion ever shone your way—if the Ring started sniffing around and putting the puzzle together—you could shift blame to Kristopher. After all, he's the crazy and tortured dark wizard with the sickle ring."

Josh's expression hadn't changed as I said any of this. He moved toward a shelf, reached up high, and pulled down a large box. "Kristopher would have been a perfect suspect. I was still working out the details, but I think it would have worked out just fine. It still might, if I need him. Funny thing, he considers me a friend. I guess we are. I honestly think he's a good person and would struggle with the thought of murdering innocents, but there's no reason why it shouldn't look as if he has."

"But you're not struggling with that."

His dark eyes met mine. "Nobody's really all that innocent, Sarah. I'm sure I don't have to tell you that. Everyone has secrets they try to hide. Darkness. There is no one without sin, especially not here in the City of Sin."

I shook my head. "You're better than this, Josh. You can stop this right now. I'll help you. It's not too late to change."

"Vladimir," he said. "Call me by my stage name now, Sarah: Vladimir Nosferatu. Josh is weak and pathetic, but Vlad is strong and fierce. He's a real warrior who does what he needs to do."

I shifted my gaze from my crushed cell phone back to his pasty face. "Don't take this the wrong way, but that's a really stupid name."

He gave me a very sinister smile. "Thank you for your opinion."

I noticed with deep dismay that the box he was opening up contained a crossbow.

"This just went on sale," he said. "It works, too. Some

might take it out hunting deer, but to give it the vampire edge necessary to be in this store, it's got thin wooden stakes included. Very effective. I've tested it before on one of the owners of that rooftop-patio blood bank." He was assembling it quickly, too. He cast another unpleasant smile in my direction. "I'll give you a chance, Sarah. Go, hide. I could navigate this store with my eyes closed, but you can at least try to get away from me."

My hands shook as I held them out in front of me. "Josh . . . don't do this. . . ."

"Consider it a chance to prove to yourself who you really are. Are you someone who accepts her fate and knows when to give up and die? If so, that will make this very simple for me. The problem you now present will be taken care of quickly. I might even make my show on time. Or will you fight to survive? Are you really the same as that friend of yours or are you your own person? Ten seconds, Sarah." He squeezed his eyes shut. "Ten . . . nine . . . eight . . ."

I wouldn't be able to get past him to get to the locked door. It wouldn't do me any good anyway, unless I managed to break it. I was stronger now compared with my previous human self, but I'd neglected to eat my spinach today to help me bust down a door right in front of a vampire with a crossbow aimed at me.

Instead, I was off the floor and tearing through the store in the opposite direction as fast as I could run. I banged my leg against a shelf and it hurt like hell. Although not nearly as much as one of those wooden stakes would hurt if it found its target.

I raced up the staircase to the second floor before he'd gotten to the count of four and I dove beneath an animatronic *Addams Family* dinner table. I didn't think this would be a good spot for very long. He'd find me. Also, it was very dusty. A sneeze felt imminent and I clamped my hands over my nose.

One good thing was that this place was huge and jam-packed full of merchandise. It was a veritable vampiric maze I could lose myself in for days and still not see everything. I had a decent view, although nothing higher than hip level from where I now crouched. A cold line of perspiration slid down my spine and I tried my best not to tremble in fear for my life.

It goes without saying, really, but this was bad. I didn't need a memo to tell me that. I'd honestly not suspected Josh—*Vlad*—for a moment. I'd been looking for people who were shady, who acted suspicious. Not someone who seemed friendly, but unlucky. I'd sensed a whole lot of good in Josh. He had a blood bank. He wanted to help make things easier for the local vampires.

Still a business, though, wasn't it? It wasn't as if he was giving the red stuff away for free. And he wanted it to be successful, just like everything else.

Two other blood banks—the strip club and the rooftop patio—had both closed up due to tragedy. Fire and murder, respectively.

He'd all but blatantly admitted to killing one of the rooftop owners with a crossbow. Did I want to lay any further bets on who might be responsible for the ultimate demise of both places? And what might be the fate of the blood banks that had just opened up to take more business away from this one?

Josh was a bad businessman, an unlucky investor, and an unrepentant killer. Not necessarily in that order. And I was currently stuck in a locked store with him on the hunt for me.

"Sarah!" I heard him on the first floor, the opposite side near the cash registers. "I'll find you!"

Was he crazy, too? Did he have some sort of split personality—Josh the nice guy and Vlad the killer? I wasn't so sure about that. I think he'd been pushed so far that he didn't know what was right and what was wrong. This? This was wrong. In case there was any doubt in the matter.

I slowly eased out a little from under the table and looked up at Morticia Addams's waxy face, but she had no words of wisdom for me. The plug to her display was pulled out from the wall socket and cast aside. She was out of commission for the day.

I really hoped only one of us got unplugged tonight.

Downstairs, when he'd talked about the two kinds of people in the world, it made me think immediately of Laura. We might look a lot alike and have been in similar situations with master vampires—on the surface, anyway. But we couldn't be more different underneath. She relied on Bernard to support her, to protect her, and yet she didn't need him for more than that. She'd had other lovers over the years. The man she'd chosen to marry was only a means to an end. A strategic decision that she'd hoped would lead to a better future as she continued on in her boat with no oars.

Bottom line, Laura didn't know what she wanted—at least not until it was taken away from her.

If Laura were here, I had no doubt at all what she would do. She would beg for her life. She would bargain. She would flirt. And then, if all of that failed, she would accept that this was the end for her because she was outmatched in strength and cunning. She would know there was no other choice for her but death.

If she'd gotten here and hidden under this table, this was where I knew she'd wait, shivering and crying, until Josh finally made his way up here, aimed his crossbow at her chest, and snuffed out a problem that had raised its tangled bed-head.

While I didn't like the situation I'd found myself in, I appreciated that it had helped me see the truth with my own two eyes.

Laura and I were nothing alike. And I sure as hell wasn't going to die here.

Well, maybe I was, but it wouldn't be through lack of trying not to.

I needed to find an exit—and there had to be another one here other than the front door customers used. The last thing I wanted to do was go mano a mano with Vladimir Nosferatu.

Which, for the record, *was* a really stupid name.

I slid out from under the table and scanned the shelves around me, searching for something that might help. It didn't take too long until I found it.

"Well, hello there, pretty," I whispered, curling my hand around a carved wooden stake. There was a pile of them and it looked like a very dangerous display to someone like me, but at the moment I was incredibly grateful for it. It was sharp. It was deadly.

It was my new best friend.

I now felt just a little less terrified.

Slowly, keeping my eyes and ears peeled for any movement or sound, I edged across the floor toward the railing overlooking the rest of the store.

Suddenly, music blasted out of the speakers so loud

I clamped my hands over my ears, narrowly avoiding stabbing myself with the stake. It was the organ music—very *Phantom of the Opera*—that usually piped into the store, but now it was way louder than normal. I couldn't hear anything else.

But, in a way, that didn't help Josh, either. If I couldn't hear him over this noise, he couldn't hear me.

Yeah, smooth move there, loser.

I headed down an aisle, keeping low. I wanted to find some sort of shield, something I could slip under my tank top to work as body armor so a thin wooden stake hurtling through the air might not kill me.

I just wished I knew where Josh was lurking right now. And with the music blasting, I could barely hear myself think.

All I focused on was my next step, keeping my eyes peeled for anything or anyone. I could get out of here. It wasn't too late for me.

I wasn't Laura DuShaw and I never wanted to be. She didn't face her problems head-on and deal with them. She avoided. She evaded. She hid.

Then again, none of her problems had been carrying a crossbow.

Where was he? Was he lurking in the shadows? Did he have me in his sights already? Or was he watching on the closed-circuit security system?

I reached the end of an aisle filled with wax fangs and vampire-themed candy. There were even tiny vials of syrup that looked like blood and cans of something called "coffin juice."

Gag.

Stake clutched tightly in my right hand, so tightly that I began to feel a blister forming, I peeked around the corner. My head ached from the music reverberating in my skull. Would a nearby store notice how strange this was? Or was this place soundproof, so nobody would notice anything but a shop that had closed up early for the night?

While I kept my attention straight forward and to the sides, I wasn't paying enough attention to what might be behind me. I didn't even hear him coming—or sense it on any level—before a hand clamped down over my mouth and an iron bar of an arm crushed across my chest, trapping my arms. I screamed, but it was muffled. I couldn't even move enough to attempt to stab at him with my stake, because he was too strong, stronger than I ever could have guessed. I was literally dragged backward into an alcove behind me, the rubber soles of my Keds squeaking against the linoleum floor as I struggled to break free.

The new area I'd found myself in was made up to look like a tiny cemetery with an iron gate and everything. All I saw was a tombstone that read: "Who Turned Out the Lights?"

He finally released me and I spun around, ready to plunge my stake deep into his chest.

Chapter 21

I stopped myself before I did any plunging.

It was Thierry.

The surprise and relief at seeing him was so big it stole my breath completely. His attention wasn't on me, though; it was on the dark store beyond. I just stared at him with shock, unable to concentrate enough over the blaring noise to figure out how this was even possible.

Then, the very next moment, the music cut out and the store was plunged into eerie silence. For a few seconds my head rang from the organ music and I heard an echoing static before it faded. It was the equivalent of my ears screaming in pain.

Thierry looked at me. "I guess he didn't like a little background noise."

I worked hard to find my voice, which I kept as quiet as his. "You're the one who turned on the speakers?"

He nodded. "I thought it might make things more difficult."

"How are you here?" Maybe I'd been knocked unconscious again and this was just another dream. "How did you know I was in trouble?"

"Your phone call. You sounded deeply distressed."

"I was. I—I am. But how did you know where to find me?"

"You told me enough. I was able to figure it out."

"You figured it out from 'Blo'?" I blinked. He would seriously kick butt at *Wheel of Fortune*.

"You mentioned Josh's name. I know he owns this place—he was your connection to Kristopher. It wasn't difficult to piece it together. I got here as quickly as I could and came in through the side door. Or—well, it's more of a side *hole* at the moment. That's where we need to get back to right now. It's our closest exit."

I reached out to touch his chest as if to prove to myself he was really here. Black suit, warm skin, slow but steady heartbeat. Check, check, and check. It still felt utterly surreal to see him in front of me right now and I could barely believe this was really happening. "Josh . . . he—he's the serial killer. He's been leaving dead bodies all over town to get publicity for himself . . . for this store. He's trying to make vampires scary again."

His expression was tense. "Did you know that when you came here?"

"No, of course not."

He sighed as he gently touched my face, his eyes searching mine. "So when you said you would go somewhere safe for an hour . . ."

I grimaced. "Trust me—my intentions were good."

"I'm sure they were. We need to leave here. Now." He reached down to take my hand in his. "Just be careful where you point that thing."

I looked at my stake. "I know. It's freaking me out, too."

Swiftly, we began moving across the second level

toward the stairs. I'd have guessed this would be the trickiest part of making our escape, but Thierry moved very fast and I had to scramble to keep up with him. Taking two stairs at a time, we were back on the main level in a matter of seconds.

Josh had still been in the store in order to turn off the music. Maybe he was gone now that he knew I wasn't alone. We moved past the coffin display room, beyond which was the Starbucks blood bank. Past more shelves and wax statues. I could see the heavy metal side door. Although it wasn't really a door anymore. It had been ripped clear off its hinges and thrown to the ground.

Sometimes Thierry surprised me by the things he could do. Door ripping definitely went in the column of "good" surprises.

A moment later, Thierry stumbled forward and let go of my hand.

That was another surprise—a bad one. Thierry never stumbled.

"Get to the exit, Sarah," he said. "Go now."

"What's wrong?"

He didn't have to answer me before I saw the problem and it made a scream catch in my throat. There was a wooden stake—a small thin one—sticking out of his back just right of his shoulder blade. No, make that three—two others were deeply embedded in each of his hamstrings. That's what tripped him up. Another stake rocketed through the air and hit him in the shoulder; it was followed in quick succession by two more that hit him in the stomach as he turned around.

Damn it. Josh was close. Close enough to see us.

Close enough to prevent us from getting anywhere near the door. And, currently, I wasn't his main target.

"Do you hear me?" Thierry growled. "Get out of here."

Instead, I grabbed hold of his arm and dragged him into the closest aisle. Then I quickly worked to yank out the stakes that were causing him pain and zapping his strength. I threw them to the side so he could start healing his injuries. I didn't have enough time to feel squeamish or second-guess what I was doing. I did, however, have plenty of time to feel terrified down to the marrow in my bones.

"Sarah, why the hell are you still here?" He sounded angry with me.

"Shut up, Thierry," I snapped, angry right back at him. It helped shove the fear to the side a little. "Just *shut up*. I'm not leaving you. What part of that do you continually fail to understand?"

He glared at me. "All of it. The exit is right there. I was blocking you so you could make a run for it."

"Yeah, blocking me with your own damn body. Nice try. But, sorry, you're not going to die for me today."

"Honestly, woman, you drive me completely crazy."

"The feeling is mutual. Now just stay right here." I could already see he was trying to get to his feet, but failing. He hadn't had enough time to heal, and those stakes were more dangerous than they looked. Wood, just like silver, would zap his strength and stamina down several notches while his body diverted its energy to heal itself. I silently thanked God that Josh seemed to be a lousy shot and had missed his heart. I didn't want to give him any more opportunities to practice his aim.

I peered around the corner to see that Josh was standing a dozen feet away in the center of the hallway blocking the exit. He hadn't come after us since he was currently having trouble with his crossbow.

"Faulty merchandise?" I asked.

His gaze tracked to me and a cold smile snaked across his face. "It's sticking a bit."

"Sorry to hear that. Maybe you can get a refund."

"I doubt it. It's out of the box. The boss here is a real jerk when it comes to returns."

"I know he's an jerk. A murderer. A real sociopath, actually. And I'd be willing to bet he's a lousy magician."

His eyes narrowed. "Maybe he's just someone who does what he has to do."

"That makes two of us."

"Your boyfriend came here to save you. Isn't that romantic?" The sarcasm dripped from every word.

"It is. And he's not my boyfriend. Despite my missing-in-action ring, he's my fiancé."

"Semantics." His grin held. He wasn't worried one little bit about any threat someone like me might pose to him. He continued fiddling with the weapon. "So did you come to any conclusions about what kind of a person you are, Sarah? A victim or a survivor?"

"I have."

"Want to share before I kill both you and your fiancé? I promise to aim for the heart this time."

"Do I want to share?" I repeated. "I'd rather have you guess."

I moved so quickly that I surprised even myself. He blinked with shock to see me suddenly standing right in front of him. He probably expected that I'd try to keep my distance from someone I considered a socio-path, for me to be on the defense rather than the offense in this particular war. It was just his bad luck that I'd been watching more than my share of the History Channel recently.

Before he had a chance to raise the crossbow again, I put every ounce of strength I had into sinking the wooden stake into his chest. Only after it had hit its tar-get did I feel the least bit guilty that it had to come to this. But I was a survivor and to survive sometimes you needed to stop acting like a victim. It was that simple.

He grimaced in pain and looked down at the stake now sticking out of his chest. Thierry had managed to drag himself out of the aisle to come to my side. He put his arm around my waist and pulled me back a bit, putting himself between me and Josh.

My hero. Even when healing up a half dozen deep puncture wounds.

Josh staggered, and then dropped to his knees. "Well played, Sarah."

My eyes burned. "You were going to kill us. You gave me no choice. I'm sorry it had to come to this."

"Yeah, me too." With his left hand, he yanked the stake out. It made a sickening smacking noise. "But I'm not sorry I don't carry stakes made of real wood. This simulated plastic is really convincing, though, isn't it? Damn, it still stings like a bitch."

He threw the bloody stake to the side and shakily got back up to his feet. Thierry pushed me backward, only we were now headed in the exact opposite direc-tion of the open door.

"So I'm guessing that you're Thierry," Josh said, now with a pained smile.

"Conversation?" Thierry asked, his voice just as pained as the other man's. "Can't say I'm in the mood."

"Be a sport."

"No, I don't think I will." Thierry's shoulders were tense and he stood tall, but I knew it was hurting him. "You threaten Sarah, I can't be a sport with you."

"It's so sweet, isn't it? Fledgling and master. Would that still be considered a May-December romance? I guess not. You're both Decembers at this very moment, since you're both about to die. I have six more stakes in here and my aim is improving, especially at this distance. I'm a fast learner." He raised his crossbow.

I held up my hand to try to stop him. "Wait . . . no! Josh, please. Talk to me. We can find another solution here, I know we can."

"You weren't willing to talk a minute ago when you stabbed that stake into my heart, were you?"

He made a good point.

I clutched Thierry's arm, which felt like steel. He was trying his best to keep me behind him, but I knew the stakelike arrows had taken it out of him—he'd been shot not once but six times, and I knew some of the wounds were bad and would take time to heal. Longer than a few minutes, at least. I managed to stand next to him before finally and successfully nudging him backward.

There had to be a way to stop Josh—to distract him. Some way to buy us some time . . .

My gaze snapped to just beyond him, farther down the hallway by the gaping open door. "You should probably know that there's an enforcer from the Ring standing directly behind you."

Josh laughed hollowly at that. "Nice try, Sarah.

Don't take another step closer to me. I have this lined up perfectly with your heart. I promise I won't miss."

Thierry's grip on my arm was firm enough to bruise. He didn't like that I was standing between him and the dude with the crossbow. Frankly, I didn't like it much, either.

I grappled to find my voice and keep it strong and loud. "You know, instead of killing those humans, you could have just taken out an ad to advertise this place. Or word of mouth is also great. Run an awesome business, word gets around. But you just weren't patient enough. You wanted easy answers."

Josh shrugged. "I did what I had to do."

"How many more murders are there going to be before you're satisfied that your campaign to scare up some business isn't working? One a day? How long before someone catches you in the act?"

"Oh, I don't know." He sounded so casual it made me shiver. "It's a nice amount of blood I've been getting. I only ever took a quick taste to sample the goods. When I could, I tried collecting the rest into containers. Importing product for a blood bank is expensive, you know. And my line of credit is currently at its max."

My stomach lurched. He'd been using the victims' blood to help stock his café all week? "You're sick."

"I was looking for the cure to this sickness." His crossbow didn't waver. "The cure was the fear I would have seen in a human customer's eyes as they wandered into the store not sure what to expect. The fear and excitement that would have opened their wallets to someone who just might be a real vampire. I like how you put it—scare up some business. That's exactly what I'm trying to do."

"The sickest thing is you didn't even do it because you're crazy. You're not out for revenge. You don't particularly hate humans. You killed all of them as a business decision."

He gave me a thin smile. "You make it sound like a bad thing."

"It is. And you're going to have to pay for it now." I shook my head. "I would have helped you, even knowing what you'd done. If you'd been the least bit sorry for it, I would have tried to find another way to end this."

His lip moved back off his teeth, baring his fangs. It wasn't a friendly expression. "You're one of the most pathetic vampires I've ever met. You have no bite at all, do you? You give other vamps a bad name. You're not a survivor, Sarah. You're a victim."

"Wrong. You're the victim here. And that bad luck of yours? It doesn't seem to be improving any time soon."

Any amusement that had been in Josh's gaze faded away. His finger tightened on the crossbow's trigger. "Good-bye, Sarah."

"Good-bye, Josh."

The crossbow went flying out of his hands before he'd gotten a shot off. It clattered to the floor. Josh turned with surprise to look behind him.

Markus Reed gave the other vampire a brief sweeping glance, from head to foot.

"Good," he said. "I'll be able to wrap this case up quickly. I really hate Vegas. You have no idea."

"Wait, what are you—?" Josh began.

He wasn't able to finish his sentence. Markus plunged his stake into the other man's chest, right to the hilt. His stake wasn't imitation wood like mine had been. It was polished silver and looked more like a cross between a stake and a scythe. Fitting, really. An enforcer seemed to be synonymous with death. He really was like a blond grim reaper.

Josh fell to his knees and touched the stake. This time he wasn't able to pull it out and grimace at the sharp but meaningless pain it caused him, like an annoying bee sting.

No more chances for redemption. No more possibilities for future business ventures that wouldn't end up in failure. He said he hated being an immortal vampire—that it was hard work with very little benefit. . . .

Well, he wouldn't have to worry about the "immortal" part anymore.

With a last hiss of breath, he collapsed to his side and didn't move again. Thanks to my morbid new talent, I knew he was dead and not faking.

I half expected him to disintegrate into the black goo I was accustomed to seeing when a vampire was staked—like Bernard. But Bernard was several hundred years old. Josh was a newbie in the grand scheme of things. His body wasn't going anywhere.

At this point, with the bad guy defeated, normally I'd be hugely relieved and throw myself into Thierry's arms, thrilled that we'd survived and all was well with the world. But when the person who saved you was someone like Markus Reed, I would save my celebrations for the moment in favor of feeling completely petrified.

Unconsciously, I'd moved to stand completely in front of Thierry. Markus noted this as he shifted his gaze from Josh to us. He didn't comment on it, but his curious expression told me he found it interesting.

Ultimately futile against someone like him, but interesting.

I pointed at the body. "He was the serial killer."

"So I gathered."

"He even admitted it. It's not even up for debate."

"I'm not debating it."

"What about his body?"

"I'll have it removed and cremated. Standard procedure." He regarded us. "You've been a wily one, Sarah. Guess I should have taken you to the airport personally. I wouldn't have left until I saw your plane leave the ground with you on it."

I cringed. "Hindsight is twenty-twenty."

"Then again, I have a funny feeling you just would have gotten on another plane and headed right back here." He cocked his head. I noticed that he wore black leather gloves. They looked like something a murderer might wear to make strangulation both comfortable and fashionable.

Thierry remained rigidly silent behind me. I pressed back against him to assure myself that he hadn't vanished into thin air. But he was still there, getting stronger by the minute. I wondered if he'd recharged enough to do that ninja move he'd done in the suite again.

"How did you know to come here?" I asked shakily.

"Thierry called me."

I gasped. "He called *you*?"

"After he spoke to you, he made a quick call to me." Markus crossed his arms. "Your fiancé cares for you very much. He was willing to give himself up in order to ensure your safety."

My mouth was dry as this new piece of info registered for me. I turned to look at Thierry. His expression was unreadable, which only made this worse. I wanted to see worry or stress or something in his gaze to help me figure out how to feel right now. Should I be relieved that Markus had stepped in and saved us? Or should I be desperately afraid that he now had Thierry in his sights after we'd almost managed to escape?

Thierry had been so close to getting away. But he'd given all of that up for me.

"What is it?" Thierry asked, meeting my eyes. "You look . . . I'm not even sure how to describe it."

"Angry, furious, frustrated . . . grateful." My voice caught before I continued. "Mad as hell. Freaked-out. Scared to death. That about covers it. You shouldn't have done this for me."

He touched my face. "Yes. I should have. And I'd do it again in an instant."

"But this means . . ." I trailed off. No, it didn't mean anything. Thierry was innocent. I spun around to face Markus. "Listen to me and listen very carefully, mister. I know you're the Ring's enforcer and that means you're some sort of scary-ass death squadron, staking whatever looks a little funny. But I don't think you're stupid."

He cocked his head. "Scary-ass death squadron?"

"Thierry is innocent. He was set up. We know that for a fact. I mean, we don't exactly have proof, since the proof is dead and gone after being mopped up last night. But it was Bernard. He hired that hunter to make an attempt on his life and frame Thierry."

"Is that so?"

"Yes!" The strain in my voice made it go pitchy and near hysterical. "But he paid up front. And the hunter—well, he's dead now, too. But he liked money. He got the money and figured he had nothing to lose. He thought it would be funny or whatever to actually kill a vampire dumb enough to pay him to stake him. Bernard hated Thierry. He wanted this treasure the two of them had locked away for ages, but Thierry refused. That's what it was all about. That's why Thierry looked guilty to you—Bernard was threatening him about this treasure and Thierry pushed back." I was desperate for this all to get through to Markus even though I knew how insanely far-fetched it all sounded. "Damn it. You have to believe me. You have to!"

Markus stood there, his arms crossed, his head tilted, and he studied me for a very long, very silent moment.

Finally he nodded. "I do believe you."

"No, you don't understand. You have to—" I blinked. "Wait. . . . What?"

"I figured it was something like that. Makes perfect sense, actually. Bernard was always a greedy bastard." The enforcer's gaze dropped to my hand. "You're not wearing your ring. I hope that doesn't mean that you've called off your engagement."

I stared at him with shock at the brisk change of subject. Had he really said he believed me? "A tattooed, tunnel-dwelling, street kid vampire named Charlotte took it as payment earlier today for saving my life."

"You really need to be careful with the vampires who choose to live underground. They're unpredictable."

My mouth hung open so wide I might start attracting small birds looking to build a nest. "What is going on here?"

"Which part?"

I turned to look at Thierry. "Did you know he'd believe me? About what I said about Bernard?"

"It's the truth."

"Yeah, but . . ." I grappled for the proper words. "But he's an enforcer."

"And he enforces vampire law when needed. He doesn't indiscriminately kill those who are only suspects."

"But did you think he'd believe us?"

"No. I was certain he'd find me guilty." Thierry glanced at Markus before returning his attention to me. "This is . . . unexpected."

"You deal with surprises way differently than I do. I think you get even calmer."

He smiled. "Or so I'd have you believe."

Before he said anything else, I threw my arms around him and hugged him very hard. He cringed a little as if it hurt him.

"Sorry." I loosened my hold and stared up into his face. "I know you're still healing."

"It's fine." He shook his head and stroked the tangled hair back from my face. His brows were drawn together and the calmness from earlier had shifted a bit to show the worry beneath. "Sarah, when you called me, the sound of your voice . . ."

I watched him carefully. "What about it?"

"All of this has just made everything very clear to me. The Ring . . . my job with them . . . it's too much. Too dangerous. I think the best answer is for you to go back home where I can be assured of your safety. I won't have much time to visit, but every day I can get away and get on a plane, I will be there with you. We can still make this work. I know we can."

He kissed me softly and I returned it, so relieved that he was okay. That I was okay. But it was me who pulled away first, now troubled. I couldn't think of a proper response to what he'd just said to me, so for once I said nothing.

"I need to work with Markus to clean up this mess and file my report with the Ring. Go back to the hotel and I'll be there as soon as I can. It's over, Sarah. You're safe. Markus believes in my innocence. Everything's better now."

Well, we were still alive. Josh was dead. Bernard had been revealed as the instigator of his own murder. And Thierry still wanted me to go back home without him, where I wouldn't get into any more trouble.

Whether it was all better was still up for debate as far as I was concerned.

Chapter 22

I returned to our suite at the Bellagio. David and Jake were still there. Word had gotten to them about what had happened and they acted sheepish around me now. Whether they felt bad for treating me like a criminal, or if it was because Thierry had easily kicked their butts, I wasn't sure, but they kept their distance and gave me some well-needed privacy. Jake even offered to go to the Glitter motel and retrieve my suitcase for me. When he returned with it, I took the time to freshen up and change clothes after having a very long, very hot shower.

It didn't wash all my cares away.

A few hours had passed since the showdown with Josh. It was going on midnight, but sleeping was the last thing on my mind. Since my latest cell phone was resting in pieces, I used the landline to make another late-night call to my best friend, Amy.

"Hey, you!" she greeted me cheerily.

"Hey yourself." Somehow, I didn't think she'd had quite the life-or-death experiences I'd had in the last day and a half. Call it a hunch. "Just wanted to touch base."

"You okay? You didn't text me back earlier."

"Yeah . . . I'm fine. I'm in Vegas right now."

"Oh my God, I love Vegas. Fun! Have you seen any shows? Cirque du Soleil is so awesome."

"Haven't really had the chance yet." I lay back on the king-sized bed and stared up at the ceiling. "I'm . . . headed back to Toronto tomorrow."

I tried to put some enthusiasm into it, but knew I failed miserably.

"You don't sound like you want to go." As bubble-headed as Amy sometimes was, she did know how to read me like a Kindle.

"I . . . I don't know. I'd thought I might be traveling for a while—with Thierry. He has a new job with the Ring that requires him to go all over the place. But it doesn't look like I'm going to go with him after all."

"I'm sorry." Her genuine compassion for my disappointment was clear in her familiar voice. "But, you know, sometimes these things happen for a reason. Maybe it just wasn't meant to be and you're on the path to even bigger and better things in the future."

I sat up and hugged a pillow to my chest. "You think?"

"Sure. If you want a change, then you should move out here with me. I could get you a job with my new company easy. And it's so much fun. Makeup application, makeovers, testing, free samples . . . it's like a dream come true. And it's got a sister company—a shoe company. I get eighty percent off designer shoes, Sarah. I could die. My feet have never been happier."

"Sounds amazing." Or, at least, I would have thought it sounded amazing once upon a time. Free makeup and deeply discounted shoes? Yes, please.

Once upon a time felt like a million years ago.

"So do it. Move out here. Take a chance, Sarah. You never know where it will lead."

"I—I don't know."

"Promise me you'll at least think about it, okay?"

I promised. She chattered on about her husband and their new city for another ten minutes before we said good-bye. I put the phone down with a heavy heart.

Change was good. I liked change. I embraced change. I welcomed change into my life.

I repeated it to myself over and over again.

There was a knock at the door. I left the bedroom and went toward it cautiously. Thierry wouldn't knock.

I looked through the peephole in the door, surprised to see Markus Reed standing there. "What do you want?"

"May I talk to you, Sarah? Privately?"

I opened the door slowly and peered out at him, scanning the hallway. "Where's Thierry?"

"He's downstairs by the pool on a conference call with some Ring elders." He shrugged. "I assume he's filling them in on what's happened here between Bernard and the serial killer case."

"You're not part of that conference call?"

"Thierry's the consultant, not me."

"Which means?"

"I don't do meetings."

The man still made me nervous. I'd always be grateful that he'd swung in to save the day, but I didn't welcome the chance to hang out with him socially. "So what's this, then?"

"This isn't an official meeting. May I come in?"

After considering it for longer than was polite, I held the door open wider. "Sure. Why not?"

He entered the hotel room and walked over toward the window to look outside. He didn't seem in any rush to speak.

"Look, Markus, I—I really want to thank you for helping us tonight. And for believing us about Bernard. This job of Thierry's is a strange one. It's hard to wrap my head around it all. I want him to reconsider. I mean, he hasn't signed the papers yet—"

"He has," Markus told me. "When we returned to the hotel. I witnessed it personally."

That deflated me immediately. "Well, he could still change his mind. Lawyers could pull apart any contract that might—"

"He signed in blood. It's binding. Trust me on that."

My shoulders slumped.

Of course. Signed in blood. What other way would a shady vampire organization have to lock an employee in for a fifty-year term than to use a little of that blood magic I'd been hearing so much about lately?

Markus studied my reaction. "You're angry with him about this."

"Yeah, you could say that. I don't understand why he'd want this. And he won't tell me, even though I feel like I have the right to know. I know they've got something on him—and he refuses to tell me what it is. Maybe it's got something to do with that stupid treasure of his that Bernard and he hid away."

"Diamonds, right?"

I looked at him with surprise. "How do you know that?"

He spread his hands. "It's my job to know everything I can."

"Must be nice to be omniscient. Maybe you could

tell me why a stash of diamonds upset Thierry so much he threatened Bernard in public. He doesn't lose his temper that badly over anything. Why are they so damn important that dangling them in front of him is enough for him to write off fifty years of his life . . . not to mention our relationship . . . to be at the Ring's beck and call?"

"He's breaking things off with you?"

"No, but . . ." I glared at him. "Why am I telling you any of this?"

"Obviously, you want to get it off your mind."

I frowned. "You can work some sort of influence over other people—you can make humans forget what they've seen. That's what I heard. Maybe you can make other vampires feel compelled to treat you like a copy of *True Confessions*."

Markus didn't confirm or deny it. His coldly handsome face was placid. I recognized that expression, since Thierry had perfected a similar one.

"So you believe that Thierry threatened Bernard's life over some treasure he valued. And the safety of this same treasure also prompted him to agree to work for the Ring."

"What else could it have been?"

He turned to the window, giving me his back. "I suppose if you don't believe Thierry values jewels that much, you might ask yourself what he *does* value. What would he put first and foremost in his life, in his world? What does he love enough to kill for? To die for? Now, *that* is a treasure worth threatening to get someone like Thierry to toe the line."

His words and what they could mean managed to render me speechless.

"This is not the reason I came here tonight, Sarah," Markus continued when my reply was utter silence. "There's something I'm very interested in getting my hands on and I believe that you can help me."

I finally found my voice. "Let me guess. Even if no one else wants them, you're after the diamonds."

He laughed. The sound was like the crack of gunfire and it made me jump. Laughter seemed like a strange thing to come out of this man. "No, diamonds hold no interest for me. As far as I'm concerned, they can stay hidden away for all eternity. Actually, I'm interested in Thierry himself."

I stared at him. "This is going to be a very awkward love triangle."

Another sharp laugh made a chill run down my spine. "*Information* about Thierry."

"What kind of information?"

"He's . . . an unusual vampire. There are many things about him that are different from others. I have a file folder three inches thick on him—including his problems with blood and his rare ability to go entirely without it."

I didn't say anything, but my mind was reeling. Thierry's blood addiction *was* unusual. It wasn't just me. Comparing him with the people at that bloodaholics meeting had made me realize this, but this was only more proof.

"He's been around for a long time," I said with a tense shrug. "I'd heard that problems with blood are par for the course."

"It's not unheard of, but it's not common, either. Those who've reached his age only need to drink rarely if they choose to, and there have been control issues in a few instances. With Thierry, his issues have been an ongoing problem that stretch back farther than you might expect—and most of this history been documented. However, there's a bit of a glitch in our files on your fiancé. Fifty years are missing from his time line in the seventeenth century and no information can be found about them. By all accounts, Thierry de Bennicoeur disappeared from the earth for that amount of time, leaving all witnesses with the impression he'd been killed. But then he returned, stating that he had no memory of his absence. Strange, don't you think?"

Uh, *yeah*. I'd say that was strange. It was also the first time I'd heard of this, not that that surprised me, since I already knew he wasn't exactly chatty about his past. But fifty years with no trace? That was a significant chunk of time, even for someone his age.

I tried my best not to give away how shocked I was at this info. "What difference does it make? Maybe he joined a monastery and then got selective amnesia after they kicked him out."

"Maybe. And I'm not saying that there will be any chance to fill in the blanks of his life, but you're close to him—closer than anyone else. If someone could find out this information and help me finally close this case file, then it would be you." He gave me a knowing look. "He *treasures* you."

I cringed at the use of the word, given what I was piecing together about what Thierry valued and what he was willing to do to ensure its safety. "Thierry's business is his business. I'm not going to pry."

"I'm not asking you to. But if you do hear anything

that might be helpful, then please pass that information along to me." He smiled a little at my reluctance. "I have something to sweeten the pot. I do you a favor and maybe you'll do one for me in return."

I was about to open my mouth and tell him it was well past time that he headed back to Grim Reaper Central when I noticed what he was holding out toward me in the palm of his hand.

My ring.

My eyes widened and I tentatively took it from him, staring at the familiar facets of the princess-cut solitaire diamond in its platinum setting. "But—but how did you—? I mean, how did you get this?"

"When I finished up with Thierry, I went for a short stroll in the tunnels. I happened along the vampire you met down there. Charlotte, right?"

Just "happened along," did he? I found that incredibly hard to believe. He'd gone down into the darkness below the city and managed to find a needle in a haystack. In less than three hours.

I stared at him, feeling sick all of a sudden. "Did . . . did you kill her?"

"Would you care if I did?"

It felt as if a hand had clutched my heart. "Yes, I damn well would care. I hated her for stealing this from me, but she saved my life. She didn't murder anyone. She was weird and creepy and had a bad attitude, but if you staked her to get this back, I—I can't wear it ever again."

I loved this ring, but if someone died for it, it would make my skin crawl to be anywhere near it. Forget Thierry's stashed diamonds, this would be my own cursed jewel I needed to stay away from.

Markus studied my face as if trying to figure me

out. I don't think he succeeded. "I didn't kill her. I let her off with a warning. I don't kill innocents, Sarah, no matter what you might believe about me. I only do what must be done."

He didn't wait for my reply. He moved toward the door, opened it up, and glanced back at me. "Remember my request. If you have any information you think might help unravel the mystery of your fiancé's past, please call me. Good night, Sarah."

The door clicked shut behind him.

I was left alone in a luxury suite at the Bellagio with a three-carat diamond engagement ring and about three million questions.

When Thierry hadn't returned half an hour later, I decided it was time for a game of hide-and-seek. He wasn't hiding very well. Downstairs, near the same spot where he'd been feuding with Bernard, he leaned against the railing near the large pool with his cell phone pressed to his ear, speaking quietly to whoever was on the other end. I waited until he finished before I went to stand next to him.

He regarded me with a smile on his handsome face. "I'm surprised you're still awake."

"When you fought with Bernard, was it because he'd just threatened to kill me if you didn't hand over your key to the safety-deposit box?"

Very rarely was I able to totally surprise him. This was one of those times.

"Sarah . . . I—"

"And is the 'offer you couldn't refuse' from the Ring that they'd snuff me out like a half-smoked cigarette if you turned down the job?"

He stared at me with shock before managing to successfully shutter his expression back to neutral. "I think your imagination is getting away from you."

"You did all of it to protect me. I'm—" It was hard for me to even say it out loud, hard for me to believe anyone would feel this way about me. "—I'm the only thing in the world that you care about that much. The only thing they can threaten to get you to do what they want."

His jaw was tight and he said nothing in reply, which was more than enough to confirm it for me. I didn't need words when I had actions as my evidence.

"I know you want me to go back to Toronto where I'll be safe. I get it, Thierry. I do. I hate it with every fiber in my being, but I get where you're coming from. If I'm not with you on your future adventures, I won't be in danger."

He nodded slowly. "That's right."

"Yeah, because I was so safe in Toronto all the time since being sired. No danger there." I didn't even try to hold the sarcasm back.

"It's for the best," he said firmly, as if he was trying to convince himself of this as well as me. "And as I said, I will visit as often as I can."

I moved toward him, pulled his arms away from their tightly crossed position, and looked up at his strained face. I took his hand in mine and placed the ring into it.

He stared down at it before his gaze flicked to mine.

"Markus went on a retrieval mission on my behalf," I explained. "Makes me think we wouldn't have gotten too far before he found us. He's that good."

"And now you're giving this back to me." It wasn't a question.

I tried to find the strength to keep going. I had to say this, all of it, all at once. "Life isn't simple or safe, Thierry. It never has been and it never will be. That's the lousy part. The good part is that I want to be with you. Not just for a little while, and not for your money and the chance at a life of leisure. I'm not Laura. I see that now so clearly, that we're nothing alike. It's made everything easier for me."

"This is easy?" He'd stopped looking directly at me, instead gazing down at the ring he held on the palm of his hand.

I took a deep breath. "No, this isn't easy. It's the hardest thing I've ever had to do. I won't go back home with the promise that you'll visit now and then. I won't agree to that. If I go back, then it's over between us. I want a future with you, but that means I want all of you. And I won't be treated like a fragile treasure you need to hide and protect. I want to be treated like an equal, like a partner. I know I'm a fraction of your age and that you've lived a long, long time and met a lot of people. You've done a lot of things." *Some*, I thought, *that you might not even remember.* "You've made some bad decisions along the way and I know you're ashamed of a lot of it. But you need to get it through your thick head—I don't care about that Thierry. I care about *this* Thierry, the one who stands in front of me. The one I want to marry."

He looked confused. "You want to marry me. Still?"

"Yes. But it's all or nothing. Either you want all of me, or you want none of me. And that's totally your decision now."

His brows were drawn tightly together. "You're saying that you would come with me on my assignments for the Ring."

"Yes."

"You'd stay by my side no matter what happens."

"Yes."

His eyes flicked to mine. "You'd accept that there are some secrets from my past that I can't share with you."

I hissed out a breath. "Yes, damn it. Now decide. Do you want me or not?"

He studied my face for so long I wasn't sure if he was ever going to speak again. A million thoughts went through his eyes as he weighed the pros and cons of my ultimatum. Would I manage to avoid danger if I went with him? Would the Ring be angry that he'd decided to do this? Did he care? Could he live without me? Could I live without him? Was it worth the trouble and worry to have me with him as he traveled the world? Would I find someone super hot and way younger than him the moment we parted?

I added that last one in just because it felt right.

"Silence, huh?" I said after enough time had elapsed that I started to sense the negative outcome of this little tête-à-tête. I tried to ignore the lump in my throat that had taken up permanent residence. "I think I get it. I won't make this more difficult than it has to be, Thierry. I'll make sure my suitcase is packed and I'll be ready to leave for the airport first thing tomorrow morning."

His expression was haunted. "You ask a lot from me, Sarah."

I raised my chin. "Damn right I do."

"I think you believe that this is simple for me. That

saying good-bye to you is not something that I hate having to do."

"And yet, here we are. I mean, I don't blame you for this. Not entirely. I know I'm a magnet for trouble, I know I'm hard to control, and sometimes I do things that are risky—to say the least. Quite frankly, I'm not totally sure why you asked me to marry you in the first place."

"You still don't know?" He let out a sharp laugh, which startled me. "To put it ineloquently, Sarah, you make me happy. You make me want to live for another six centuries, provided that you're by my side. I want nothing more than that—not since nearly the first moment we met."

The heavy elephant lounging on my heart since he'd said I had to go back home shifted its big butt a little. This was what I needed to hear, what I'd been so thirsty for.

But then I frowned. "Wait a minute. *Nearly* the first moment we met?"

His lips quirked. "I'll admit it did take me a few days to recognize your particular . . . charms."

I couldn't help but laugh a little at that. "Ditto."

He stared down at the ring he now held between his thumb and index finger. "Are you absolutely certain about this?"

"I don't know. Ask me and I'll tell you."

That earned me a wry look. "You're not making this easy for me."

I shook my head. "Not a chance."

His expression grew tense again. "I didn't want you to go back home without me. But I thought it was the right decision. I wanted you to be safe, even if I went about it the wrong way. You believe me to be so worldly, but when it comes to matters like this, I find myself at a severe disadvantage."

I waited, not wanting to say anything to interrupt him. I just focused on trying to keep breathing.

His jaw tightened and his forehead furrowed. He was still fighting some sort of tug-of-war inside of himself. Maybe it was a devil-on-one-shoulder, angel-on-the-other situation. I let him battle it out without comment. I'd already had my say.

Finally, his gaze met mine and held. "Marry me, Sarah. Be with me always."

A smile slowly crept onto my face and with it came deep relief and such happiness I didn't think I could contain it. I held out my hand to him. "Yes, Thierry, I'll marry you."

He mirrored my smile, so wide that I could see his fangs. He was about to slide the ring back on my finger where it belonged, when he stopped and gave me a look that could only be described as mischievous. "Before I make this official, I have one condition of my own."

I blinked. "And what's that?"

He told me. It took only a minute for me to agree.

He'd met all of my demands; the least I could do was meet one of his.

Chapter 23

Since I was a kid, I'd always dreamed of a huge wedding, one where I wore a big, princess ball gown and there was a five-course meal, and I had a half dozen attendants. Since getting engaged, I'd been worried that I wouldn't be able to get all my friends and family together in one place for a wedding. I now knew that was impossible.

And I didn't really care.

I didn't need the huge guest list, the ridiculously expensive gown, the string quartet, the trained doves (because there had to be doves).

Now I knew that was all window dressing to what I really wanted.

My conditions were met—I would travel with Thierry as he began his job as consultant for the Ring. While he hadn't officially confirmed it, I knew the only reason he'd taken the job or threatened Bernard's life was because they'd threatened mine. But what better way for him to keep an eye on me than if I was by his side?

I could have moved to Vancouver and started a new life like Amy suggested. But I didn't want that. I already had exactly what I wanted. And the best part? I now knew without a doubt that he wanted me, too.

Thierry's condition was this: If I wanted to marry him, then I needed to put my money where my mouth was. Now. Did I really want to be committed to a six-centuries-old master vampire with a shady new job and an even shadier past? Did I trust him enough to give him my hand in marriage, binding us together from this day forward?

The answer was an unequivocal Y-E-S.

So here we were. In a Las Vegas wedding chapel called the Love Shack.

I wore a sparkly off-white shift dress and gold pumps I'd bought only this morning. Thierry wore—*shocker*—a black Hugo Boss suit.

No family or old friends in attendance. Instead, we had new friends: Charles and Victoria.

I'd been happy to hear that she wouldn't have to do any more pageants or adopt a life of crime to make a living. On the conference call last night, Thierry had been authorized to hire her on as a noncontracted undercover "child" agent for the Ring for occasional missions. Since she'd wanted to try acting, she was thrilled for the opportunity to stretch her theatrical legs in a potentially beneficial way. And also make a very generous paycheck.

Charles was our official witness and Victoria was our flower girl—and unofficial maid of honor. She wore her prettiest and frilliest pink dress for the occasion. It did smell a little bit like cigarette smoke, but I was willing to overlook that.

"Do you, Sarah, take Thierry as your hunka-hunka-burning-love husband from this day forward until death do you part?"

Thierry grimaced a little at that. I watched him with

amusement. This had been his idea, after all. And I had to admit, I was the one who'd insisted on the "Love Me Tender" ceremony.

I looked from the Elvis impersonator's gold lamé suit and long black sideburns to Thierry. He stood next to me, holding my hands, and he studied me as if he still expected me to change my mind and go running for the hills at any given moment.

"I do," I said firmly.

"And do you, Thierry, take Sarah as your jailhouse-rockin' wife, from this day forward until death do you part?"

"I do," he said firmly, holding my gaze.

"Then by the power vested in me by the state of Nevada, I now pronounce you husband and wife. May you never be lonesome tonight or move into a heart-break hotel again. Thierry, it's now or never. You may kiss your beautiful bride."

Instead of cringing again at our spectacularly cheesy (and completely awesome) ceremony, Thierry focused all his attention on me. I grinned at him as if shocked that this had actually happened without the world exploding right in the middle of it.

"We're married," I told him.

"We are. I love you, Sarah."

My heart swelled. "I love you, too."

He cupped my face between his hands and kissed me. I wrapped my arms around him, almost losing my hold on my small bouquet of red roses and baby's breath—which was a thirty-dollar wedding package add-on. We'd kissed plenty of times over the months since we first met, but this one felt different. It was the first kiss in the next chapter of our lives.

Despite any questions I had, secrets he had, or promises I'd made to curious parties, Thierry had just made me the happiest woman on earth. And I was going to try my very best to return the favor.

I honestly had no idea whatsoever what tomorrow might bring—or the day, week, year, decade, or even century after that. But, really, why spend time worrying about the future when the present was this bloody fabulous?

Turn the page for a sneak peek at the next exciting Immortality Bites mystery,

BLED & BREAKFAST

Coming soon from Obsidian.

Crystal balls have a lot in common with eyeballs. They both have the power to reveal hidden truths. That is, if you're brave enough to look deeply.

This occurred to me as I sat in a quaint fortune-telling café called the Mystic Maison, across the table from two sets of eyes and one crystal ball.

The first pair of eyes was clear blue and smiling, set into the pleasant face of a woman in her late fifties. She wore the expected outfit of a fortune-teller—colorful blue and green robes embroidered with gold stars and moons, as well as a jade green turban that mostly encased her jet black hair. With a glance into her eyes, I could tell that she was both friendly and earnest.

She believed she could tell my future while I waited for my coffee order. Whether she really could was currently up for debate.

"You're new in town," the woman, who'd already introduced herself as Madame LaPorte, said as she gazed into the crystal ball in the middle of the small round table, covered by a red tablecloth. The conversations of others in the busy café buzzed all around, and coffee, tea, and freshly baked cinnamon pastries pleasantly scented the air.

"Just arrived," I confirmed.

"And you're here . . . not purely for a vacation, but for business."

"That's right."

A small frown creased the skin between her thin, penciled-in brows. "However, you do hope this trip will serve two purposes—business *and* pleasure. This is also your honeymoon. Am I right?"

I sent a sidelong glance toward the other pair of eyes watching this reading with interest. These eyes were the gray of a winter sky. At first glance, they were cold. At second glance, colder.

At third glance . . . I didn't think they were cold at all.

To say I was fond of these particular wintry eyes would be an understatement.

"A resort in Hawaii would have been our first choice," Thierry said, giving me a wry look. "But a hotel room in Salem will suffice."

"Palm trees and hula dancers," I said with a shrug. "Who needs 'em?"

Only a day and a half after we'd gotten married in Las Vegas in a whirlwind ceremony that involved an Elvis impersonator and some really cheesy but fabulous vows, Thierry had been notified of his next assignment. That call put us on a flight from Vegas to Boston. From there, we rented a car that brought us the rest of the way to Salem—and *bam*. Here we were.

No rest for the wicked. And, really, with so many airplanes in my future now that I'd happily committed myself body and soul to being both Thierry's wife and his assistant in his job as a consultant for the Ring— the official vampire council—I was going to have to figure out a way to get over my fear of flying.

Since we were currently in Salem, maybe I'd learn how to ride a broomstick.

Madame LaPorte wasn't a witch, nor did I think she had any clear vision of the future, crystal balls or otherwise. So how did she know this about us?

Easy enough to figure out. I'd noticed Thierry fiddling with his plain gold wedding band—which he'd insisted on wearing even though he never wore any other jewelry. You can't teach an old dog new tricks. Master vampires . . . well, they were very much the same thing. That he was willing to try to adjust to anything outside of his comfort zone to make his fledgling vampire wife happy made me . . . very happy.

Giddy might be a better word for it, actually.

But the fiddling was a definite tell that Madame LaPorte had picked up on. Newlyweds, table for two.

She gazed deep into the crystal ball. "I see wonderful things for your future. Every day you spend together will be filled with adventure and romance."

I tried not to smile too widely at that. "Good to know."

Thierry gave me another glance as I slid my hand over his. "Enjoying your complimentary fortune so far, Sarah?"

I nodded. "Any fortune that isn't one of doom and gloom is much appreciated."

Madame LaPorte raised her eyebrows. "I don't give bad fortunes. Who wants unhappy news—especially at such an exciting time of your life with your young and handsome husband?

Handsome, most definitely—Thierry was tall, broad-shouldered, with dark hair and those piercing gray eyes that more often than not took my breath completely away when he looked at me. But young? It was a good sign that this fortune-teller wasn't quite as universally insightful as she would have liked us to believe. Thierry might physically look as though he was only in his mid-thirties, but tack on another six centuries and you'd be in the right ballpark. This particular ballpark had been around since medieval times—and I'm not talking about the theme restaurant with jousting actors and wenches delivering ale and turkey drumsticks.

At twenty-eight, I was practically an amoeba when it came to life and experience compared to Thierry. But, as they say, opposites attract. There weren't too many couples—fanged or otherwise—more opposite than the two of us.

I was about to reply to Madame LaPorte when I felt something strange—a sensation of cold fingers trailing down my spine. I tightened my grip on Thierry's hand and turned slowly in my chair to glance over my shoulder across the café.

Someone was watching me from the archway leading into the gift shop area. A man with dark hair and black eyes. His attention was focused on me like a laser beam. His gaze was cold, hard, and endlessly unpleasant.

"Who's that guy?" I whispered, turning back around.

"Who do you mean?" Madame LaPorte asked.

"The tall, pale man standing over there with cheekbones sharp enough to cut glass. He's giving me the creeps."

She frowned, glancing over in the direction I nodded. "There's no one there."

I turned back around slowly, surprised that she was right. "Where did he go?"

"There was no one there to begin with," Thierry said, his brow furrowed. He didn't say it like he doubted I saw anything. More that he was confused by why he *hadn't*.

"Hmm. Could be you caught a glimpse of the Maison's ghost," Madame LaPorte said lightly. "Lucky you. He doesn't make an appearance for just anyone."

My gaze shot to hers. "There are ghosts here? Are you serious?"

"No . . . *ghost*. Singular. While there are admittedly many rumored ghosts in Salem, this is the only one that's ever been of any real importance." She smiled. "Exciting, isn't it?"

"Yeah," I agreed half-heartedly. "Hooray."

We really should have gone to Hawaii.

"You believe there's a ghost haunting this café?" Thierry asked.

She brightened even more. "With all my heart."

"Most spirits lose their ties to the world of the living after three days. How long has this one been here?"

"There have been sightings of Malik for over three hundred years. Not just at the Maison, either. All over Salem."

"Malik." I repeated the name. It didn't sound nearly as friendly as Casper. "Who was he?"

"A witch-hunter." Madame LaPorte's expression turned serious, but I could tell that she loved sharing this subject matter. "Murdered by a witch during the trials. She trapped his spirit here forevermore."

"Forevermore?" I repeated. Not exactly a word you heard every day. But it did add some drama.

"And then some." She sighed. "Unfortunately, I've never been lucky enough to see him. Then again, we don't know for sure that's who you saw, do we? It could simply have been a customer who slipped into the next room."

Then, after wishing us a pleasant visit to town, Madame LaPorte excused herself so she could go give another table a free and pleasant—but quick and generic—fortune while they waited for their order.

Adventure and romance. I did like the sound of that.

The waitress brought over our mugs of coffee a moment later.

I glanced at Thierry as I stirred two teaspoons of sugar into my Hazelnut blend. "The ghost of a witch-hunter named Malik was just giving me the furry eyeballs from across the room. Should I freak out now or save it for later?"

He raised a dark eyebrow. "Better than a vampire hunter."

"I appreciate you taking this seriously."

A smile played at his lips as he gave me a slight shrug. "If that is indeed who you saw, you must remember that a ghost's affect on the living is negligible at best. Even if the rumor's true and you did see this particular witch-hunter, it's nothing to concern yourself with. He can't do you—or anyone else—any harm."

I took a sip of my coffee, successfully calmed by his calmness. "I'm surprised you didn't see him, too. If he's really a ghost, that is."

"Me too."

Thierry and I might be opposites in many ways, but we did share a special skill that only a small percentage of vampires possessed. We could see ghosts and also sense the departing spirit of someone after death. But ghosts weren't exactly commonplace. Something would either have to trap them here on earth or they would have to be summoned by a psychic with very strong skills—and psychics like that were as rare as finding a nun in a string bikini.

Bottom line, ghosts weren't lurking on every street corner. Thankfully.

"Here he is," Thierry said, rising from the table. Any amusement on his face from earlier faded. "Let me do the talking, Sarah. Owen is not someone I want you to have much contact with."

That was rather ominous. "Noted. I'll play the part of the mute brunette."

We'd been asked to meet a vampire at this café upon our arrival named Owen Brumley, whom Thierry already knew from years ago. Owen was to give us an overview of the problem Thierry (and I) had been sent to check out.

That was the job of a consultant. Quite simple, really. If there was a vampire-related issue that drew the Ring's attention, they sent someone like Thierry to assess the situation. From what I'd deduced, it seemed as if the Ring was mostly interested in keeping the existence of vampires a big secret from humans—worldwide. Anything that risked that secret needed attention and a swift resolution.

The Ring also had their own police force, called enforcers. Or perhaps *assassins* would be a better descriptor. They were vampires who were also vampire *hunters*. They took care of problems if and when they escalated.

Just because vampires didn't automatically become evil fiends after sprouting fangs and developing a thirst for blood, it didn't mean we were all good, either. I'd met a bad one recently—a serial killer who'd nearly added Thierry and me to his list of victims. But he'd been stopped. Permanently.

Sarah Dearly lives to bite another day.

That was just a joke, of course. I rarely do more than nibble.

I'd met a few people from Thierry's very long and—at times—notorious past. So far, they were mostly horrible people who disliked him due to some lingering grudge. My hopes that Owen would be different were modest at best.

"Thierry de Bennicoeur . . . ," Owen began as I tensely watched him approach the table from the corner of my eye. "It's been a hell of a long time, dude."

I blinked. *Dude?*

I turned fully to get a look at this vampire as he clasped Thierry's hand and shook it vigorously.

"Good to see you again, Owen," Thierry said.

Owen Brumley looked a whole lot like a male model crossed with an A-list actor. With blond hair and flashing green eyes, he was at least six-three, and had the muscled physique of a personal trainer. Standing next to my already extremely GQ-esque husband . . . it was quite a sight.

Holy hotness, Batman. Times two.

I didn't know why this surprised me. I'd met my share of good-looking vampires since I was sired into a life of fangs, blood, and nonreflection by the ultimate blind date from hell seven months ago.

"And this"—Owen flashed me a killer smile that revealed the small but pointy tips to his fangs— "must be Sarah Dearly."

"However did you guess?" said the previously mute brunette.

"Thierry told me over the phone that you were drop-dead gorgeous. Call it a hunch."

I glanced at Thierry with surprise. "You actually used the words *drop-dead gorgeous* to describe me?"

He was the only one of us who wasn't smiling. "I certainly could have. However, Owen sometimes tends to make things up to be amusing. This is one of those times."

It wasn't said with fondness.

Call me crazy, but I had a pretty good hunch why Thierry didn't want me to have much to do with Owen. The guy was a serious lady-killer. However, with that leering edge to his gaze, it didn't make me want to start swooning over his good looks, even though every other woman in the café was currently checking him out with blatant interest.

"Hey, Owen," a blonde said with a sultry smile as she moved past us on her way to the counter.

"Lydia," he said smoothly. "Looking good today."

She giggled. "You too."

When she was out of earshot, Owen turned to me and whispered conspiratorially, "But not nearly as good as *you* look, Sarah."

I think I was the only woman within a thirty-foot radius who wasn't drooling right now. Still, I would reserve my judgment for when I'd known this guy for more than two minutes. First impressions could sometimes be deceiving. "Gee, thanks."

Thierry's expression had darkened and he gestured for Owen to take a seat. "Why don't we get to the point?"

Owen slid into a chair. "No small talk for an old pal? Thierry, you haven't changed at all over the years, have you?"

"I've changed," he said tightly. "More than I ever would have thought possible, actually."

Owen's gaze flicked to me again. "Maybe you're right. And what a wonderful change it is. Tell me, Sarah, how on earth do you put up with Monsieur de Bennicoeur's dour ways? You must feel as if you've married a high school principal."

I shrugged. "Guess that's my type. The dourer the better, I say."

"I'm not dour," Thierry said dourly.

Owen grinned. "Congratulations on your nuptials, by the way. I think it's fantastic."

"Do you?" Thierry gave him a skeptical look before his expression finally eased. "Well, thank you. I appreciate that."

"Can't believe you also committed yourself to the Ring, though. They must have had some serious duress involved to get you back into the fold. When I finished my term with them I was happy to finally be free. But good luck to you."

Thierry didn't reply to this and I wasn't going to touch this subject with a ten-foot wooden stake. In a nutshell, the Ring—while a necessary entity—was a shadowy and mysterious organization that did shadowy and mysterious things. Thierry had been an original founder but left a century ago to pursue other interests. Very recently—like less than a week ago— he'd taken a job as a consultant—a job that required him to sign on the dotted line. In blood. It was part of a blood-magic spell that bound him to the Ring for the next fifty years.

He'd done it because they'd threatened to kill me if he didn't. So yeah, *duress* was a good word. He had yet to admit this to me in so many words, but I knew it was the truth. He'd sacrificed his own future to save my life and he'd never wanted me to know.

It made my heart swell every time I thought about it. I would love him forevermore for that. For-ever-more.

And I didn't trust the Ring as far as I could throw them. I had a very good memory, and this matter, as far as I was concerned, was nowhere near resolved.

"So . . . ," I said after silence fell at the table. "What's happening in Salem? You're the guy with all the answers, apparently."

Owen gestured for an eager waitress to bring him a cup of coffee. "Not all the answers, I'm afraid."

"All I was told was that there have been some disappearances," Thierry said. "Here in Salem. Tell us more."

He nodded. "A few vampires have gone missing while visiting town. Nobody would have thought anything strange about it, but they've been clustered, all in less than a month. One of these vampires is the mistress of a Ring elder, thus the quick response."

"Do you suspect vampire hunters?"

"No. At least, I don't think so. Hunters steer clear of Salem. That's why I like it here so much."

I frowned. "Why do they stay away from here? They seem to congregate everywhere else to make our lives difficult."

"Likely the threat of witches," Thierry said, glancing at my surprised reaction. "Hunters are a superstitious lot. Witches are bad luck for them. Also, crossing paths with a witch-hunter would be dangerous for everyone involved."

I thought it through, still disturbed by the idea of witches and witch-hunters, let alone regular hunters. "Okay. So it would be like turf wars—*West Side Story* without the singing."

"Something like that. Or at least that's what they try to avoid. Other towns that are rumored to be homes to covens are treated much the same way. The world of witches and the world of vampires rarely cross paths."

"So there *are* witches in Salem," I said. For this I looked at Owen for the answer. After all, he lived here.

"Some," he agreed. "But no megas."

At my confused look, Thierry took over. "A mega is the unofficial term vampires use for a very powerful witch who can do magic without a grimoire, a book of spells. These witches are rare."

"And luckily, none are currently living in Salem," Owen added. "Just the harmless ones who like to do simple spells and cook up magical recipes. There are many peaceful Wiccans here, too. And, of course, there are the ones who only *think* they're witches. They usually wear the pointy hats."

When I thought of Salem, of course I thought of witches. I'd loved watching reruns of *Bewitched* when I was a kid—had the nose twitch down pat. This town was ready, willing, and able to appeal to that particular tourist expectation. There was even a statue of Elizabeth Montgomery herself I'd seen as we'd driven to the café.

But *mega*-witch? Kind of like an alpha werewolf, I figured—the leader, the most powerful one. Only . . . minus the hairballs.

"You said one of the missing vampires is the mistress of a Ring elder," Thierry said, helping to get us back on topic.

Owen nodded. "That's right."

"If there aren't any hunters in town, maybe nothing bad happened to her," I reasoned. "Maybe she was tired of being his mistress and took off with someone else."

"Maybe," Owen allowed, then cleared his throat. He wasn't looking directly at us anymore; instead, he was staring over at the coffee bar with its glass displays of baked goods.

Thierry watched him carefully, his arms crossed over his chest. "Let me guess. You were involved with her."

"I'm not really sure I'd say that one night constitutes *involved*." He shrugged. "There's a popular karaoke bar that I go to all the time, and let's just say that Monique knew how to sing Beyoncé like nobody's business. I had to have her."

"You slept with the mistress of a Ring elder." I put it into words. Although it didn't surprise me at all to learn that this guy favored one-night stands.

He didn't look the least bit guilty about it. "What can I say? For a three-hundred-year-old woman she was unbelievable beautiful. Like a Victoria's Secret model. But she's gone—just disappeared."

"And the other two?" Thierry asked.

"A regular vamp couple passing through town with no Ring affiliation. I met them. Nice." He cleared his throat again. "Really nice."

Something about the way he said it . . . "How well did you know them?"

"Uh . . . let's just say that some couples like to experiment when they're on vacation. And if they happen to suggest that I join them, what am I supposed to say? No?"

I could safely say I'd now known him long enough to make a non-first-impression impression. Owen Brumley—a vampire of amazing looks and indeterminable age—was the town slut.

"So what you're saying is that three vampires have gone missing while traveling through Salem," Thierry said evenly, "and all three of them had spent a night with you."

Owen took the mug of coffee from the passing waitress's tray and gave her a flirtatious grin before she moved away. "Basically. And just for the record, I had nothing to do with their disappearances."

I exchanged a look with Thierry. There was no accusation in his gaze toward Owen at these revelations. Nor was there any surprise. None at all.

"Does the Ring know any of this?" I asked. "That you were, um, *intimately* involved with them?"

"Are you kidding?" He gave me a stunned look, then turned to Thierry. "If Franklin found out about me and Monique . . . he'd probably have me staked. And it was *nothing*. A momentary dalliance."

Thierry let out a humorless snort. "You're right. He wouldn't be pleased. I believe you also had an affair with his second wife, if I'm not mistaken. During the Civil War?"

Owen took another sip of his coffee. "Whatever. It's not like it's relevant. Three vamps are now missing without a trace. That's all I know. Now it's your job to find out what happened to them."

"And you?" I asked. "What are you going to do?"

"Whatever I like. As usual." He gave me another leering look. "I can show you around town if Thierry's too busy. It would be my pleasure to get to know you better."

"I don't think so," I said. "You're not nearly dour enough for me to spend more than a few minutes with. No offense."

I heard another snort from Thierry's direction. This one held way more humor than the last.

If he'd even been the least bit concerned that I'd be taken in by this shiny but vapid vampire, then he needed to think again. I mean, please.

"We need a suggestion for a hotel," Thierry said. "Can you help?"

Owen had brushed off my dismissal without even an ounce of ill will, which I had to respect. His smile hadn't even wavered. "Of course. But you don't want a hotel. I know a great bed-and-breakfast that would be perfect for you."

A bed-and-breakfast sounded wonderful, actually. I'd never stayed in one before. And Salem—witches or not—seemed like the perfect spot for a casual but fun honeymoon, even if we had to take care of some business as well.

"Lead the way," I said.

Just before I followed Owen and Thierry through the swinging glass door, I had that strange shivery feeling again. I stopped and turned to look.

The pale, dark-haired man was back, and he stood a dozen feet away, staring at me. I met his black eyes directly and felt frozen in place by the coldness in his gaze.

"Soon," he said, his voice deep and scary and as icy as his eyes. Then the corner of his mouth turned up into a sinister smile.

The next moment he disappeared into thin air.

I shuddered.

Yeah. That was definitely a ghost. And one that nobody else seemed able to see.

Lucky me.